BROKEN TRUST

GEORGE ENCIZO

ISBN: 9781642370935
ISBN: 9781642370928
Library of Congress Control Number: 2018941601

Printed in the United States of America

Book design by Elizabeth Babski
Cover Photos Courtesy: Florida Memory.com

BROKEN TRUST

GEORGE ENCIZO

gatekeeper press
Columbus, Ohio

Also by George Encizo

Descent Into Hell
Baxter House
The Farber Legacy
Blocker's Bluff

For Karen, John, and Kristen

CHAPTER 1

FOUR HOURS INTO OUR SHIFT and already it was a busy afternoon. Five emergency calls. The last one was a gunshot victim. We did our best to stop the bleeding, then got him on the gurney, into the ambulance and rushed to the hospital. On the way, he began bleeding profusely. I worked feverishly to stop the bleeding, but it was difficult. I had blood on my hands, some on my uniform and the floor. Unfortunately, the wound was so severe that by the time we got him to the ER, he bled out and died. After we returned from the hospital, we used the time to clean the ambulance and put everything back in proper order in the event of another call.

I'd already showered and change uniforms.

The temperature was in the mid-sixties, pleasant for a February afternoon in Tallahassee, Florida. By nightfall, it would probably be in the forties.

As my partner and I were straightening out the rear of the ambulance, my phone rang. I stepped out of the vehicle to answer it. I recognized the number. It was my mother.

"Hey, Mom, what's up?" I could hear her breathing. She doesn't jog as I do, so it wasn't from that. I waited. "Mom, are you there?"

"Yes," she said. "It's..."

"It's what, Mom?"

"It's your grandfather." She sounded worried. "I had to rush him to the doctor."

I stiffened. "Why?" I worried it might be something serious. Something that would require me to rush to the doctor's office.

If it was and I didn't get there in time, I might never have the opportunity to say goodbye to him. I said a silent prayer that it wasn't.

"I was checking his blood pressure like I always do. His face was bright red, and his pressure was too high." I could tell she paused to take a deep breath. It's how she calmed herself. "Your grandfather said he was fine, but then he clutched his heart. I did as you told me. I gave him an aspirin and then rushed him to the doctor."

Thank goodness Mom followed what I'd taught her.

Where my grandfather lived, there wasn't a hospital. Folks had to go north to Thomasville, Georgia or come east to Tallahassee.

"He's not?" I asked.

"No, he's still with the doctor. But I'm worried, Erica."

I was worried, too. "I'll get there as soon as I can."

I looked at my partner. He mouthed, "Do what you have to."

"Wait," Mom said. "He's coming out with the doctor. Let me find out what it was." I barely heard her mumble an obscenity. "That crazy old man is smiling. I swear I'm gonna kill him."

I breathed deeply. I was relieved. Thank God my grandfather was okay. At least I hoped he was.

"Erica, he's fine. It was hypertension. The doctor gave him medication for it and wrote a prescription. He has to take two pills every day. I'll take care of filling the prescription and get him started on his meds." Then I heard her say, "Like it or not, you crazy old fool."

I breathed a sigh of relief. Grandpa meant a lot to me. He raised me as a teenager. Were it not for him and my grandmother, my mother and I might not have gotten over the death of my father. And I might have become an unruly teenager.

"You don't have to rush here, Erica. I've got it under control."

"Okay. But let me know if he gives you any trouble." Mom said she would, and we said goodbye.

"Everything okay?" my partner asked.

"Yeah. My grandfather gave my mother a scare." He gave me one, too, but I was certain he could tell. "It's okay now. Let's finish up before dinner."

We'd barely got through dinner when we got a call. Two teenagers were fighting and did a number on each other—nothing serious. We cleaned their wounds and sent them off in a patrol car. Their parents would deal with the police. We were back at the station within an hour.

Later that night at a little past nine, less than three hours until our shift ended at midnight, my partner and I were returning from a call in the Killearn Lakes area that turned out to be nothing serious when we were told to respond to a 911 call in Bradfordville.

A ninety-one-year-old woman had tripped and fallen in her home. The woman was unconscious when we arrived on the scene. We attempted to resuscitate her; unfortunately, we were unsuccessful.

We listened as the granddaughter sobbed and told us they'd been going through old photos, and her grandmother had just started talking about her life as a young girl during the forties. When she got up to go to the bathroom, that's when the accident occurred.

The granddaughter's voice resonated weariness and sorrow. I wasn't the least surprised. I'd feel the same way.

"I wish I had taken the time in the past to listen to my grandmother when she reminisced," she said, "but I was too wrapped up in my own world to care about my grandmother's ramblings. If only I'd taken the time to make recordings or taken notes, I could pass them on to my children and grandchildren." Her eyes were shut, holding back tears. "Now, all I have are sketchy tidbits and the photos," her voice cracked, "and the lasting memory of seeing my grandmother wheeled out of her house in a body bag."

It made me think of my grandfather, and my mother's earlier call. I'd be devastated if something like that happened to him.

After that call, we thought the rest of the night would go by without another incident. But on the way back to the station, we got another call. What a night we were having.

A frantic wife said her husband was having difficulty breathing.

When we arrived at the scene, the wife met us at the front door and led us to the living room where her husband was lying on the sofa. She said they were watching television when he suddenly grasped his throat and said he couldn't breathe. As we worked on the husband, I noticed the wife clutch her chest and drop to the floor. My partner continued tending to the husband as I rushed to her.

She'd just fainted, and I was able to revive her. She said when she saw us working on her husband, she thought she was about to lose the love of her life. Fortunately, her husband didn't die. It was nothing more than a panic attack brought on by indigestion.

The woman, seventy-nine, and her husband, eighty-one, reminded me of my grandparents, especially my grandfather. They thanked us, but not before making us look through their photo album filled with memories of their fifty-five years together.

Fortunately, that last call was it for the night. We made sure the ambulance was in order for the next shift, then clocked out. I left the station house feeling stressed out.

I was on my way home when I got a call on my cell phone.

"Hey, babe, how was your shift?" my boyfriend asked.

"Awful."

"Well, it's over. Go home and get some sleep."

"After the night I had, I don't think I'll be able to sleep."

"You will don't fret. I gotta go. We just got a call. Talk to you when I see you."

Just like him. To leave me hanging.

CHAPTER 2

PULLING INTO MY DRIVEWAY, I saw the front porch. It reminded me of my grandparents' front porch. They'd be waiting for me whenever I got home with open arms and warm hugs. It warmed my heart knowing they were inside waiting for me.

Unfortunately, there was no one inside my house waiting. And that made my anxiety worse.

I'm Erica Blass. I live with my boyfriend, Aaron Dawson. We are both thirty-four and paramedics. I did three years as an ER nurse at a Tallahassee hospital but decided it was too heart-rending watching doctors lose the battle to save a life, so I became a paramedic.

Aaron worked for the City of Tallahassee, and I worked for Leon County. Four years ago, in 2012, we bought a townhouse together in Tallahassee. We'd talked about marriage and children, but with our schedules it just didn't seem the right time.

After entering the house, I grabbed a beer from the fridge and sat down. I wasn't ready to climb into bed yet, especially alone. Those incidents still had me feeling angst.

Mom's call about Grandpa earlier in the day, and the grandmother incident, had me in a funk. There was no way I'd fall asleep. I sat there with my beer and tousled my hair. I don't know how long I was at the kitchen table, but when the first blush of dawn filtered through the window blinds, I looked at the microwave clock. I had less than six hours until my next shift at noon.

I'd finished off three pots of coffee. An empty cup and a cinnamon-apple muffin were still on the table. I should have showered and gone to bed as soon as I got home. Instead, I'd spent hours worrying about my grandfather.

I needed a shower, and, more importantly, some sack time. I got up from the table and went into the bedroom. I wasn't about to miss the chance to catch a shower and a nap.

The next afternoon, I made a call to Grandpa.

"Hey, kiddo, what's up?" He sounded like his old self.

"What's up? What's up with you?"

"Ah, your mother called you."

"She was worried about you," I said. "So am I."

"I'm fine. Don't fret about me. Your mother checked on me. So did my neighbor. Between the two of them, they got me covered. Worry about yourself."

Just like him to be concerned about me. Knowing he was in good hands, I relaxed.

"I'll worry about you. And just to be safe, I'll call you every day."

"Make it once a week, and I'll answer the phone when you call."

I shook my head. Just like him to be difficult.

"Make it twice a week, and you got a deal."

"Deal," he said.

"Love you, Grandpa."

"Same here," he said, and we ended our conversation.

Saturday evening, Aaron and I were sitting in the living room enjoying a pizza. I decided to mention the incidents to him. Especially, the one about the granddaughter, and how I'd be devastated if I'd lost my grandfather.

Aaron understood as his grandparents had died when he was in college. He wished he had taken the time to listen to his grandfather when he talked about his life as a boy. Unfortunately, like that granddaughter, he hadn't spent the time. Now he regretted it. I felt sorry for him.

"Do you know anything about your grandfather's teenage years?" Aaron asked.

I shook my head. "Nothing," I said. "But he knows all about mine."

"Maybe you should talk to him." Aaron touched his temple. "I got an idea. Why don't you talk to him, get him to tell you about them, and then write a book about him?"

"Write a book about him? Are you crazy? I know nothing about writing a book."

Aaron grinned. "You could learn."

"Learn? Me? Get serious." I hadn't written anything meaningful since term papers over a decade ago in college. My writing consisted of texts, emails, shopping lists, and accident reports. I'd heard stories about writers who'd spent years working on a manuscript and died before they finished it. And here Aaron was suggesting I write a book.

That was two months ago. Since then Aaron had pestered me until I relented. He nagged and nagged me to write my grandfather's story. I secretly thought he hoped it would occupy so much of my time that he wouldn't have to attend any more theatre performances.

I remember he said, "The season tickets were a bad idea, and subscribing to the opera was also a waste of time."

I was concerned that something could happen to my grandfather, and I might never get the opportunity to learn about his adolescence. I just couldn't let that happen. If it did, I'd be heartbroken as would my mother. I knew I had to put aside my insecurity and lack of experience and write something. Maybe a book.

My grandfather, Francis David Teague, hadn't invented the light bulb, flown around the world solo, climbed Mount Everest, landed on the moon, or discovered the cure for cancer. In fact, he hadn't done anything noteworthy. He was special to me, though. Grandpa was an ornery old man with a quirky sense of humor, which I probably inherited from him, and he could be a downright pain in the ass sometimes. But, I loved that pain in the ass.

At my grandfather's age, I didn't expect he would remember much from his pre-adult years. What I remembered from my childhood came from the thousands of pictures my mother had saved over the years. My parents were obsessed with the camera and had boxes and boxes of pictures of me. They even had one of me sitting on my potty-chair. How embarrassing was that?

I enrolled in a three-week course for beginning writers at the library. After reading the course description, I realized the journey would be littered with volcanos ready to bury me under an endless cycle of rewrite after rewrite.

I had submitted a few short stories and got horrible comments from the instructor. I asked her what I could do to improve. After she politely told me to take up finger painting, I decided to scrap the writing idea. But Aaron urged me to continue. He offered to buy me some books on the craft of writing and even agreed to pay for a writing coach to save me from yanking my hair out.

I dearly loved my grandfather and because I feared that something could take him away from me, and I'd never have the chance to learn about his adolescence—that would always be in the back of my mind and haunt me—I decided I'd approach my grandfather.

If Aaron was willing to assist me and provide me help, I'd take the chance.

"I'll do it with the condition you help me. No way I'm doing it myself."

Aaron crossed his heart. "I promise I'll be there every step of the way." Then he held his hand up. "Except when you ask your grandfather. You're on your own there. Besides, how hard was it to tell him we were moving in together?"

I turned my head. I didn't want to make eye contact with him.

"You didn't tell him, did you?"

My chin trembled. "I meant to. I just never got around to telling him."

Aaron clenched his jaw. "That's why I'm not going with you when you talk to your grandfather. But afterward, I'll provide moral support."

"Coward. Just wait, I'll do it." I let out a huge sigh. "You'll see. I know a few magic tricks. I could pull a rabbit out of my hat. And you better be there for me for moral support. I'll need it if he says yes." Aaron laughed.

I hoped I'd see too because honestly, I didn't know any magic tricks.

CHAPTER 3

FRIDAY MORNING, I MADE THE trip to my grandfather's house in Monticello. Grandpa lived alone in the same one-story house where my mother grew up and I spent my teenage years.

Monticello was a rural city in North Florida and the county seat of Jefferson County with a population of about three thousand. It was a small working-class town that was once a supply center for surrounding farms. As I passed through downtown, I drove beneath canopied streets and by several homes, now B&Bs, that dated back to before the Civil War.

When I arrived, I pulled into the driveway and sat a moment. Like I used to when I came to visit on college weekends. I used that moment to cherish the greeting my grandparents always gave me—warm smiles, sweet kisses, and big hugs. I wiped a tear away, got out of the car, and walked into the house.

Grandpa was out back on his screen porch sitting in his rocker with his morning cup of coffee and the newspaper. He only read the sports pages and comics and did the crossword puzzle. The rest of the paper he considered a waste of his time. Since I don't read the newspaper, I'm not one to agree or disagree.

I learned a long time ago that you don't just strike up a conversation with Grandpa when he's on the porch. He might be engrossed in a sports article or the comics. Or he may be asleep. When he was ready, he'd acknowledge you.

I sat next to him in one of the three rockers surrounding the coffee table. My grandmother used to sit with him in one of the rockers. The other one was always for me. I had fond memories of sitting with him on the porch as a teenager. He'd engage me in conversations about local events, how my grades were, who I was dating and what I had planned for my future.

Grandpa always had a word of wisdom and always had something funny to say. I leaned over and kissed him on the cheek.

He put the paper down and turned his head. "You again."

"Yes, me again," I echoed. "Who'd you think it was?"

He leaned back in the rocker. "So, what do you want this time? Money, advice or just sit and BS?"

It was how he'd greeted me when I was younger. Most times I answered BS, but this time I had a purpose.

"I need a favor." I'd asked for favors numerous times and he'd always given them to me, but this was different.

"Now what have you done? Did you get another speeding ticket?"

I smiled. "Nothing that exciting, but first I have to get something from the kitchen."

I went into the kitchen and poured myself a cup of coffee. His breakfast dish, fork, and knife were drying in the drainer. Grandpa had a dishwasher, but he didn't believe in using more than one dish, bowl and silverware setting for all his meals. Apparently, that habit hadn't died even though a lady came in once a week to clean the house and do his laundry.

I grabbed my cup and a small box, then went back to the porch and sat next to him. The morning sun felt good and the view of his gardens was fabulous. His backyard was a sanctuary for nature's creatures. Different species of birds congregated around the feeders and the birdbaths. Butterflies fluttered across the yard, occasionally hovering over his red, pink, lavender and purple Pentas—a sparkling star-shaped cluster of flowers—to enjoy their nectar. When I retire, I hope I'm fortunate enough to have a backyard like his. Sitting on the porch was Grandpa's way of communing with nature.

Grandpa saw the box. "What's the box for?"

"It's for you. Open it." Inside the box was my magic trick.

He grabbed the box. "It's from a doughnut shop." He opened the box and his eyes bulged. "Dang, it's a Bavarian cream. My favorite. You remembered."

"Yep, today's April sixth. Happy Birthday. You're eighty-six today."

"Hey, you're not supposed to give away someone's age, you scallywag."

"Too late, matey." Grandpa was like a kid when it came to Bavarian cream. Before I could say another word, the doughnut was gone. Just like a kid, he used his shirt sleeve to wipe his mouth.

Grandpa stood five-foot-ten and weighed one hundred sixty-five pounds according to his last doctor's report. He wore jeans around the house, but in the warm months he favored shorts and sneakers, always sneakers. T-shirts were his favorite except when a shirt was required.

Grandpa rubbed his hand over his nearly bald head. His glasses resting comfortably on his nose. He licked his lips, snatching a smidge of Bavarian cream from the corner and took a sip of his coffee.

"So, what do you want?"

I fingered the necklace he'd given me when I graduated nursing school and took a deep breath. Maybe it was a mistake to do this. I had no experience at writing a book.

"Damn, girl, get on with it."

Those were the same words he said before I told him I was no longer going to make the daily commute to Tallahassee and had decided to get an apartment there. We argued about it, and he threatened to disown me if I did. I had countered that he didn't own me and I was a grown woman not some high school kid. If he wanted to disown me, go ahead, but he'd never see me again.

Fortunately, my grandmother intervened and offered a compromise. I could get an apartment as long as I came home on weekends. My grandmother convinced him he should accept the compromise. We both agreed, except my acceptance came with the right to bring my dirty laundry with me. Grandpa agreed to my counteroffer as long as I did my laundry, not my grandmother. The first two months, I came home every weekend. The month after that it was every other weekend and then once a month. But I was always there for Sunday dinner.

Grandpa narrowed his eyes. "Well, you got something to say or not?"

All those doubts bubbled back up. I just had to say it. What could he do, throw me out of the house or threaten to disown me?

"I want to write a book about you."

Grandpa set his cup on the coffee table, raised his eyebrows, and cocked his head. "You what?"

"You heard me; I want to write a book about you."

"Why? There's nothing special about me. I'm just a simple man."

I twisted my watch, bit my lip, and continued. "You're not a simple man, Grandpa. You're special."

He waved my remark away. "Like hell I am."

"Grandpa, you're special to Mom and me."

"Pfft."

"When Dad died, you were like a father to me. You went with me to all my school events, you taught me to drive, and every year you took me to the Watermelon Festival. Heck, you even screened my dates."

"Good thing considering some of the clowns you brought home."

I giggled. "I never got the chance to find out. They didn't want to go back out with me after meeting you."

His eyes twinkled.

"There was one date that was the best of all—the father-daughter dance."

He touched my hand. "We sure wowed them on the dance floor, didn't we?"

"We sure did." I'll never forget that night. I felt like Cinderella at the ball. "After Dad died…I don't know how we'd have survived without you and Grandma."

"That's what families do. You and your mother would have done the same for your grandmother or me."

He reached out and brushed a tear from my eye with his thumb. I rubbed my face against his hand, remembering how he did that when I was a teenager. Whenever I felt sad, alone or disappointed over something, Grandpa stroked my face and I felt comforted and loved.

"That's why I want to write your story. I know a lot about your adult life from Grandma and Mom. I want to write about your boyhood. What it was like being a teenager in the forties. What do you say, Grandpa, will you let me?"

He rubbed the back of his head. "Let me give it some thought. When do you want an answer?"

I wanted to say right now but knew better. "Is a day or two too soon?"

He locked his fingers together and placed his hands on his stomach—a good sign. "Okay, I thought about it. I'll let you."

"You will?" Grandpa never decided so quickly. Something else must be going on that he's not telling me.

"Yes, but I have some conditions."

I knew it. Grandpa always had conditions. "What conditions? And don't make them so difficult I can't meet them."

There it was, his devious smile. They were going to be difficult.

"First off, you write what I tell you and nothing more. If you don't like what I tell you, we can discuss it, maybe. Second, I'm going to tell you some things that I've never told anyone, not even your grandmother or your mother. You have to write them whether you want to or not. Third, when I'm not up to reminiscing, we just talk about what's happening in your and your mother's life." He stared at me. "Understood?"

"Okay, anything else?"

"When I feel like it, you pour me a shot of whiskey from the bottle I keep hidden." He pointed his finger at me. "And you don't tell your grandmother where I hide it. Is that clear?"

"Grandma? Ugh. Right, Grandpa. I'll keep that in mind the next time I do a séance."

I studied his face to see if he was kidding. Didn't seem so. Except, Grandma had died five years ago and he hadn't had a drop of whiskey since her funeral. After the funeral he had emptied that bottle into the sink. I needed to tell Mom about this. If it were just a slip of the tongue, I'd let it go. But if it was something more, maybe I picked the right time to write his memoir.

I drew my fingers across my lips. "Clear as a bell. Trust me; it will be our secret, and if anyone breaks a secret they're a scallywag." It was how he taught me to keep secrets when I was a little girl.

"And you don't want to be a scallywag, aye, matey?"

I remember the first time he told me that. It was after Grandma caught him giving me a taste of whiskey and told me to say it was Coca-Cola. I took a sip, and my throat felt like it was on fire. When the drop hit my stomach, I thought it would burst into flames.

Grandma didn't scold us. Instead, she laughed. "Serves you right, scalawag. Maybe you won't do it again."

I never touched another drop of whiskey after that.

"So, are you ready to start?"

I gulped. "You mean right now?"

"Of course, right now. You haven't changed your mind, have you?"

"No, it's just that I'm not prepared. I have some things to do first. We'll start the next time I visit." I checked my phone for my schedule. The next available day was in a week. "How about next Tuesday? I'm off then."

"I'll have my secretary check my schedule, and if it's okay she'll call you." He smiled. "Oh, what the heck. Next Tuesday's okay."

CHAPTER 4

A WEEK LATER, I HAD my notebook, a pocket recorder, and several pens in a backpack. I also had my cell phone fully charged, just in case. I was nervous as a schoolgirl on her first day but excited, too. I was finally going to start my book. Well, start the research for it.

I pulled into Grandpa's driveway and hesitated. He wouldn't change his mind, would he? No, Grandpa was dependable. But he may not even remember our conversation. And, his remark about Grandma had me worried.

With my backpack in hand, I used my key, went to the kitchen, and poured a cup of coffee. Then I stepped onto the porch. Grandpa was reading the sports page.

"Morning, Grandpa, you ready to start?"

He put the paper down, gestured for me to sit, and rubbed his hands down his pant legs. He was nervous. It wasn't a good sign.

"I don't feel like reminiscing today."

Grandpa had either forgotten or changed his mind, and there wasn't going to be a book. If he'd forgotten, then there was more to his remark about Grandma.

"Does that mean you no longer want me to do this?"

"I just don't feel like doing it today, that's all." He gestured to the chair again. "Just relax and enjoy the morning with me."

I sat and took a sip of my coffee. When I was a teenager, we'd sit a spell then he'd say, "Let's do something, Erica. We need to stay busy." We'd get up and go into the garage where he'd teach me about the different tools he had and the proper way to use them. And he taught me how to change the oil, spark plugs, and the filter on his truck. He'd say, "One day this truck will be yours, and you need to know how to take care of it." He taught me how to drive the truck, and believe it or not; I still own it. It's a classic now. Since my place doesn't have a garage, I keep it in his.

It wasn't long before Grandpa got bored as I'd hoped he would.

"You wanna go for a walk?" he asked. "If the neighbors don't see me take my usual walk, they'll knock on the door and ask if I'm okay. What do you say?"

"I'd love to."

He stood. "First, I have to make a pit stop. Three cups of coffee will do it every time." He winked at me. "You wait here. I'll be right back."

"Got nowhere else to go."

While he was gone, I reached into my backpack, took out the recorder, and put it in my pocket. I also opened my notebook to the notes I'd made from old conversations with my mother. According to her, Grandpa had been drafted to serve in the Korean War but never spoke about the experience. I wouldn't inquire about it and would only write about it if he wanted me to. He married my grandmother after the war, and they had my mother. Grandpa graduated from college using the GI Bill. My mother didn't know where he worked when she was a kid.

"Okay, kiddo, you ready to go?"

"I have a better idea, Grandpa. Why don't we take the truck for a ride around town? It's been a while since we did. What do you say?"

His eyes lit up. "That sounds better than a walk. Who drives?"

He hadn't had a driver's license in years. Grandpa voluntarily gave it up not long after Grandma died. But he always asked.

"Nice try. I'm driving and no argument."

Grandpa nudged my arm. "I had to ask, kiddo."

Grandpa's 1957 green Chevrolet pickup truck was in pristine condition. I helped him take care of it until he gave it to me and then I took care of it myself. When I was a kid, working on the truck was his way of getting me out of the funk I was in from being uprooted and moved in with a pair of senior citizens. I was belligerent, angry at my father for dying and leaving me without his shoulder to cry on. Grandpa would invite me to join him in the garage as he tinkered with the truck. Eventually, my anger subsided and I took an interest in working on the truck. Of course, once the truck was mine, he supervised its maintenance. Well, he said he enjoyed watching the kid do as he taught her. I didn't mind because I enjoyed his company and sharing those moments with him. Plus, he was a great gofer and kept our cups filled with fresh coffee.

I washed and polished the truck twice a year, especially in spring after the pollen had quit falling like rain. He nagged me until I finished the job. I firmly believed it was his way of getting me to visit, although he knew I would. It was one of the reasons I loved him.

I put the garage door up and we climbed into the truck.

"You know when I first bought this truck, I didn't have a garage door opener. I had to open the door by hand and then close it after I drove out of the garage. Many times, I left the doors open, so did most of my neighbors." Grandpa shook his head. "It's a damn shame you can't do that now." He pointed a finger at me. "If it weren't for you and your mother planting a seed in your grandmother, I still wouldn't have an opener. The three of you ganged up on me and made me get one."

"It made life easier." I backed out of the garage. "Where to first?"

"Turn right." I did as he asked and drove beneath the canopy of spring leaves. We passed a few houses, and he pointed at a gray one on our right. "That's where the widow Hillenberg lives. She's a nice lady but a bit nosy, and she cleans my house once a week."

I smiled. "I know, and you're lucky she does."

He turned and gave me a cool stare. "Yeah, well, I pay her enough."

I almost laughed as I knew she did it out of the goodness of her heart, plus my mother and I paid her a stipend and reimbursed her for the groceries. Annamarie Hillenberg is seventy-four and was a close friend of my grandmother. I think that friendship was why she looked after Grandpa. But she tended to pry at times. Grandpa didn't have a mortgage and what few bills he had were automatically paid from his bank account where his Social Security and pension checks were deposited.

"She hangs around for lunch and brings liverwurst." Grandpa pinched his nose. "Damn stuff smells and looks like dog food. I hate it."

"You don't have to eat it."

"I don't, but she does."

Mrs. Hillenberg came out of her house, sat in a rocker, and waved to us. We waved back.

"She'll sit there every morning until I walk by and say hello." Grandpa turned, grinned and winked. "I think she has a crush on me. Don't tell your grandmother."

Again, he spoke as though she were still alive. It made me wonder if there was more to it. I'd have to discuss it with my mother.

"I won't. It'll be our secret."

"When you get to the next street, turn left."

I made a left, and when we passed a one-story yellow house with a porch and a carport on the side, Grandpa pointed to it.

"Slow down. It's the house that I lived in as a boy." He pointed to the next one. "And that's where the Sherens lived. That's another story. Maybe I'll tell you about them." I was curious about his comment about the neighbors and it being another story. Good thing I'd turned the recorder on when we left the house. I'd have the neighbors' name as a reference.

He shook his head and breathed a heavy sigh. It reminded me when he was disappointed that I hadn't made the honor role in high school. "It was white when we lived there, and there wasn't a carport just a dirt driveway where my father parked his truck. And the Sherens' house was a different color, too." There was that look again, as if the neighborhood had disappointed him. "The whole neighborhood has changed."

"Everything changes, Grandpa."

A tiny tear dripped down his cheek. "Whatever." Then he rubbed his chin. "Let's go by the old bottling company."

"Did your dad work there?"

"No, he worked as a mechanic at the Chevrolet store. Hardly anyone worked at the bottling company." Grandpa stared out the window a minute, and I didn't say anything. After a minute, he said, "My mother tried, but they didn't hire women. But that's part of that other story." He blew out a frustrated breath as if I'd argued with him. "Oh, hell, I'll tell you that story when the time comes."

That other story had me really intrigued, and I couldn't wait to hear it.

We drove by what used to be the bottling company. There wasn't much to see. A sign reading, Jimmy's Auto & Jason's Tires, had long since replaced the bottling company's logo. They'd always schlepped tires, but old timers knew what it once was. When I had a chance, I'd go to the library and see if there was anything useful about the building and the bottling company. Then I'd use what Grandpa told me and verify it.

Grandpa continued. "I'd only been inside it once and don't remember much." He waved his hand. We'd been driving around town for thirty minutes and I was starting to feel hungry. "Okay, I've seen enough. Let's go to lunch."

I sensed there was more to the story about the bottling company, my great-grandmother, and those neighbors. In time, I was sure he'd tell me.

"Where do you want to go for lunch?"

He scratched his chin, contemplating. Or maybe he was confused. I waited as he deliberated.

Grandpa rubbed his forehead. "Oh, hell, any place in town is okay."

I pulled into a nearby parking lot, turned around, drove west on Washington Street, through the roundabout, and past the courthouse. I was about to park in front of Terry's Bakery when he put his hands up.

"No, not this place!"

I braked. Fortunately, there was no one behind me. Grandpa's objection caught me by surprise. I'd chosen the place because I thought it would be nostalgic since in the past when I'd visited my grandparents, we often ate lunch there. Grandma said it was a favorite of theirs because inevitably there would be someone there they knew who would join them for lunch. I'd hoped maybe we'd meet someone from Grandpa's past to cheer him up. But now I was dismayed.

Grandpa explained. "This was the last place that your grandmother and I had lunch before…"

That made sense. He'd told Mom and me at Grandma's wake that they had lunch there and that later in the evening, Grandma said she was tired and turned in early. The next morning Grandpa discovered that she had passed peacefully during the night. I was going to suggest an alternative place.

"Forget about lunch. I ain't hungry. Let's go home."

I jog in the mornings, and my metabolism requires regular intervals of nourishment. I needed food. I considered a fast-food drive-thru but didn't want to go against his wishes.

"Maybe there's something in the refrigerator, and we can have sandwiches. How's that sound?"

He crossed his arms over his stomach and looked down. "There's probably some American cheese leftover if you want to make yourself a sandwich."

Cheese sandwich. It would have to do. I let his silence on the drive home be his way of reliving that less than happy memory.

When we returned home, Grandpa went out onto the porch, slouched in his rocker, and looked forlornly at the gardens he and Grandma had created. I made two sandwiches, poured two glasses of lemonade, put everything on a tray, and joined him.

He looked at the sandwich and waved his hand. "If you don't mind, I'd rather be alone."

"Sure. I'll leave yours here, and I'll eat in the kitchen. When I finish, I'll clean up after myself and leave. I'll call you when I can come back. That okay with you?"

"Whatever." Disappointed at the turn of events, I stood to go. I felt guilty for steering up memories that made him sad. I was also frustrated that I hadn't accomplished anything and concerned that Grandpa wouldn't want me to come back and write his story. Grandpa reached for my hand. "Wait, before you leave, would you go to the hall closet? There's a box in there. Would you get it down for me?"

I imagined the hall closet crammed with boxes. "How will I know which one?"

"It's the one with *Memory Box* written on it. Put it on the kitchen table."

After I ate, I got the box from the closet, set it on the kitchen table, and then left. The drive home was somber because I worried I had upset Grandpa.

GEORGE ENCIZO

CHAPTER 5

WHEN I RETURNED HOME, I realized that I had left my backpack at Grandpa's house. Also, I still had the recorder in my pocket, and it was turned on. I took it from my pocket, turned it off, put new batteries in it, and set it on the kitchen table. Grandpa's nostalgic memories could wait for another time. For now, I wanted to do some research about the sites we saw and those neighbors.

Unfortunately, there was nothing on Google useful about the Sherens. There were other Sherens listed, but none from Florida. Facebook had the same results. As for the bottling company and the Chevrolet dealer, I'd need to visit the library.

I considered calling my mother and telling her about my visit and what happened with Grandpa but decided not to. No need to worry her. I'd tell her another time when I had something more pleasant to say and add as a side comment. Maybe I'd discuss it with Aaron and see what he thought. After all, he'd inspired me to take on this task of telling Grandpa's story. After today, I wondered just how daunting it was going to be, but I wasn't backing down. I was doing this as much for Grandpa as for Mom and me. The book would be a lasting memory for us. It was another reason I wanted to write Grandpa's story.

Which brought me back to calling my mother. I decided it would be best to update her on what had taken place since I last spoke to her, but not about when we started to go to lunch.

My mother's name is Marion Blass. She was named after my great-grandmother. When I'd first told her of my plans to write the book, she didn't think he would be receptive. She said he never talked about his youth, not to her, and rarely to my grandmother. She vaguely remembered a few snippets from my great-grandmother but not enough to be of help.

"I can't believe he's telling you things," she said that day on the phone. "You always could work wonders with him."

"I think it was the other way around."

"Whatever. Erica, you should ask your grandfather about his memory box."

"Memory box? What's that?" She had piqued my curiosity.

"My parents kept a box full of pictures, letters, and mementos. Mom let me look through it with her once. You'd be surprised what's in that box. It might also be helpful for your book if your grandfather lets you look in it." She scratched behind her ear thinking of something. "Oh, you should visit the library and speak with the ladies of the Genealogical Society. They might be helpful. Annamarie used to be a member."

"Thanks, Mom, I will, and maybe Grandpa will let me see that memory box." I didn't tell her that the box I got from Grandpa's closet had *Memory Box* written on it.

"Maybe, but don't get your hopes up," she said. "Good luck."

The next week I called Grandpa to ask if I could come to his house to pick up where we left off. I feared he'd changed his mind since my last visit.

"What took you so long to call? Did you change your mind about writing my story?"

Well, that was a surprise.

"I was just waiting until I had a day off," I said. "Can we do it this Wednesday?"

"Sure, and bring that boyfriend of yours. What's his name?"

He'd never asked for me to bring Aaron, so I wondered why he wanted to see him. "His name's Aaron. If he has the day off, I'll bring him. But why?"

"No reason in particular, just bring him. Okay, kiddo?"

"Okay. I'll see you Wednesday."

Now I had to ask Aaron if he would come with me. I knew he had the day off and was considering going fishing Wednesday. Aaron worked twenty-four-hour shifts with forty-eight hours off. I worked four consecutive twelve-hour shifts with two days off. There was no reason he should say no. After all, the book idea was his idea, and he promised to support me.

That night when Aaron came home from work, I snuggled up with him in front of the TV after dinner. He put a movie on—one that said nudity and sex for mature audiences only. Great. It was just the thing to set the stage for my request. As the movie unfolded and the actors were engrossed in sex, I placed my hand on his thigh and rubbed it.

"Damn, babe, what are you trying to do?"

I gave him my sultry smile. "Want to take this to the bedroom?" He had never said no when I asked him, so I expected he wouldn't this time.

He put his hand on my cheek, gently rubbed it, then pulled my head to him and kissed me hard on the mouth. My hands started tingling.

Aaron scooped me up in his arms and carried me to the bedroom. Needless to say, when I asked him to go with me to my grandfather's, he gave me an unequivocal yes.

Wednesday morning, Aaron and I headed for Monticello. First, we made a special stop at Dunkin Donuts. We took Centerville Road instead of I-10 and 90 because it was a canopied roadway winding through the countryside past several churches, small farms, ranches, and even a Tallahassee Fire Station.

When we arrived, I parked in Grandpa's driveway. "I really appreciate this, babe."

He brushed the back of his hand over my cheek and gave me a silly grin. "You know I'd do anything for you."

My face felt comfortably warm, and I almost shed a tear. "And I'd do the same for you. You're the best."

He made a coy smile. "Wanna make out before we go inside?"

Any other time I would have said yes but not in broad daylight in my grandfather's driveway. My reaction must have shown on my face.

"Just kidding." He winked. "We better go in."

Damn, if only it were dark. We got out of the car and walked up to the front door.

"I better ring the bell in case he's in the bathroom or asleep. And, remember, we go at his speed. When he's ready, he'll talk. Just be patient." Aaron bit his lip. I rang the bell several times before I heard Grandpa.

"Hold your horses, dammit, I'm coming." Grandpa opened the door and shook his head. "Oh, it's you. I was in the bathroom. I thought it was Annamarie." He grinned at Aaron. "You must be the boyfriend." Grandpa extended his hand. "I'm Francis, pleased to meet you." Aaron shook hands with him, but before Aaron could introduce himself, Grandpa followed with, "Both of you come on in." We followed Grandpa into the house. "You want coffee? There's a fresh pot in the kitchen. Help yourself."

Aaron said no. Grandpa eyed him suspiciously because he had declined coffee. I said yes and went to get a cup.

"Bring me a cup. The kid and I will wait on the porch. Come on, fella, follow me."

Aaron looked at me with fear. I knew he'd never felt fear facing a horrible accident scene. Well, Grandpa probably seemed as scary as a cataclysmic explosion. I waved, mouthed go, and he followed Grandpa onto the porch.

I poured two cups of coffee and joined Grandpa and Aaron. Grandpa sat in his chair. Scattered on the table were several pictures. Aaron stood nearby, arms crossed and leaning against the wall as if he thought the chair might swallow him.

"Is he gonna stand there all the time? Damn, boy if you do you'll collapse sooner or later." Grandpa motioned to a rocker. "Pull that chair over and join us. I won't bite."

Aaron did as he was told. The poor guy wasn't used to Grandpa's ways.

I handed Grandpa his coffee and sat.

He sipped his coffee and set his cup on the table. Then he picked up the crossword page from the newspaper and his pencil.

"What's an eight-letter word for a combination of contradictory words?"

Aaron and I raised our eyebrows at each other.

Aaron put two fingers to his forehead. Then he pointed them in the air. "Oxymoron," he replied.

Grandpa lowered his glasses and penciled in the letters. "Damn, boy, you're good." Then he smiled at me. "He's a keeper, kiddo."

I smiled back. "Yup, he sure is. What's with all the pictures?"

"There from the memory box you got down for me. I thought if I looked through it, I'd find some pictures that would help me remember some things."

"Did they help?"

Grandpa tilted his head. "Some, but trying to remember what happened eighty-something years ago was like trying to remember the first sentence I spoke." He grinned. "I probably said something like, 'Get this shitty diaper off me.'"

Aaron and I laughed.

"And I'm positive I peed and shit in my diaper like most infants, and I crawled before walking into places I wasn't supposed to. Anyway, the whole decade of the thirties was a blur to me."

"That's okay, Grandpa. Remember whatever you can" The memory box was next to Grandpa on the floor. "What else was in the box?"

"Just some things your grandmother and I collected over the years. Your mother came by and told me I should let you look in it. There are some things I think you could use for that book. You're still going to write it, aren't you?"

I couldn't resist tapping him on the arm. "Why do you think we're here?"

He rubbed his arm as though I had struck him hard. "Ouch. Watch it, kiddo." He glanced at Aaron then back at me. "I don't know. Maybe you came so he could ask me for your hand in marriage."

Aaron bolted upright as though he'd just been kicked in the ass.

I held a hand up to him. "Grandpa, we talked about this several times in the past. You're embarrassing him. Apologize. Now, Grandpa."

"I'm sorry. I was just hoping that…"

Aaron raised a hand. "No need to apologize, Mr. Teague." He smiled at me. "We'll get around to it one day."

Oh my gosh, my heart started racing, my face turned red and I placed my hand over my heart. Aaron winked at me, and I knew he meant it.

Grandpa interrupted my reverie. "Can we get on with the book?"

I took a deep breath to control myself. "Show me what's in the box."

Grandpa reached into the box and shoved aside a stack of letters with string wrapped around it.

"Ooh, what are those?"

"Nothing. There's no reason for you to see those letters. You don't need them." His jaw clenched, and I wondered why he seemed annoyed. "I forgot they were there." Next, he took out some more photographs and then adjusted his glasses. "Ah, these are what I wanted to show you." He went through the pictures and selected several. "Look, this is me as a boy. I think it was in 1942." He peered at it more closely. "Yes, it was. See I'm standing by an airplane." He handed me the picture.

It was black and white and yellowed with age.

"I forget who took it, but it was the day we went to the Army Day at Dale Mabry."

"What was Army Day?" I handed the picture to Aaron.

"It was a day for family and guests to visit with the soldiers and pilots at Dale Mabry Field. You probably didn't know that there was once a major military installation in Tallahassee where pilots trained. The Tuskegee Airmen trained there as did some from other countries." He selected another. "This was me with an army officer." Grandpa's face beamed. Then he handed me another. "And this one is my parents and me in front of our house. The one we drove by." He rubbed a finger over it, and his eyes brightened. I could tell by his expression that he adored his parents. He handed me some of the pictures. "Here you look at these and see if they're helpful." Grandpa grabbed his cup, took a sip of coffee, and sat back in his chair.

I went through the pictures and stopped when I came to one of a man and woman. The man wore a suit and the woman a dress that fell below her knees. She was attractive, and he was good looking. Her hair was similar to my great-grandmother's style. It reminded me of Betty Grable in old movies and her famous pompadour.

"Who were these people, Grandpa?"

I handed him the photograph. He looked at it, frowned, rubbed his jaw, and seemed uncertain. "They're the Sherens. They lived next door to us."

I picked out a picture of two women in bathing suits. "Who were these two babes?

He grabbed the picture from me. "Hey, watch what you say. That's my mother and the next-door neighbor." Then he smiled. "You ready to hear what I have to say?"

CHAPTER 6

THE THIRTIES WERE A BLUR, but I bet I was like any other toddler who after learning to feed himself, dumped his dish on himself, placed it on his head, and smiled for the camera. And, as a wily two-year-old, I had my parents chasing me around the house trying to prevent me from doing something that would kill me.

When I was old enough to start school, Herbie Levay, the kid who lived next door, started too. We walked together with our mothers behind us. After school, we'd play in front of his house and dare each other to eat dirt. It tasted almost as bad as what came out someone's heinie, but I didn't know because I never tasted that. Herbie may have. Nobody could pick a booger bigger than we could. We also climbed the neighbors' trees and rubbed sticks on their fences. He was the only kid in the neighborhood my age. There were a couple of high school kids who would graduate soon. Herbie and his family moved to Thomasville in 1939 when we were in fourth grade. I became the only kid my age, and king of the block.

After Herbie and his family moved out, the Sherens moved in. They didn't have any children. Mrs. Sheren worked in an office, at least I thought she did. She was always dressed up and wore a big red ribbon in her hair. Her name was Violet. I remember the name because we had wild violets growing in our garden. Often, I picked them, put them in water, and put the glass on the kitchen table for my mother. Mom would lean down and kiss me on the forehead. I also sold them to the neighbor ladies for a penny a bunch.

Like the flowers she was named after, Violet was pretty too. I don't remember Mr. Sheren's name. I didn't care much for him. I think he was a traveling salesman because he was out of town a lot. He could have been a gangster because he always wore pinstriped suits.

On my tenth birthday, I got a new bike with a basket so I could ride it to school. Mom also got one, and hers had a basket, too. My mother baked cookies, cakes, and pies to sell to some of the rich folk and a few stores in town. Now that we both had bikes, I could accompany her. I used to roller skate through town, but now I could ride my bike. I loved it, except when I rode on Cherry Street. I always rode my fastest and didn't look over my shoulder at the water tower behind me. I thought it was going to fall and land on top of me. One day, when I was brave enough, I was going to climb it.

After Mom and I had made her deliveries, we'd have lunch at Paul's Café. When we returned home, Mom would put some of her earnings in a cookie jar. She'd keep the rest for herself.

"For a rainy day, Francis," she'd say. Then she'd give me a nickel and say, "Someday you'll have your own cookie jar."

What my mother didn't know was that I had an old coffee can in my desk drawer where I put the nickels and other coins my parents gave me. My desk wasn't fancy, just a simple wooden one my father had made from scrap lumber. On the desk stood a small lamp so I could do my homework. Like Mom and Dad had, a crucifix hung on the wall above the desk.

We lived on a tree-lined street and had electricity because we were fortunate to live close enough to town. Those less fortunate used kerosene lamps. We were lucky to have four seasons with brutal summers, staggering humidity, and an enormous number of mosquitos and chiggers. Fall was mild and brought a bit of fall color. Occasionally, the winter was cold but rarely freezing.

Spring was my most favorite season, mostly because it meant school would soon be over and when I rode my bike home from school, I'd smell the confederate jasmine vines on the neighbors' fences. Those vines smelled like the perfume Mom wore to church on Sundays. Spring also brought all those different color daylilies blooming everywhere, and the red, white and pink azaleas, too.

Our front yard was small, and Mom claimed a corner of it. Dad made a wooden sign, painted it white, wrote *MOM'S GARDEN* on it and stuck it in the ground. I'd come home from school, listen to Mom humming as she worked in her garden. She seemed peaceful and at ease as she tended to it. Mom's daily prayer was, "Be at peace within and all around you." That was how I learned the meaning of contentment.

Mom often asked me to go with her to the grocery store so we could both put bags in our baskets. It made it easier for Dad because he worked all day. The stores weren't open at night. He gave me a nickel every time I helped Mom.

After the Sherens moved in, my parents became friendly with them. They didn't go to our church. We were Catholic and went to St. Margaret's. I don't know what religion they were.

Occasionally on Saturday nights, the Sherens would come over and the adults would play card games while I listened to the radio. On the Saturday nights they didn't play cards, my parents would take me to the picture show. After the show, we'd go to the Davis drugstore for ice cream.

Eventually, the Sherens convinced my parents to go with them to the honky tonk to dance. They agreed, but Dad insisted he and Mom go in his truck so I wouldn't be home alone too late. It was a condition my mother reluctantly agreed to. I didn't mind being left alone because I could listen to whatever I wanted to on the radio, but mostly *Superman, The Lone Ranger, The Green Hornet, Dick Tracy, and Gangbusters.*

I was asleep when my parents came home, but I heard them laughing as they came in the house. Mom said, "Stop, Frank, you'll wake Francis up." Heck, I was already awake. The next morning, they were all smiles and lovey-dovey. Eventually, my parents agreed to go with the Sherens in his Super Deluxe Ford with running boards.

In the summer on Sundays after church, my parents and I would pile into the truck and go to Lloyd Creek. That's where Dad taught me how to swim. Occasionally, on Saturdays, my parents would give me a quarter and send me off to the picture show for the matinee. They showed all my favorites—*Gene Autrey, Roy Rogers. Hop-along Cassidy*, and if I was lucky, *The Lone Ranger*. A quarter was enough to see the film and buy candy. I think they were trying to make a brother or sister for me. Unfortunately, my mother couldn't get pregnant, so that left my parents with just wonder boy—me.

My fifth-grade teacher's name was Miss Lucy. She was so pretty, even prettier than Mrs. Sheren, maybe even Mom. Miss Lucy would read us stories during class. My favorite was *Adventures of Huckleberry Finn* by Mark Twain. I'd rest my elbows on my desk, place my chin on my fists, and pretend I was Huck. Miss Lucy was mesmerizing. I always made sure I said good morning and goodbye to her, and I said it with the biggest smile that I could muster—maybe even big enough to stuff a watermelon in my mouth. When she returned my greeting with a smile, my heart beat faster. I wished she could be my teacher forever.

When my parents and the Sherens were out on Saturday nights in Mr. Sheren's car, I'd climb into Dad's truck and pretend I was driving Miss Lucy to the picture show and all the kids in my class were jealous. I even pretended to put my arm around her like Dad did with Mom.

For Christmas, I wrapped two cookies and gave them to Miss Lucy as my special present. I'd hoped that she would pretend there was mistletoe above us and kiss me. Sadly, it didn't happen. I'd miss her during Christmas vacation.

We shared Thanksgiving and Christmas dinner with the Sherens. Mom did the cooking because Mrs. Sheren wasn't much of a cook, but she did help with setting the table and doing the dishes. Dad and Mr. Sheren listened to the radio and talked about sports. My father was a mechanic at the Chevrolet store, so they didn't have anything in common about work to discuss. The Sherens went on vacation for New Year's, so we celebrated without them.

CHAPTER 7

FOR MY ELEVENTH BIRTHDAY IN 1941, I asked my Dad to teach me how to drive. Actually, I nagged him until he agreed but he had one condition. I had to go with him to work and watch while he worked on the cars at the Chevrolet store. If I was going to learn to drive his truck, I had to learn how to take care of it. Dad worked Saturday mornings, and the owner agreed to let him bring me. He had me stand near him while he worked under the hood of several cars. I learned a lot that day.

The manager of the store, Mr. Coogins, was thrilled at how attentive I was and took a liking to me. When he asked me my name, I said, Frankie.

"No, what's your real name?"

I hesitated, so my Dad said, "Francis, but he likes to be called Frankie."

"Why? There's nothing wrong with the name Francis. Lots of famous people were named Francis."

"Really, there were famous people with my name?

"Really. Let's see there was St. Francis Xavier, Francis Bacon, and Francis Scott Key, who wrote the national anthem. And Saint Francis of Assisi. Maybe one day you'll be famous, too, Francis."

Well, that made my day and my father's, too.

No longer would I care when the kids in my class teased me about my name. But to make sure they stopped, the next time they did I walked up to the biggest kid, Coley Parkes, clenched my fists and got in his face.

"You gonna do something about it, Coleman?" Damn, if that's boy's face didn't turn the color of a tomato when I addressed him by his given name. His head was round like a basketball and he had blond hair that barely covered his head. Even our teacher called him Coleman.

He stepped back and put his hands up. "Ah, come on, Frankie. We was just teasing. We won't do it anymore." Then he put his hand out, and we shook.

From then on, everyone called me Frankie except one girl. She always wore a pink ribbon in her hair and insisted on calling me Francis. She still does.

Two weeks later, Dad took me to work with him.

When Mr. Coogins saw me, he asked, "How old are you, Francis?"

"Eleven, sir."

"Eleven, huh. When you turn twelve, Francis, you come see me. I could use someone to sweep the floors and keep the store tidy."

"Thank you, sir, I will." Both Dad and I were thrilled.

That afternoon, my father showed me how to shift gears, which was the gas pedal and which was the brake. Then he taught me how to check the oil, test the battery, and change the spark plugs. Eventually, he let me start the engine. Every Saturday after work, he taught me more and more until he finally trusted me to back the truck onto the street. Mom was so frightened, she turned her back and went into the house before I hit the end of the driveway. Dad and I started going out in the country, where he let me drive.

Once, when we were driving in the country, I asked him who taught him to drive. Was it his father?

"No, Francis, it wasn't. My father died in the first World War. My mother never recovered from the trauma of his death and left me with my grandparents. They had a farm in Alabama." Dad rubbed the back of his neck.

"How'd you end up in Monticello?"

"When I turned eighteen, I left the farm, ended up in Tallahassee, where I got a job at an automobile store. Later, I met your mother, and we got married. I met Mr. Coogins on a lunchbreak at a diner. He offered me a job and assistance buying a house. I accepted and we moved to Monticello, purchased our house, and settled down to raise a family. Soon after, you came along."

The next time my parents went dancing with the Sherens, I drove the truck around town pretending Miss Lucy and me were on a date. I stayed off Main Street to avoid the police.

I wasn't much worried about getting caught by the police as there were only two officers and one police car. They didn't have uniforms, just badges, and there wasn't a police station. The officers mostly walked downtown. Folks would call the operator if there was a problem and then the bells on the telephone poles would ring. The officers would go into a nearby store and would be told where to go.

At the end of the school year, I said goodbye to Miss Lucy. It was both a sad and eventful day for me. I waited until all the other kids said their goodbyes and left. Then I walked up to her desk and tried but couldn't get my mouth to say anything.

"What is it, Francis?" Miss Lucy always addressed me by my given name.

"Um."

"It's okay. I know what you want to say."

"No, wait. I have this for you." I plucked a rose from my book bag that I had picked from a neighbor's garden. I handed it to her. It was wilted from being in my bag all day and not being in water. "I'm gonna miss... I mean, I'm going to miss having you as my teacher, Miss Lucy." With Miss Lucy using correct grammar was important.

She took the rose and smiled. "It's beautiful. Thank you, Francis." Then surprised me by leaning down and kissing me on my forehead.

I'm sure I blushed. I know I almost peed my pants as I turned and ran out of the room.

Saturday night when I took my weekly bath, I made sure not to get any soap or water on my forehead. I wanted that kiss to last a lifetime.

Our backyard garden was where we grew tomatoes, potatoes, and other vegetables. We also had snakes. Mom was afraid of them and would have me chase or kill them. Most were the long black garden ones which were harmless. We had a chicken coop with five hens and a productive rooster that woke us in the morning. It woke us at night to alert us when a coon or a fox wandered into the yard. When that happened, with the rooster and the hens cackling, we had no choice but to see what the disturbance was. Dad didn't own a gun, but he had a baseball bat and a bucket full of rocks. The rocks usually scared the animal away, and we could go back to sleep. Dad built a chicken-wire fence around the coop that was high enough to keep out the critters, but they still wandered into the yard. Another thing we had to worry about was the deer because they'd eat the vegetables. The best we could do was cover the garden with chicken wire. Dad said it was a pain in the patoot. But the garden meant we always had fresh vegetables, and the coop meant we always had fresh eggs. Most of our neighbors had such gardens. It wouldn't be long before they were known as Victory Gardens.

I was working in the yard with my mother and wiped the sweat off of my forehead with the back of my hand leaving a smudge of dirt. When we finished, Mom washed it off and suddenly Miss Lucy's kiss was gone. But I never forgot that kiss.

Besides helping my mother with her deliveries during the summer months, I was responsible for caring for the garden. My reward was a nickel a week that I could spend on whatever I wanted at Candy Jones Candy Store. I didn't put the nickel in my coffee can. Instead, I spent it. Candy Jones, the owner, was always delighted to see me. He'd always give me an extra stick of bubblegum and say, "Mind you, don't tell anyone or I won't do it anymore." I never did.

At night, I chased fireflies and caught them in a jar. I caught enough then sat on the porch and used the jar as my light. There wasn't a whole lot for me to do in the neighborhood since I was the only kid my age.

Once in a while on a Saturday night, my parents and me would pile into Dad's 1935 Chevy pickup truck and drive to Walker's Horse and Mule Barn where folks would come to trade or just to visit. Nearby, there was an empty lot full of mules and wagons. Saturday night, the stores in town stayed open late so folks could shop at the fish market, any of the three drugstores or let their kids visit Candy Jones Candy Store.

When school started, I met my sixth-grade teacher, Mrs. Devaney. She was nice like Miss Lucy, but not as pretty. None of my teachers were as pretty as Miss Lucy. Mrs. Devaney also gave more homework. It was nothing I couldn't handle. She would often challenge us with math questions. Mrs. Devaney would write a problem on the chalkboard and we'd have to solve it. The first one to bring the correct answer to her was rewarded with a gold star. I received several gold stars that year because I liked math. I'd occasionally walk by Miss Lucy's class and wave to her.

My parents weren't going dancing with the Sherens that much because Mr. Sheren was frequently out of town on business. At least that's what Mrs. Sheren said. My mother felt sorry for her being all alone, so Mom invited her to dinner a few times a week. Mrs. Sheren asked me to call her Violet. Mom said I could, so I did.

I was looking forward to Christmas and the Erector Set that I'd seen in the Sears Catalogue Wish Book. Violet and Mr. Sheren shared Thanksgiving dinner with us. Mom wanted to put our Christmas tree up early, so Dad and I drove to the Monticello Nursery Company the first Saturday in December to select a tree. We found a great one, and Dad paid two dollars for it. We tossed the tree into the back of the truck, brought it home and left it by the back of the house in a bucket of water. We planned on putting the tree up on Wednesday evening the following week. It would be a grand celebration with my mother's cookies and a mincemeat pie. Mr. Sheren was out of town on business, so Violet was invited to help decorate. We had only two sets of lights for a six-foot tree, but my mother and I made strings of popcorn as garland and Violet was going to bring some ornaments.

Unfortunately, on Sunday morning, some country I never heard of bombed a place called Pearl Harbor. We didn't learn about it until the next day. We read it in the Monticello News. President Roosevelt asked Congress to declare war. We listened to his speech on the radio.

In school the next day, Mrs. Devaney tried her best to explain what happened and showed us on the map where Japan and Pearl Harbor were. She also pointed out Germany and Italy because those two countries also declared war on us. America was now at war, and boys and men were eager to fight.

Even with the terrible news, my mother said we would still celebrate the holiday. And we'd start it off with a tree trimming party that included eggnog, cookies, and pies. She also said we'd sing along to Christmas music on the phonograph. Violet arrived with a flask and poured something in her eggnog.

Mom looked at me, at Dad, then back at me. Even I knew when Mom gave you that look, you don't argue with her. Dad didn't. But, his jaw clenched and his chest expanded. I knew when he did that, the teapot was about to boil over. Dad didn't allow whiskey in our house. He looked at Mom. She shook her head. I guess because it was Christmas he said nothing, but I could tell he was angry.

Afterward, my father said we had to be ready for big changes.

CHAPTER 8

I WAS TAKING NOTES FURIOUSLY, even though my recorder was picking up all of Grandpa's words. I didn't want to miss a single nuance.

Aaron looked content slumped back in his rocker with his eyes closed. I figured he was imagining the world Grandpa described. Just like I was.

Suddenly, Grandpa sat back in his chair and sighed. "All this reminiscing is exhausting. Can we take a break?"

He'd given me way more than I expected. "Sure, if you'd like. We can continue another day. Besides, I have to go to work later."

"That's good, because I'm gonna take a nap. Leave the box, and I'll go through it and see if anything helps me remember more."

I placed my recorder and the pads of notes in my backpack. We said goodbye to Grandpa and left. The temperature had risen slightly as we got in the car and I drove away.

"Let's see your notes." Aaron showed me his notebook. "Four words, that's all the notes you took?" I had pages and pages of notes plus my recorder, but all he had was *1940, Violet and Miss Lucy*.

His grin widened. "I couldn't help it. I was fascinated. Did you see the way he smiled when he talked about Violet?"

"You noticed, too?" I shook my head. "Judging by her picture, she was a looker."

Aaron grinned. "How about the way he eyed his teacher. Miss Lucy must have been some looker."

"Did you eyeball any of your elementary school teachers?"

He blushed. "Guilty as charged. You know, your great-grandmother was a hottie, too." He rubbed my thigh. "Guess that's where you got your good looks."

I looked at his hand. I knew what he was thinking, and if it were any other time, I might take him up on his offer. "If you're hoping for something when we get home, you're out of luck because I have to go to work."

He patted my thigh—which usually made me give in. "Shoot, I forgot. But don't plan on an early bedtime when you get home." Then he winked. "Did you notice how your grandfather always called his parents Mom and Dad, not Ma and Pa like on the Waltons?"

"Guess you can't believe everything you see on television."

"Or in movies and books," he said. "So, what's next?"

"I think tomorrow I'll come back and visit the library and see if there are any old photographs from the 1940s. Maybe I'll get lucky and meet someone who was alive then."

Aaron's smile told me he approved.

"I can't come with you. I'm going fishing with the guys." He leaned closer and kissed me. His way of begging for me to let him go fishing.

"Enjoy your fishing."

"Thanks, babe. You're unbelievable, you know that?"

I elbowed him and gave him the biggest smile I had to offer. "Of course, I do."

The next morning, Aaron kissed me goodbye and left to meet his buddies. After breakfast, I made the trip to the Monticello library where I met Mrs. Hensen, the head librarian. She told me that some of the members of the Genealogical Society were in their office around the corner and down the hallway.

I followed her directions to the door with the gray sign protruding over it with black letters that read *Genealogy*. I knocked and a familiar voice called out, "Come in."

I opened the door, stepped in, and was surprised to see who belonged to the familiar voice.

"Erica, what brings you here?" asked Annamarie, the widow who cleans Grandpa's house. She was seventy-eight, had short gray hair and wore a print top, Capri jeans, flats, and walked with an air of sophistication about her.

Besides Annamarie, there were six others. Five women and a gentleman. Three of the women were on computers. The office was slightly larger than a bedroom but large enough for file cabinets, a bank of computers, and a conference table.

I smiled when they all looked my way. I felt like the time Gina Amendola invited me to her house for dinner. Besides her parents and brothers, her aunts and uncles had been there. Gina's aunts eyed me like an intruder.

"I'm researching for a book I'm writing."

Annamarie reached out and touched my arm. "The one about your grandfather." My mouth fell open. "He told me about it. In fact, he asked me if I thought he should let you do it. Naturally, I said yes."

I did a double take.

My mouth fell open. Well how about that? Grandpa never said he talked to Annamarie about the book.

"He didn't tell you, did he. Why am I not surprised?"

I shook my head. "Why am I not?"

Annamarie waved her hand. "Let me introduce you to our members. Folks, this is Erica. She's writing a book about her grandfather, Francis Teague, about his life in the forties."

Suddenly they were all over me like Gina's aunts and uncles, piling my plate to the ceiling with everything and anything that was on the table. I half expected to hear someone yell, *Mangiare, mangiare.*

"Most of us are younger than your grandfather," said the only gentleman in the room. "I don't know what help we can be."

"Maybe you were, Ronnie, but not me," said a brown-haired elderly lady who stepped in front of Ronnie. "Besides, you lived in Lloyd. Young lady, I was born in the thirties, and I knew your grandfather." Grandpa hadn't mentioned her. I wonder why. "My name is Rosalind Pruting. Call me Rosie. Francis and I were in the same class, both elementary school and high school." I saw a twinkle in her eye, and I adored the little pink bow that she had in her hair. "I had a crush on him in high school." I don't think I'd ever seen such a smile as she had on her face. "But he was interested in a cheerleader. I was in the band, and she and I rode the school bus together." I sensed the disappointment in her voice.

"Your grandfather was on the football team and one game when the coach called him to go in on offense, he tripped over his own feet and landed flat on his face in front of the cheerleaders." Another huge smile. "Guess whose feet he fell on? That cheerleader's." Everyone laughed, including me. "Anyway, Monday in class your grandfather was so embarrassed he hid in the back of the classroom, and that was the end of any chances with that cheerleader. Don't tell him I said so." Rosie winked at me. "We became friends, but I won't tell you what happened after we did. Let your grandfather tell you." Then she smiled and winked in a way no woman her age should ever smile and wink. At anybody.

There's no way I would tell Grandpa. "Don't worry, Rosie, I won't."

"So, how can we help you?" asked Annamarie.

"Grandpa's telling me about his life in the forties. I want some info about that time, maybe some pictures to look at to see what the town was like back then. Anything would be helpful."

Rosie walked to a cabinet, pulled out a blue notebook, opened it, and handed it to me. "These are articles written by folks who lived in and around Monticello in the forties and later. You're welcome to look through them and take notes."

I glanced at the newspaper articles. Most were written during the past ten years. Some were about the fifties, but most were about the forties. The ones from the forties talked about the town and about their experiences living there. I took a pad and pen from my backpack and made notes.

"These are wonderful. There's so much here. Thanks, Rosie."

A bespectacled lady, gray-haired with a tinge of blonde, and a heart-warming smile like my grandmother introduced herself. "I'm Leena, the society's editor. We've got yearbooks, too, if you want to look through them."

"Not yet. I'll come back when I get that far." I thought about some of the landmarks Grandpa mentioned. "Was there really a water tower and a Paul's Café?"

Leena's eyes glowed. "There sure was, both are long gone. Paul's was near the Sinclair Store, and the water tower was at the corner of North Cherry and East Pearl Streets."

Suddenly, everyone started talking about the old town. I had a hard time keeping up. I pulled out my recorder, turned it on, and took copious notes. One woman showed me a picture on her iPad of a street scene with the water tower in the background. She also gave me a website to look for other photographs. I was overwhelmed by the information.

I looked at the wall clock. I'd been there three hours. "Ladies and gentleman, I appreciate your help, but unfortunately I have to go to work this afternoon, so I have to leave. But I'm sure I'll be back after I sort through the information."

"Did we overwhelm you?" asked Ronnie.

I grinned, considered fibbing but knew they'd see right through me. "Kind of."

"Well, it's not every day we get to reminisce like this," Ronnie replied.

"I appreciate you all taking the time with me. Thank you." I packed up my backpack and gave each of them my card—which had just my name and phone number. Aaron had suggested I have them made.

"We enjoyed it," said Leena. "Here's my card." She handed me her card, and I felt embarrassed at how professional it was as compared to mine. I was also surprised to learn that she was an author and a historian. "Don't be alarmed," she said. "I only published one book."

We both grinned and shook hands.

"Thanks, Leena. Bye, all." With the knowledge that I had met a real author, I started to leave feeling a little embarrassed.

"Erica, wait," said Annamarie. "I'll walk you out."

I felt a slight increase in my pulse and was curious why she wanted to go with me. "Sure," I said.

Once we were in the hallway, Annamarie looked right then left as though she were searching for someone. "Erica, are you sure all this isn't too much for your grandfather?"

I appreciated her concern, but it was none of her business. Annamarie could be nosey at times. "Why?"

She leaned closer. "Because I've noticed he sometimes forgets things. Nothing major just little things. I worry about him."

I was concerned, too, but she didn't need to know that. I'd already made a note of it. "Thanks for telling me. I'll watch for it, but Grandpa seems to enjoy going down memory lane. If I see anything that might seem serious, I'll discuss it with my mother." I gave her a cheerful smile and added, "I appreciate your concern. Now I really have to be on my way."

Annamarie stiffened, and I was worried I might have offended her. "Sorry to have bothered you. Take care." I smiled, turned and left.

Later that night when I returned from work, I told Aaron about my trip to the library. He was fascinated by what I'd learned. After listening to my tale, he kissed me and then surprised me.

"Listen, babe; I enjoyed hearing your grandfather's story so much that I want to continue going with you. But…"

Okay, what's his *but* going to be? I wasn't compromising morals if that's what he wanted.

"You have to go back when we both have a day off. What do you think?"

"Really? That's your but?"

"Really. I even mentioned it to some of the guys, and get this? The guys were so thrilled that I was learning something about the forties when their grandparents grew up that a couple asked if they could go with us to meet your grandfather."

I placed my hands on my hips, my chest heaved, and I gritted my teeth. Aaron stepped back and stretched his palms out. "You did what?"

"I didn't reveal anything. I just mentioned when the story takes place, that's all." He raised his hand and gave me a shit-eating grin. "Honestly. So, do we go together or do I have to stay home?"

I shook my head. There was no way I could be annoyed with him after seeing the expression on his face. "You can come. We'll arrange our days off and go together." I glared at him. "But, no buddies and no telling them anything. Grandpa's story is not for public knowledge. Understood?"

"Understood."

When I called Grandpa to set up our next visit, he sounded worried.

"I thought you gave up on me, kiddo."

"I was waiting until Aaron and I had the same days off. We'll be there tomorrow."

"You're bringing the boyfriend again? Good, I might have a few chores for him." Grandpa cleared his throat as only an old man could do and hesitated. "Oh, and we have to take a walk first thing. Last time the neighbors were at my door because they hadn't seen me out for my walk."

"No problem."

The next day we arrived at Grandpa's, went for a walk, waved to the neighbors, and then sat with coffee on the back porch. Aaron was relieved that Grandpa had changed his mind about the chores especially since he was so eager to listen.

"Okay. Turn your recorder on and get ready to take notes." He looked over at Aaron. "I don't suppose you're going to take any notes."

Aaron held his pad up and grinned.

"Good, now let's begin."

CHAPTER 9

AFTER THE CHRISTMAS AND NEW Year's holidays, my parents and the Sherens went back to dancing on Saturday nights. But they'd only gone a few times when my mother said she just didn't feel right partying while there was a war on and men were away from home fighting. Plus, she wasn't pleased with the ideas Mr. Sheren was putting in my father's head. I'd overheard him hinting at enlisting, and suggesting Dad join up too. Once when my parents came home, I heard them arguing.

"Frank, listen to yourself. You've got a family, and you're not a young man like those who've enlisted."

"But I feel like I'm not doing anything for my country sitting at home."

"You're taking care of your family. We're your responsibility."

Dad muttered something under his breath.

"Forget it," Mom said. "I'm going to bed. Maybe you should sleep on the couch."

I'd never heard my mother talk like that to my father.

A few weeks later, Mr. Sheren suggested they dance at home instead of going to the honkey-tonk. He'd brought home a copy of Glenn Miller's *Chattanooga Choo Choo*—which they played on the phonograph. Mom was satisfied, but the Sherens still went dancing without my parents. They went to Ma Barnes, a dance club on the edge of town that my parents would never visit. Every third Saturday, the Sherens came to our house to dance. Mr. Sheren brought other records with him. Sadly, for me it meant the end of me driving Miss Lucy around town.

The country went on "war time"—which meant we had to push our clocks ahead one hour. Everyone did it because it was the law.

On Army Day, April 6, we all piled into Mr. Sheren's car, and he drove to Tallahassee to the public open house at Dale Mabry Field. I remember the date because it was my twelfth birthday and my father let me take the day off from school. Both he and Mr. Sheren had the day off from work. We joined thousands as we watched from the car as the naval planes flew over the field. Next, we rode in military trucks to tour hangars, buildings and airplanes. We also got to talk with soldiers and take pictures with them. It was a grand day, and we were glad we were part of the celebration.

On the drive home, Mr. Sheren took Centerville Road—an unpaved road—and stopped at Bradley's Country Store, a barn-like structure with a covered porch and tin roof. It was on Moccasin Gap Road—also an unpaved road. He stopped for gas and something to eat. Dad purchased meat to store in our icebox for meals. The ladies strolled the aisles. Mom bought some jams and grits. Violet purchased some sweets. Mr. Sheren bought a sausage dog and finished it before we were back on the road.

"Frank, have you thought about enlisting to fight the Japs and the Gerries," asked Mr. Sheren.

I sat in the back seat between Mom and Violet. Dad glanced over his shoulder at Mom. Her face reddened.

"I don't want to talk about it." He looked at me, then at Mom. She gave him her look. When she does that, it means she was angry and don't argue with her. I was too. I didn't want my dad to enlist.

"Marion doesn't want me to. How about Violet? What's she think?"

"She got no say."

Violet shook her head and startled me when she grabbed my knee. I felt her nails dig into my skin when she squeezed. Best I could figure, she did it because she was angry and used my knee to keep from speaking her mind.

"No more talk about it," Dad said.

Mr. Sheren drove us home. He parked in his driveway, and my parents and me went home. Mom prepared dinner. Dad sat on the porch. I listened to the radio. We ate dinner that night in silence.

In the days ahead, my parents continued bickering about Dad wanting to enlist. Eventually, they stopped arguing—mostly because Dad went and joined anyway. My father was proud and stubborn. When he had a problem, if something needed fixing or he had concerns about what might happen down the road, he'd go at it like a man on a mission.

Mr. Sheren also enlisted. He joined the army, and Dad joined the navy. They both joined around the time an eighteen-year-old kid named Boots Thomas enlisted in the marines. Mom had hoped the navy would reject Dad because of his age. He was thirty-five, a year older than Mom. But the navy was in desperate need of ship mechanics. With my father's experience as an auto mechanic, they were eager to hire him.

Mom was somewhat relieved that he would be on a ship and not in combat like Mr. Sheren might be. Violet wasn't the least bit pleased that he was going off to war. She and my mother would often console each other.

When the time came for Dad to leave, we walked him to the Greyhound bus station on West Washington Street. The service station had a large canopy allowing the bus to pull in under it. The driver said he would wait while we said our goodbyes. My parents hugged and kissed. Mom didn't want to let him go.

Then Dad took me aside and hoisted me over his head. He was six feet tall and extremely muscular, I felt like I was king of the mountain. No one could knock me off.

"Damn, Francis, you're too big for me to do this. There was a time when I could lift you up on my shoulders and carry you around like I was your private train. Not anymore, though. How much do you weigh?"

"I don't know. Maybe eighty pounds."

Dad laughed and set me down. He placed his hands on my shoulders. "Listen, son, while I'm gone, you have to be the man of the house and look after your mother. Help her with her chores, do your own, and watch over the house. I'm counting on you."

"Don't worry, Dad; I'll make you proud. But on one condition."

He rubbed his hand through his hair. "What's that?"

I glanced at Mom, and she waved the back of her hand. "You promise you'll stay safe and come back home to Mom and me. You gotta promise us, Dad."

He looked at my mother, and she had tears in her eyes.

"Damn, boy, I'll do the best I can."

I crossed my arms and shouted, "No, Dad, it's not enough. You have to promise." I wasn't going to let him leave Mom and me without promising. We might never see him again.

Dad looked at Mom, saw the tears in her eyes, and rubbed his jaw. He looked at me then back at Mom. I hoped he was rethinking the idea of going off to war.

"Damn, you sure make it hard for me. Okay."

"Okay, what?"

"I'll stay safe and come back in one piece. I promise."

I wrapped my arms around him and squeezed him tight. It wasn't what I'd hoped to hear, but it would have to do. My eyes felt wet, so I quickly wiped them. I didn't want Dad to think I wouldn't be the man he wanted me to be.

Other passengers on the bus were watching out the windows. The driver said he had to get on the road, so Dad boarded.

The last thing my father did before leaving was to whisper in my ear, "Teach your mother to drive."

Right, like Mom would let me teach her to drive. She'd always declined when Dad tried to teach her. I just nodded my head and promised Dad I'd do it. How, I had no idea.

Dad boarded the bus, and Mom and I watched as it drove away.

That bus was just a bucket of steel and rubber, but still, it was the interloper that crumbled the foundation from under my mother's feet, leaving her without a pillar to hold up the structure she and Dad had built together. It left my mother naked without support to care for the child they raised together. I understood my father felt a sense of duty to his country, but he also had an obligation to the woman who comforted him in time of need, bore him a child, cared for us both and made our home a castle. I wanted to pick up some rocks and throw them at that God-awful bucket.

And what about me? Who was going to provide the foundation that I would need to get through the world that lay ahead? Damn that bucket of steel and rubber, and damn my father for leaving my mother alone.

Mom's hand trembled as I held it. Her other hand held a tissue that she used to dry her flood of tears. God forgive me for cursing my father. My mother didn't deserve to be left with a broken heart, worried that she might never see her man again. And neither did I. It wasn't fair, it wasn't right that we should be left to face what lurked in the shadows at night. No, Dad, it just wasn't right.

Gradually, the bucket disappeared until it was gone leaving a void in our world. Dark clouds hovered above. It was quiet, eerily, and an eeriness penetrated our inner-being robbing it of all hope and replacing it with despair. It was eerily quiet like the somber silence after death.

We were so preoccupied with our tears of despair that we hadn't realized God was sharing a wave of sympathy with us. If I could speak to him, I'd ask why he'd done this to us? We didn't deserve this punishment, and I was mad at him for doing it. My Dad had done it, but God should have stopped him, and now Mom was immersed in sorrow. Maybe I should throw rocks at

God. Mom wiped the backs of her hands across her eyes and grasped her crucifix.

"You folks need a ride? It's awfully wet out there."

I wanted to take her in my arms and console her, but when Mr. Kelsey, who worked at the courthouse, offered us a ride, I had to hide my tears.

"If it's not a bother," Mom replied.

Mr. Kelsey raised a hand. "No, bother at all. My car's ready to go. Let me pay my bill, and then I'll take you home." He looked in the direction the bus went. "Frank really left, huh?" One of the advantages—and disadvantages—of living in a small town was that almost everyone knew you and your business.

"Yes, sir, Mr. Kelsey," I replied. He shook his head and then went into the station, paid his bill, and drove us home.

When we arrived, Mr. Kelsey turned to Mom. "Should you need any help, don't be afraid to ask."

My mother nodded and forced a smile. We got out of the car, and Mr. Kelsey waved and drove off.

Dad was really gone, and my mother and me were alone to fend for ourselves. That night, I heard a shrill from Mom's bedroom. I wished I could comfort her. As I lay on my bed, I stared up at the ceiling, said a prayer for Dad, but also cursed him for what he did to Mom. I cursed God, too, and would never forgive him for the pain he caused my mother. Sunday when we went to church, Mom said a silent prayer for Dad. I glared at the crucifix above the altar, and although I tried, I just couldn't find forgiveness in my heart for what God had done to my Mom.

Fortunately, Dad was frugal, the mortgage was paid off, and he'd put money aside in case of an emergency. We had funds to last a while. He also kept an envelope marked "Seed Money." We knew what that meant. My mother also had the money she saved from her baked goods sales, and I had my can of nickels.

Violet was alone, too, but at least she had a job to support herself, unlike my mother.

Mom still baked and made her deliveries, but at night I'd hear her crying. Dad hadn't prepared me for dealing with my mother's loneliness. I covered my head with my pillow hoping it would go away—but it didn't.

Mornings, I was up before the sun, fed the chickens and greeted the milkman—just like my father used to. I made my breakfast and packed my lunch for school. For dinner, I ate macaroni and cheese, which became my staple during the war years. I worked the garden and tended the chickens. I let a few hens hatch their eggs so we'd have more chickens. As an older hen stopped producing—just like my father—I wrung its neck and butchered it for meals.

One night when my mother was in her bedroom with the door closed, I decided to check on Violet to see how she was doing. I snuck out of the house and walked next door. Violet's kitchen light was on, so I knocked on the door.

"Come in, the door's unlocked," she called out.

I opened the door and stepped in. Violet was sitting at the kitchen table with a drink in hand. An open bottle of whiskey sat on the table. Whatever she put on her eyes ran down her cheeks, and she looked like a clown in the circus.

"Frankie boy, you come to check on old Violet?" Her words were slurred.

"Yes, ma'am."

"I ain't no ma'am. Come over here."

I hesitated, concerned she might do something. What I didn't know. I'd never been in her house before.

"Come on, don't be afraid. I won't bite." Violet cocked her head and pinched her thumb and finger together. "Well, maybe just a teensy little bite. Come on, Frankie boy."

I tentatively walked over.

She grabbed my arm and ran her hand over my bicep. "You have muscles just like your daddy. Want to drink with me?"

"I'm not old enough."

She stroked my arm. "Sure, you are. Come, sit down with Violet. Can't you see I'm lonely since my man left me? Please, Frankie."

The only other women who'd touched me were Mom and Miss Lucy, but I never felt like I did at that moment. And being next to her in her loneliness wouldn't be proper for a boy of twelve. She might do something that she'd probably regret, assuming she remembered. I knew I'd remember and then I'd have to keep it a secret from Mom, and I couldn't do that. Although tempting, it was time for me to act like a gentleman.

"Violet, I think you've had too much to drink."

"You think so?"

"Maybe you should take a bath. You'll feel better." I thought about what I said and decided she might want me to take one with her. "Better yet, maybe you should lie down. You'll feel better in the morning."

She took a sip and waved her other hand at me. "You're no fun. Okay, maybe I'd best lie down. Wanna join me?"

"You go ahead, I'll put your glass in the sink."

"Okie dokie." She stood, steadied herself by placing a hand on the table, and then danced off to her bedroom singing the words to *Chattanooga Choo Choo*.

I watched as her hips and arms swayed. The way she bounced off the doorway, I figured, maybe I'd better follow and make sure she got into bed. When I entered her bedroom, the essence of her permeated the room. Her room looked like a hurricane had blown through it. Clothes, including some unmentionable, were scattered on the floor. I wasn't about to touch any of them. Being there felt strange, almost like being in the girl's bathroom at school.

Violet was face down on the bed, still dressed. She must have passed out too fast to get undressed. Her feet dangled over the edge. I grabbed her ankles. They were slender and soft to the touch. I lifted her legs onto her bed, a bed I shouldn't have been near. I knew this was improper, but I also knew I was trying to do the right thing. Violet stirred, her buttock moved from side to side, and I watched to be certain she was asleep, not dead. I knew I shouldn't have, but I gazed at her shapely body. Next, I covered her, backed out of her room, and took one more glance at her covered form.

Violet's kitchen was a disaster. I washed the dirty dishes, put them in a rack to dry, grabbed a broom and swept the floor. I didn't want to leave without making sure Violet was okay, so I tiptoed into her bedroom and checked on her. Fortunately, she was snoring softly. Back in the kitchen, I grabbed the garbage bag, turned the light off, locked the door, and slipped out of the house.

I was just a twelve year-old kid with two lonely women who needed help, and I had no idea what I could do for them. Nothing I learned in school or read in books had prepared me for this. I'd never been a father or a husband. I barely had any friends. Dad shouldn't have piled this burden on me. If he'd stayed home, I wouldn't have been in this predicament. It wasn't right, it wasn't what a kid my age should be expected to deal with, especially alone. What was a kid supposed to do?

CHAPTER 10

AARON SCRIBBLED IN HIS NOTEBOOK. Hopefully, it was something I could use. He sat back in his rocker and looked at his pad. He seemed satisfied with whatever he'd written. I was considering how Grandpa felt after his father left, and him and his mother being alone to fend for themselves. And him being alone with Violet. Although tempted, Grandpa acted like a gentleman. I was proud of him.

"Whew, how'd I do, kiddo? Did you get a lot?"

"You did good, Grandpa. I'm surprised by how much you remembered."

He tapped his forehead with a finger. "There's still a lot of marbles in here. But I could use a break."

I could use one, too. He'd talked through lunch, and I was sure Aaron was hungry. Grandpa's comments about how he felt when his father joined the war resonated with me.

After my father died of pancreatic cancer when I was eleven years old, I became angry, too. I took my frustration out on everyone and anything. I even considered running away from home. But I had my grandparents, and Grandpa's patience and understanding got me over my anger.

"We can come back tomorrow," I said. "If that's okay with you?"

He thrust his chest out. "That would be great. I've got so much to tell you." He picked up the memory box and rifled through it. Finally, he pulled out a photo and handed it to me. "See this one?"

It was a photo of a boy standing next to a soldier in front of an airplane.

"That's me on Army Day."

I looked at the photo. It was black and white and yellowed with age. The soldier towered over him. Grandpa was smiling. He pointed his thumb at the plane behind him. I showed it to Aaron. He smiled.

Grandpa handed me the box. "See if there are any pictures you're interested in hearing about."

I combed through it. I noticed the stack of letters he'd tried to hide from me the other day was missing. "What this one?" It was a photo of two women. I handed it to him.

"That's my mother and Violet. There's also one of her somewhere in there with me. I'll see if I can find it."

I smiled. "I'd like to see it. Can I fix you something to eat?"

"Annamarie will be by later. I'm gonna take a nap. You two go on." He pointed at Aaron. "He looks like he's starved."

Aaron grinned.

"Okay," I said. "We'd better get going. We'll see you in the morning."

"Not too early. I need to take a walk so the neighbors see I'm still alive."

We climbed into my car, and I drove off. "Man, that Violet was something. It sounded like she was a wild one," said Aaron.

"I'll say."

Aaron tilted his head toward me. "Do you think she?"

"She what? You better not mean what I'm thinking." If she tried to seduce my grandfather, I was sure he wouldn't let her.

"I was just curious. Say, what's an Erector Set?"

"It was a boy thing. You'd build things like bridges, buildings, and such." I elbowed him. "Even I knew that, and I'm a girl."

"Well, I'm not up on my forties lingo. I thought the Lone Ranger was a Johnny Depp movie."

I shook my head. I couldn't believe how uninformed he was. "For a guy, you missed out on a lot."

"I guess so."

"What were you scribbling in your notebook?" He showed it to me. "An airplane?"

"It's' to remind me to Google Dale Mabry Field and Army Day."

I made a left onto Moccasin Gap Road.

"You doubt my grandfather's words? I already did that." He was about to tear the page out. "Keep it. Maybe I'll use it in the book."

His eyes lit up. "Really?"

"You doubt my words?" Aaron waved me off.

We were approaching Bradley's Country Store.

"You think they were in business in the forties?" he asked.

I turned into the parking lot and pointed to their sign. "Again, you doubt my grandfather's words. The sign says since 1927— proves they were."

CHAPTER 11

LATER THAT NIGHT, MY MOTHER called and asked if I'd gone to see Grandpa. I could tell by the way she asked that there was something wrong.

"He seemed fine. Is there a problem?"

"Annamarie called and was in tears. She'd made dinner for him and after dessert they were discussing going to the Senior Center. Anyway, she was teasing him about a woman named Rosie who goes there on Fridays with her husband, and it annoyed him."

I almost dropped the phone. "What did he say?"

"According to Annamarie, he ordered her out. After all she's done for him. Can you believe that old man?"

"No, Mom, I can't."

Grandpa could be ornery, but I'd never known him to be insulting on purpose, especially to a woman. He couldn't lose Annamarie. He needed her to care for him and his home.

I worried it could be another sign of deteriorating health. Hopefully, this wasn't the start of Alzheimer's. Maybe he was tired and irritable from talking all day. I'd have to watch for mood swings. And I probably should be careful not to exhaust him. I don't want to be the cause of something happening—something terrible, something that would take him from me.

"Annamarie's done. She's not going to help him anymore."

It was bad, terribly bad. If Annamarie quit looking out for him, what would we do?

Mom sighed. "I called him and told him he'd better apologize to her first thing in the morning and told him if he didn't, we'd put him in a nursing home. I think I scared him."

I was sure she did. "Should I ask him about it when I go tomorrow?"

"See if he brings it up first. If not, you might as well. And, Erica, be sure and mention the nursing home if he hasn't apologized yet. It's the only way to make that damn fool understand. You let me know what he says tomorrow. If he did apologize, I'll call her and see if I can change her mind. Otherwise, we have no choice."

"Okay," Wow, I hated to think of putting Grandpa in a nursing home.

Aaron and I returned the next day with a box of Dunkin Donuts, a bribe in case I had to persuade him to apologize to Annamarie. As we pulled into Grandpa's driveway, he was coming out of Annamarie's house. We waited on the sidewalk.

"Morning, Grandpa. Did you take your walk?"

He pulled at his ear. "I had to stop at Annamarie's to straighten something out." He waved his hand. "It was nothing, just a misunderstanding. You ready for another history lesson?"

I assumed he'd apologized, and I wouldn't have to threaten to put him in a nursing home. Thank goodness, he listened to Mom. Now, he could enjoy his doughnuts.

"We're ready when you are."

"Then let's get started." He pointed at the box in Aaron's hand. "Better have a jelly doughnut and a Bavarian cream."

"Got both," Aaron said. "Personally, I like the ones with powdered sugar."

Grandpa smiled. "Let's go inside and have coffee and doughnuts."

Inside, Aaron set the box of doughnuts on the kitchen table. I made a fresh pot of coffee and then we all sat on the porch. As Aaron and Grandpa munched on their doughnuts, I opened my backpack and took out the recorder, a pad, and a pen.

"Whenever you're ready, Grandpa."

CHAPTER 12

E VENTUALLY, MY MOTHER AND VIOLET got on with life. Thank goodness for me because then I was able to get back to being a kid again. Almost.

Rationing was already in effect, and we had to stand in line like everyone else to get our ration books. We conserved as best we could. With the extra hour of daylight, we kept the lights off, and like those who lived far from the city, we started using kerosene lamps. We'd listen to the radio once a week. Mom listened to the news report about the war, and I listened to *The Green Hornet* or *The Lone Ranger*.

The school teachers were in charge of issuing ration books. Mrs. Devaney handed me our "sugar books," which limited the amount of sugar we could purchase. Less sugar meant less income because Mom couldn't bake enough products to supply all her customers.

Rationing of gasoline meant I couldn't drive Dad's truck on pretend dates with Miss Lucy. I had to conserve gas so I could teach Mom to drive. Mom continued making her deliveries by bicycle. The government imposed a national speed limit of thirty-five miles per hour, but no one drove that fast around town anyway.

We had a girl in my class named Mika Takada. She was a sweet oriental girl with long black hair and a warm smile. I always said hello to her. One day, she didn't come to class and then I never saw her again. We figured maybe her family moved away.

On the last day of school before summer vacation, I said goodbye to Miss Lucy. She called me into her classroom and asked how my father was doing.

How was he doing? I had no idea, and it bothered me. I could have told her, and I knew she would understand how I felt. But I'd already burdened Miss Lucy with enough of my troubles. Especially, that time when I threw up in front of the class almost spraying my lunch on her desk. I wanted to storm out of class and run home. But I stayed in class and endured the teasing from my classmates, except from one girl. Miss Lucy sent me to the boy's room to wash my face and rinse out my mouth. After class, she told me not to worry everyone got sick at one time or another. I felt like I had a second mother.

"We haven't heard from him yet, but I'm sure he's okay."

"I'm sure you'll hear from him soon, Francis. How's your mother?"

I'd told Miss Lucy that my Mom had a hard time after Dad left. I needed someone to talk to, and, Miss Lucy was very understanding.

"It's a little tight with sugar rationing, but we'll manage."

She put a hand on my arm and I got so lightheaded, I thought I was going to faint.

"I'm glad. Have a fun vacation, Francis."

I strolled out of her classroom and down the hall to the exit.

Mr. Coogins, the manager of the Chevrolet store, had told me that when I turned twelve, I should go see him about a job. Since school was over, I decided to take him up on his offer. I rode my bike into town, rested it against the dealership, and went inside. Unfortunately, when I got there, things had changed.

Mr. Coogins shook his head when he saw me. "With rationing, there are no sales, and folks aren't bringing their vehicles in for repair. They're keeping their old cars and fixing them by themselves. I had to let a couple of men go. I felt bad being as how they were family men. If it weren't for the Sinclair store, I'd have to close up shop." He put his hand on my shoulder. "I'd like to hire you, but I'm afraid I can't. I guess things must be tough at home with your father away and your mother's bake sales off." Mr. Coogins' wife was one of Mom's customers.

"We're managing. Any suggestions for where I might find some work, even if it's part-time?"

"I don't think anyone in town is hiring."

I lowered my head and took a deep breath. "You know any place my mother could get work?"

Mr. Coogins rubbed his chin. "Does your mother drive?"

I bit my lip. "No, sir. Before he left for the navy, my Dad told me I had to teach her."

Mr. Coogins rubbed the back of his head. "Well, you best do as your father told you." He scratched his head like he was pondering something. "Hmm, I just might know where she could get work if she's willing to clean up other people's messes."

I wasn't sure what he meant, and I didn't know if my mother would be willing. We'd never talked about her getting a job.

"I don't think she'd mind."

Mr. Coogins narrowed his eyes. He looked like he didn't believe me.

"Tell you what. You ask your mother. If she's interested, tell her to come see me." He shook his finger as though scolding me. "You best do as you father told you and teach your mother to drive."

I was about to jump up and down but thought better of it. "Thank you, Mr. Coogins. I'm going home right now and ask her."

Mr. Coogins chuckled. "You go do that."

I hopped on my bike and rode home without a clue as to how I'd talk Mom into talking with Mr. Coogins about cleaning other peoples' messes. Thinking about teaching her to drive put my stomach in a knot.

At dinner that night, I decided to bring up the subject of her getting a job.

I rubbed the back of my head and tried to calm the butterflies in my stomach.

"Mom, I talked to Mr. Coogins today." When she looked at me, I saw the circles under her eyes.

"Does he have a job for you?"

"He's not hiring." I swallowed hard. "I asked him if he knew where you could get work."

"You did what? Why, Francis?"

"Because I know how difficult our situation is. I was trying to help."

She laid a hand on her heart and lowered her voice. "Francis, I appreciate you trying to help, but somehow we'll manage. You shouldn't worry about our situation. It's not your responsibility."

"But Mr. Coogins said he might have something for you. He said for you to go see him."

I thought she'd get angry. She speared a hunk of Spam and lifted it to her mouth. But she paused halfway there. "What kind of something?"

At least she was curious, not angry.

Before I could answer, Violet knocked on the door and entered without being invited in. She'd been doing that lately.

"I'm sorry," Violet said. "I thought dinner was over. I'll come back."

Before Mom could reply, I said, "Come on in, Violet. Mom and me were just finishing." Maybe Violet could help me talk Mom into it.

My mother narrowed her eyes, but I ignored her.

"Might as well join us for dessert, Violet," Mom said. "You're already here."

Violet's face lit up. "Don't mind if I do. I didn't have dinner, but I'd love dessert." She took a seat.

Mom cleared the table of our dinner dishes, cut three slices of pie, set them on the table, and sat down.

"Did I interrupt your conversation?" Violet asked.

She did, but I was grateful because maybe Violet would be an ally.

"No," I said. "I was just telling Mom that Mr. Coogins might have work for her." My stomach quivered. "If she's willing to clean up other peoples' messes."

Mom's mouth fell open. "What did you say?"

I ignored her. "Mr. Coogins said if you don't mind cleaning up other peoples' mess…"

"Are you serious, Francis? I have enough cleaning up our house. Why would I want to clean someone else's?"

"Because we need the money, that's why." I wasn't going to back down. "I can clean the house for you. I already clean my room, take care of the garden, feed the chickens, and work on Dad's truck. At least hear what Mr. Coogins has to say. Please, Mom."

Before my mother could answer, Violet jumped in. "He's right, Marion. You should at least hear what he has to say." Then matter-of-factly she added, "If I can clean up someone else's mess, why can't you?"

Both Mom and I were shocked. We thought since she always left her house dressed up with a ribbon in her hair, that she worked in an office.

"I thought you were a secretary," asked Mom.

Violet grinned. "That's what I wanted everyone to believe. I change clothes when I get to work and before I come home." She cocked her head and put her hand on her hairdo. "A girl has to keep up appearances." She dropped her hand and her expression fell as she studied my mother. "You're not disappointed, are you?"

Mom hesitated. I worried she might tell Violet to get out of our house, and I'd lose an ally.

Mom rubbed her chest. "I'm just sorry you weren't honest with me since I trusted you."

Violet placed her hand on her chest. "I hadn't meant to break your trust. I wanted to, but he told me not to. I'll never lie to you again."

I looked back and forth between the women before setting my gaze on Mom. "What about Mr. Coogins offer?" I asked. "Will you at least consider it?"

Mom pursed her lips. "I'll talk to him."

Thank goodness, she'd at least talk to him.

"But if I get a job, you're going to clean the house, Francis. I want your word."

I wanted to shout but thought better of it. "I will, Mom, I promise. But please don't make me clean the toilets. Please."

Mom and Violet laughed. "Maybe," Mom replied.

Now, all I had left was to teach Mom to drive. Hopefully I had the courage to convince her to let me.

The next afternoon, Mom rode her bicycle into town and to the Chevrolet store to speak with Mr. Coogins.

I eagerly waited for her to come home. Unfortunately, when she did, she said, "Not now, Francis, I'll tell you after dinner."

After dinner? How was I supposed to wait until then?

"You go get us a chicken," she said. "I'll pick some vegetables, and I'll make us a chicken stew. We'll have enough for the next couple of days." Then she gave me a warm smile. "I'll bake some cookies, too."

My mother wanted to make a stew; I wanted to know what happened. I guess making cookies was her way of placating me. I waited impatiently for dinner. Finally, Mom filled our bowls and we sat. Then, of all the times for her to show up, Violet burst into the kitchen without bothering to knock.

"Okay, Marion, I want to hear what happened. Did you take the job?"

"Have you had dinner?"

Violet sniffed the air. "Not yet, I was hoping..."

Mom shook her head, and I wanted to tell Violet to go home.

"Sit down. I'll fix you a bowl," said Mom.

With her soup in front of her, Violet picked up her spoon then hesitated. I did, too. We were both eager to hear what happened.

"Okay, if you two aren't going to eat, then I might as well tell you what happened. When I got there, Mr. Coogins stood in the doorway looking up and down the street. Maybe looking for customers. I got off my bike and with it beside me strolled up to him."

"What did he say, Mom?"

"He knows a lady who needs a housekeeper and asked if I was interested."

Violet swiveled in her chair and crossed her legs. I leaned forward.

Mom's eyes sparkled. "I said I might be."

She might be? What kind of answer was that? I guess she was being stubborn.

"He called Mrs. Coogins on the telephone, and she came and got me. She took me to Mrs. Atkinson's house on Palmer Mill Road. She's a widow lady. Her husband left her enough money to live comfortably, and she wanted someone to keep house for her Monday, Wednesday, and Friday. Mrs. Atkinson wanted a colored lady, but Mrs. Coogins convinced her to offer me the job."

Mom stood and leaned against the counter. Violet drummed her finger nails on the table. I wanted to pull my hair out.

"Mrs. Atkinson offered me the job. I'd work from eight to five and get paid six dollars a day."

"Did you say yes?"

Mom clapped her hands together and smiled. I thought she was going to jump up and down.

"I did. She has an electric dishwasher, an electric washing machine and dryer. On Tuesdays and Thursdays, I can make my baked goods sales." She focused on Violet, and I thought maybe I saw tears in her eyes. "Francis and I will be able to get by on my earnings."

Violet stood and hugged my mother. I wanted to shove her aside so I could do the same.

"Six dollars a day is a lot, Marion. I only get paid five dollars. I can drive you to work if you want me to."

"I don't mind taking my bike. Besides, you have to conserve gas. But if the weather is fowl, you can take me."

We ate dinner and then had cookies for dessert. I went to the living room to listen to the *Green Hornet* on the radio, and Mom and Violet talked in the kitchen. I secretly listened.

I overheard Mom tell Violet that while she was talking to Mr. Coogins, he looked her up and down.

Mom was a good-looking woman, and I guess that's why Mr. Coogins did what he did.

"What did you do?" asked Violet.

"I just grinned and told him to take his eyes off me."

Violet smiled. "You are a looker, Marion. What happened after that?"

"His face looked like a tomato."

Mom and Violet giggled.

CHAPTER 13

AS USUAL, GRANDPA'S STORY HAD pulled me in, but he seemed to fade the last few minutes and I wasn't surprised when he leaned back and sighed. In fact, I was about to suggest we take a break. I didn't want a repeat of what had happened with Annamarie.

"Grandpa, maybe we should break for lunch. What do you think?"

He leaned back and rubbed his hands over his eyes. "All this reminiscing is exhausting."

Aaron looked like he could use a break, too.

"I'll send Aaron out for sandwiches. Anything special you want?"

Grandpa scratched his head and focused on Aaron. "Stop at one of those fast food places and get me a cheeseburger, fries, and a shake."

Oh boy. If I let Aaron buy him that for lunch and my mother found out, I'd be in deep shit.

"What about your cholesterol, Grandpa?"

He shushed me. "I got pills for that and, besides, I've had enough of Annamarie's healthy meals. I wanna eat like Aaron does."

Aaron sunk in his chair. How did my grandfather know about Aaron's bad eating habits? Was he guessing? Truth be told, I liked cheeseburgers and fries, too. Aaron raised his brows. His look said, *please.*

"Okay. Aaron, as long as we're blowing it, you might as well get shakes, too. And hurry back."

Aaron was on his way out when Grandpa called, "Make sure they're cheeseburgers,"

Aaron pumped his fist, smiled, and left.

Grandpa and I chatted about nothing as I got up my nerve. Finally, I brought up the subject of Annamarie.

"How are things with you and Annamarie? We noticed you were coming from her house when we got here."

His face turned red, and he glared at me. "You talked to your mother, didn't you?" "She called me last night."

Grandpa clenched his jaw. "What did she tell you?"

I had to make Grandpa understand that Mom and I had his best interests at heart.

"She told me what you said. That wasn't nice, Grandpa." I moved my chair closer to his. "If you lose Annamarie, you know what happens don't you?" I placed my hand on his wrist. "Mom and I will have no other choice than to…"

"No, no, you don't have to." His face turned ashen. "I already apologized to her." A small tear filled his eye. He wiped it away. "We're going to the Senior Center together Friday and having lunch." He sniffed, seemed to force a smile. "There'll be someone there I haven't seen since your grandmother passed away."

I had an idea who she was but wasn't going to pry.

Grandpa covered my hand with his. "Honestly, everything's okay. Annamarie and I

talked about getting her some help. You and your mother think I could afford a cleaning lady, say twice a month?

I put my arm around him and kissed him. "I'll talk to Mom. I'm sure you can. I love you, Grandpa."

He placed his hand on my cheek. "I love you, too, kiddo. You proud of me?"

I was more than proud of him—I was ecstatic. And I was glad the nursing home wasn't an option. Mom would be happy, too, and I'm sure she'd agree to the cleaning lady.

"More than proud."

Aaron shouted from the kitchen, "Lunch is here. Come and get it."

You want to eat here," I asked Grandpa. He nodded toward the kitchen.

"We're coming," I shouted.

Aaron had already started on his fries. The aroma of the meal had my mouth watering. Grandpa started on his cheeseburger first. I did, too. A fly on the wall would have thought we were a trio of teenagers rushing to finish lunch before returning to class.

After lunch, Aaron cleaned the table. We settled on the porch with the remainder of our shakes. Aaron was eager to hear more from Grandpa.

Grandpa sipped on his shake and then began.

CHAPTER 14

IT WAS LATE JULY, AND Mom had been working her job at the Widow Atkinson's house for three weeks. She rode her bike when the weather was good. When it wasn't, Violet drove her there and back. It gave me an idea how I might approach Mom about teaching her to drive. Instead of Violet taking her, I could. And when she learned to drive, she could drive herself. I decided to wait until the perfect time to approach her.

While Mom was at work, I cleaned the house—everything except for the bathroom and Mom's room, which was off limits. Mom had graciously agreed to clean the bathroom for me. In addition to my cleaning, I had other chores like tending to the garden, the chickens, making my own meals, and shopping for Mom.

We finally got a letter from Dad. I took the letter out of the box. I ran my finger over the address. All it said was, Dad's name and *FPO New York, N.Y.* The letter was addressed to Mom and me, and I knew I couldn't open it without her. She was still at work. I set it on the kitchen table and went to my room to do my homework.

I went back and picked up the envelope and considered opening it anyway. Just then, Mom came home.

As soon as she came through the door, I shouted, "Mom, Mom, we got a letter from Dad!"

She grabbed the letter from my hand and tore it open. I saw a tear trickle down her cheek.

"Finally, Francis, I hope he's okay." She read the letter to herself then read it to me. Most of it anyway. She said some of it was just for her.

Dad was on a battleship somewhere in the Pacific Ocean but couldn't tell us where. He wasn't sure how long the letter would take to get to us as mail was slow on the ship. Mom checked the date on his letter. It was dated over a month before. Dad said he would write as often as he could and hoped we'd get his letters before the war ended. Dad also wrote that he had arranged to have most of his pay sent home. He wouldn't need much onboard the ship. And on shore, he didn't plan on doing any carousing with his crew mates. It might take a while before the money arrived as he had to sign for his pay with the paymaster, and he wasn't always available at sea.

We laughed when he wrote that most of his crew mates were barely out of high school. They called him, "the old man." The crew chief was older than Dad, a seasoned sailor, and a mechanic. The crew referred to the chief as, "Granpappy." Then he added a PS. *Tell Francis to keep the promise he made to me.*

"What promise, Francis?"

"Dad wants me to teach you to drive the truck," I blurted.

"He wants you to do what?"

I had hoped to tell her when the time was right, but Dad changed everything. Mom's reaction made me wonder if she'd refuse like she always did with Dad, and I wouldn't be able to keep my promise. I felt a knot in my stomach.

"Is he out of his mind? He wants you to teach me?"

"I can do it. I know how to drive the truck. I've driven it around town."

Her jaw dropped. "When?"

Time to confess.

"Ever since Dad taught me. When you and he went dancing, I used to take the truck for a drive. Sometimes I drove around town when you were making deliveries."

"Do you hear what you're saying, Francis?" She picked up the letter. "You don't have a license. What if the police saw you or the home guard. They'd report you. Then what would you do?"

I couldn't help grinning. "Neither one of the two police officers are ever around and they're hardly ever around when I'm out driving. Neither is the home guard. I'm careful, Mom."

Mom shook her head. "What am I supposed to do with you?"

"Let me teach you to drive, so when it rains you won't need to impose on Violet, and you can make your deliveries with the truck instead of your bike. And I can go with you."

Then I added another thought. "We'll be able to go to Lloyd Creek on Sundays after church and go swimming. You could invite Violet if you want. Come on, Mom. Dad wants me to."

She shook her head again and wrapped her arms around me. "I'm supposed to be the one teaching you things. Not the other way around."

She hugged me so tight I could barely breathe. "We'd be teaching each other. When I'm old enough to get a license, you can go with me if Dad's not home by then."

Mom stepped back and grabbed my shoulders. "He'll be home, don't you worry." Then she smiled. "Okay, you can teach me to drive." She held up her hand. "But, I'll still ride my bike. We have to conserve gas, and Lloyd Creek will have to be a rare occasion. When do we start?"

"First you have to learn about caring for the truck, just like Dad taught me. Then I'll teach you to drive."

"You mean I have to change the oil and all those other things your Dad did?"

"Dad made me, so I'm making you."

She shook her head. "Okay, we'll do it your way."

"Dad's way. We'll start tomorrow."

The next day, we spent an hour going over the mechanics of the truck. Mom was a good learner and grasped what I taught her quickly. For several days, we worked on the mechanics and then I had her sit behind the steering wheel to get the feel of it. I showed her how to shift gears and which pedals were what. Once she had those mastered, I told her to start the engine. Mom turned white, and I thought she would give up right that second, but she didn't. Instead she focused so hard, it was like the truck was in trouble and cranked it on.

When the engine rumbled, she grinned as if she invented the thing.

Next, I had her back a few feet in the driveway.

"I'm afraid I'll hit something."

I looked behind us, and I had her look, too. There was nothing but gravel. "You can do it, Mom. It's only a few feet."

She gripped the steering wheel so tightly, her knuckles turned white. Then she shifted gears and pressed the gas pedal. The truck lurched forward. "Oh, dear Lord," she screamed.

"Brake, Mom."

She hit the brake, and the truck slammed to a stop.

I breathed a sigh of relief that we hadn't barreled into the chicken coop. "Now shift into neutral." She did. "Breathe, Mom."

Mom took a deep breath. "Okay, I'm ready."

She tried it again and succeeded in driving a few yards.

Before long, she was backing down the driveway and then driving back near the side door. When she was comfortable with it, I figured it was time to go all out and have her drive around the neighborhood.

Mom's hands trembled. "I'm not sure I'm ready for this."

"Just go slowly." Mom backed to the end of the driveway. I looked left and then right. "There's nobody on the street, just us. Give it a try." I added a little begging to my voice. "Please."

Mom smiled and shook her head. "You're just like your father. Let's hope I don't crash the truck."

I beamed with pride that she said I was just like Dad.

"You won't. Now go for it."

She backed onto the street, turned right, and drove down the block. "I'm doing it, Francis. I'm driving." Mom's excitement was like on Christmas when Dad gave her a box of sweets.

Violet went with my mother to get her license. Now that Mom was legally driving, we decided to go to Lloyd and go swimming. Mom invited Violet, so I had to sit between the two of them.

Violet squeezed my knee and smiled. "This is going to be fun, Frankie boy."

I hated when she called me that. I ignored her. It was just Violet being Violet.

Once we arrived at the creek, I shed my trousers, shoes, shirt, and dove into the water in my bathing suit. Mom and Violet both wore short one-piece bathing suits. Mom's was blue and Violet's was bright yellow. They donned their bathing caps. When Mom was close enough, I splashed her. She splashed me back, and then the three of us splashed each other. Mom and Violet were having a great time, splashing each other and laughing. It warmed my heart. They seemed to have no thought of their men being off fighting the war.

We were back home that evening when Mom said, "Francis, that was the best day I've had in a very long time. Thank you. But…" There was that but again. "The truck stays in the driveway for now. We've already used too much gas."

Although disappointed, I beamed with pride. "You're welcome, Mom."

Mom was happy. Unfortunately, for me, my driving days were over. I could only dream about dates with Miss Lucy. That night I did and slept soundly. I suspected Mom did, too.

The new school year had begun. I was in junior high school. My seventh-grade teacher wasn't as pretty as Miss Lucy nor Mrs. Devaney. In fact, she was much older than both of them.

With fall and winter approaching, I had to harvest what vegetables were still in the garden and prepare the soil for winter planting. Including school, I worked from sunup to sundown.

We got another letter from Dad right before Halloween. Mom read me some of it. The parts she didn't read me made her tear up.

Violet tried to get my mother to go out dancing with her on Saturday nights, but Mom refused. She didn't feel it was right with Dad and Mr. Sheren away.

Mom invited Violet for Thanksgiving dinner. We didn't have a turkey; we had a chicken from our coop.

With Christmas several weeks away, Mom said she didn't think we could afford a tree and presents, but we'd make do the best we could. She'd bake pies and cookies, and once again I'd butcher a chicken. She asked if it would be okay to invite Violet. I didn't want to say yes but felt it wouldn't be right to say no and have Violet be alone on Christmas day. So I said yes.

I sensed Mom invited Violet because she was lonely and missed Dad. I couldn't replace Dad, but I had to do something that might bring joy to Mom.

If Dad was here, he'd buy Mom a Christmas tree, so I decided I'd surprise her with one. I grabbed my nickel can and drove the truck to the nursery where Dad and me always bought a tree. When I pulled up and parked, the owner eyed me suspiciously.

"That your truck?" he asked.

"Yes, sir."

He rubbed his chin. "You don't look old enough to drive. How old are you?"

"Old enough."

He shook his head. "What brings you here?

I reached for my nickel can and got out of the truck. "I need a Christmas tree. It's for my Mom."

"Your mom, huh? Where's your dad?"

"He's off fighting the war." I'm usually patient, but he was starting to annoy me. "Why you asking so many questions? I just want a tree."

"Sassy, ain't you? Just like my youngest. Okay, how much you got to spend?"

"How much is a tree?"

He scratched his chin. "You know my youngest boy is in the army, and he's fighting, too. Wait here I'll be right back."

I was still concerned that he might arrest me and hold me for the police. He certainly was big enough, even bigger than Dad. If I tried to run, he'd probably grab me by the collar, lift me off my feet, and dangle me midair. My worry ended when he returned with a tree and tossed it into the back of the truck. It wasn't as big as the ones Dad and me always bought, but it was a Christmas tree.

Then he reached into the nickel can and took out five coins.

"This should be enough." He smiled. "You and your mom have a Merry Christmas. Go now, go on home before I change my mind."

I thanked him and smiled all the way home. I was sure Dad was proud of me. When I got home, I set the tree against the side of the house and filled a bucket with water. I put the tree in it to let it absorb water until we would put it up and decorate it.

When Mom saw the tree, she was so overwhelmed with joy that she lifted all ninety pounds of me over her head.

"Oh, Francis, this is wonderful. I don't know where you got it, and I don't care. Your father would be proud of you."

"Mom, put me down before one of us gets hurt."

She set me down and laughed. "This is going to be the best Christmas, Francis. I just know it will."

Violet came and help set the tree up and decorate it. With only one strand of lights, we had to make the best of them. Violet and me made garland from the popcorn Mom made. We sang along to Christmas carols on the phonograph, and I danced with Mom and Violet. Mom and Violet also danced together.

The three of us celebrated Christmas together. As New Year's Eve approached, Violet again tried to convince my mother to go dancing with her. Mom finally agreed, and they went out New Year's Eve to a jook joint frequented by soldiers.

While Mom and Violet were out, I listened to the radio and pretended that Miss Lucy was listening with me. At midnight, I imagined kissing her and saying Happy New Year. Then I went to bed.

I was awakened by the light from Violet's headlights. I got up and glanced out the window. Mom and Violet got out of the car. Mom walked around to Violet's side. She expected Violet was going to say goodnight again. Without warning, Violet took Mom in her arms and kissed her. I guessed Mom could taste the alcohol on her breath. I expected Mom would slap Violet, but instead she stepped back and walked home. Violet danced into her house.

CHAPTER 15

WHEN GRANDPA STOPPED TALKING, I stretched and met Aaron's eyes. He looked ready to go home. I was, too.

Grandpa picked up his shake and slurped the remains of it. "Tastes just like when I was a kid."

I touched his arm. "I'm glad you enjoyed it." I felt a rush of affection and squeezed Grandpa's arm.

I met his eyes with my brows lifted. "I'm glad you enjoyed yours, too," he said. "Listen, kiddo, can we take this up another day? I feel like a nap. Do you mind?"

We'd almost passed the entire afternoon listening to him. "How about I come back next week on my day off?"

"Sounds like a plan to me."

"Erica, can you give us a minute?" Aaron asked.

My brows rose. What was he up to? "Sure, we can talk in the kitchen. We'll be right back, Grandpa." We grabbed the empty food wrappers and left Grandpa.

"Take your time," Grandpa said.

In the kitchen I narrowed my eyes. "What's up?"

"Listen, babe. I love listening to you grandfather about his past. Can you hold off until I can come back with you? Please."

"You're really into this, aren't you?"

He put his hands together as though praying. "I am. So, what do you say? Will you wait, please, please? I'll make it up to you, I promise."

Aaron had a way of making me give in when he begged. With Aaron, I don't have my grandfathers' genes when it came to negotiating.

I explained to Grandpa that we had to check our schedules to see when we both could come back, and he was agreeable.

"Kid's into this, isn't he?" Grandpa said with a huge smile.

"What can I tell you," I said. "He's enthralled by your story."

As soon as we left Grandpa's house, I called my mother.

"How did it go today?" she asked.

She couldn't see the smile on my face. "Grandpa apologized to Annamarie."

"I know she called me. Said he was in tears. Can you believe that stubborn old fool broke down crying?"

I wasn't that surprised since he'd shed a tear when he told me he apologized.

"Annamarie asked if it was possible to get him a cleaning lady twice a month. It's getting to be too much for her."

"What do you think?" I asked.

"He can afford it. I'll take care of it. How's the book coming?"

"It's coming. Grandpa remembers a lot, and Aaron and I are enjoying listening to his stories."

"Good. I'm happy for you. Any chance Aaron will…"

"Mom, don't ask." She'd asked the question. How many times did I have to tell her I had no idea when or if Aaron would propose."

Mom just laughed. "Never mind, then. I'll let you go. Say hello to Aaron."

Aaron's first day off was the following Tuesday. I suggested we wait until he had a chance to sleep—but he didn't want to wait any longer. I called Grandpa and told him when we would visit him.

When I got home from work Sunday, I found him at the dining room table, his laptop in front of him, and a sheepish look on his face.

"Hope you don't mind. I downloaded the recordings onto my laptop and burned a CD. With the help of your notes, I made a rough outline of all your grandfather had told us so far including dates and events in chronological order.

"What else have you done?" I asked.

"I went on Amazon and purchased three books for you. One about the craft of writing, one about the first fifteen pages, and one about plot and structure. I looked through them before I bought them. Erica, they're awesome." He threw his hands in the air as though he'd scored a touchdown. "You're gonna be a bestselling author."

"Yeah, right."

"Never can tell."

I backed up and crossed my arms. What was he thinking?

"You have to start sometime."

Aha, I knew he was up to something. "I already did. Last week."

His brows shot up. "You did? Let me see what you wrote."

"You doubt me?"

Aaron set his legs apart, put his hands on his hips, and stood straight as a board. He looked like a drill sergeant addressing his troops.

"Let me see it." He nodded toward the computer.

I rocked in place and wiped sweat from my brow.

"Now, Erica."

I sat at the computer and pointed the arrow to *my files*. When the list came up, I pointed to the one marked *Grandpa's Story*.

"See, I started."

He crossed his arms.

"Open it."

I rubbed my chin.

"I said open it."

I left clicked and the file opened.

Aaron peered over my shoulder and read what I'd written. "Chapter one? That's all you wrote?"

"I said I started. I didn't say I wrote anything."

He shook his head.

"I'm gonna call that writing coach and make an appointment for you. She'll get you started. And no argument. Understood?"

"Understood." I didn't dare argue. Would a soldier argue with his drill sergeant when given a command?

Tuesday morning, we left for Monticello. I felt bad for Aaron since he had been up all night. But I'm sure he'd been able to nap periodically during his shift.

Grandpa was sitting on the front porch eagerly awaiting us.

"Did you bring doughnuts?" he asked with a huge smile.

Aaron lifted the Dunkin Donuts box.

Grandpa waved a finger. "You the man, Aaron."

They were like two kids. "Okay, already. Let's go inside."

After coffee, on the screened porch, I turned on the recorder and with pen and pad prepared for another round of my grandfather's life.

Grandpa held up a hand. "Before we begin there's something I have to tell you."

My heart started pounding. Was he going say this was the last time that he'd talk about his life because the stress from remembering was too much? If he did, that would be the end of the book? Oh, I hoped not.

"Both of you listen carefully. You're going to hear more things that I've kept secret." I narrowed my eyes. What did he mean by kept secret? "But if you're going to write about my life in the forties, then you have to hear them. You have my permission to add or delete whatever you think is best." Then he smiled, and my heartbeat returned to normal. "After all, if you're gonna write a bestselling novel, you might as well get it right." He laughed.

Aaron and I joined him, though I have to admit my laugh was a little forced. What was he about to tell us? I pushed away my worries.

"Don't worry, I'll make sure to make you look good no matter what you tell us."

"Good. Now, are you ready?"

"Have at it."

CHAPTER 16

I OFFICIALLY BECAME A TEENAGER WHEN I turned thirteen in April 6, 1943. But being a teenager wasn't the most exciting thing that happened. The Lone Ranger and Tonto appeared in the movies and on the radio. Quaker Oats and Tootsie Rolls were popular. Tootsie Rolls, especially at the movies.

More importantly, we got more letters from Dad and the money he had taken from his paycheck started arriving. With the extra money, Mom splurged, and we had Spam and eggs for breakfast three times a week. Of course, the eggs were from our chicken coop, and the Spam we had left over we ate for lunch or dinner.

After school, some of my classmates and me played war using sticks as rifles and our fingers as pistols. We chose sides and took turns as Gerries or Japs against the GIs. Let me tell you, the Gerries and the Japs went down easy. I was disappointed we never played any naval games. Since Dad was in the navy, I would've liked to play a sailor.

I became friendly with Coleman, even though we had argued in the past. We talked about playing catch at my house. He was supposed to come over Saturday morning. I mowed what little lawn we had with the push mower, picked up the trash, and made sure the yard was spotless. Mom baked cookies for the occasion. Coleman was to arrive at ten-thirty. I waited until noon, but he never showed. I hadn't been that heartbroken since Dad went off to the navy.

Mom did her best to console me. She took me in her arms.

"Maybe he forgot."

I didn't believe for one minute that Coleman had forgotten. I was positive he was just being mean.

I got over Coleman's meanness, and the next week in school I avoided him. I even considered knocking his block off just for good measure. But my parents had taught me to turn the other cheek when someone crossed you. The next time we played dodgeball, I made sure I was on the opposite side as Coleman. I took every advantage to pound him with the ball and when I did, I laughed. The big baby cried when I called him dodgeball head.

I worked hard at taking care of the garden, the chickens, and Dad's truck. I had to make sure the truck was in good working condition in case Mom wanted to take it to work or take us swimming or to the movies.

We stopped going to the movies on Saturday nights because the newsreel about the war bothered Mom. The last time we went that year, we'd seen *The Song of Bernadette*, which was really good. But that night when she thought I was asleep, I heard her crying in her bedroom. I knew the pictures we'd seen in the newsreel had bothered her, so I decided not to ask to go to the movies again. The next Saturday, we went for ice cream and strolled around town.

Mom was always tired when she came home from work, so I made sure dinner was ready. I'd be tired too if I had to walk to work every day like she did. Even though we were no longer going to the movies, I still heard her in her room at night crying. She must have missed Dad. There was nothing I could do for her. Friday nights should have been a blessing for her because she had the entire weekend off, but they weren't.

Violet convinced Mom to go dancing with her again on Saturday night. Mom was hesitant, but I convinced her she needed a night out.

Saturday night, Mom and Violet went dancing. While they were out, I drove the truck around the block several times. I knew

I shouldn't have because we were conserving gas, but I wanted to get more practice in before I got my learner's permit. I'd saved enough money to pay for it myself and planned on surprising Mom when I got it.

I was home way before Mom and listened to Dick Tracy on the radio and read some Red Ryder comic books. I dozed off on the couch but woke up when I heard someone outside talking. I figured it might be Mom and Violet, so I went to the window to check.

Mom and Violet were dancing by Violet's car. They must have had a great night out and didn't want it to end. Violet held my mother in her arms, and they swayed back and forth. What I saw next, I've never told anyone. Definitely not my father. Violet pulled Mom close and kissed her. I expected Mom would walk away like that last time. Instead, she kissed Violet. Then Violet kissed Mom again and then took her by the hand and led Mom into the house.

I went to my bedroom and laid in bed wondering what was happening. I heard Mom come home. She was humming when she came into the house.

I looked at the clock on my desk. Mom had been at Violet's almost two hours. I covered my head with my blanket and pretended to be asleep. Mom looked in on me and then went to her room.

In the morning, I awoke to the smell of Spam and eggs. I joined Mom for breakfast, but I didn't mention what I'd seen. If Mom was happy, then whatever happened last night was none of my business.

A month later after school, I went to the courthouse and got my learner's permit. That night, I showed it to Mom.

"Francis, how did you get that? You're not old enough."

I thrust my chest out and grinned. "I'm thirteen and went and got it myself. Now I can drive the truck when you're with me, and we don't have to worry about a policeman. I can drive when we go to Lloyd to swim, and I can take you shopping."

"You're thirteen already?" She placed her hands on her cheeks. "Has it been that long since your father..." Her eyes filled with tears.

"Don't cry, Mom. The war will be over soon, and he'll be home." I wrapped my arms around her and let her cry on my shoulder.

When she finished, Mom wiped her cheeks and touched her palm to my face.

"You've grown so much. Your father would be proud of you." Then she smiled. "You really are the man of the house."

We received another letter from Dad. It was just a paragraph, but he packed a lot into that paragraph. I could tell because after reading it, Mom held it against her heart and smiled. Dad always included a line that asked about me and that I must be all grown up.

Mom wanted to write Dad a letter, but she didn't know where to send it. She asked the mail carrier, but he wasn't sure either. He suggested she write a paragraph or two, put the letter in an envelope, and address it to Dad care of *FPO New York, N.Y,* same as Dad's return address. The mail carrier said he would send it to the war department—maybe they could get it to him—but he couldn't promise and hoped for the best.

Mom wrote the letter and added two lines from me. *I miss you Dad. Hurry home.* Next time the mail carrier came, I gave it to him.

On the last day of school, I stopped by Miss Lucy's classroom to say goodbye. She was sitting on the edge of her desk with her face buried in her hands. She may have been exhausted from a difficult day or maybe she was preventing herself from fainting because she had low blood sugar. I quietly approached and heard what sounded like a kitten when it lost its mother. A kitten I could deal with, but she wasn't a kitten. She was Miss Lucy. On the floor by her feet was a telegram. I picked it up.

"Are you okay, Miss Lucy?" I asked. "You dropped this." I held the telegraph out to her.

She looked up, startled, and wiped her eyes with her hands. Her eyes were red and the shadow she used on them was dripping down her cheeks. Miss Lucy always kept a box of Kleenex on her desk, so I grabbed one and offered it to her.

"Thank you, Francis." She took the telegram from me. "My fiancé is missing in action." She reached for another tissue and wiped more tears.

I wasn't sure what missing in action meant, but I suspected it wasn't good. "I'm sure they'll find him." Then without thinking, I put my hand on her shoulder. I'd never touched a woman except for Mom and Violet. Miss Lucy's shoulder felt like a marshmallow.

It may not have been proper to do that, but I considered Miss Lucy as my best friend, and I wanted to let her know that I was there for her.

She put her hand on mine. It was warm to the touch, just like my mother's. It gave me goosebumps all over. She looked at me with a smile like my Mom's, a smile that could melt ice on a cold day.

"Thank you. Francis. Let's hope so."

I wanted to take her in my arms like I did my mother but decided I best not in case another teacher saw us.

"I gotta go home now. Will you be okay?"

She smiled. "Yes. You have a nice summer."

"You, too." I left the classroom with a tear in my eye.

As I walked home, I had a strange feeling that someone was following me. I'd stop, turn around, and look behind me, but there was no one. I repeated it several times—with the same result. Using my super powers, I whirled on my heels and low and behold there was a small dog following me. I had no clue as to what kind it was. Best I could say, it was a small mutt and covered with dirt.

I expected it would run off, but instead the dog sat and whimpered. I carefully approached it, bent over and touched the top of its head.

"Are you lost, little dog?"

It whimpered and offered me its paw.

"Where's your home?" Of course, it didn't answer me. I didn't have to be a dog owner to know it wouldn't. "I have to go home now, so you go on home, too. Shoo." The dog sat, looked up at me and whined. "Dang, dog, I can't take you with me. Mom won't let me have a dog."

It wagged its tail.

"Okay, but Mom's probably not gonna let you stay." We started walking home, but soon I heard a mewling cry and turned around. "What's the matter?" The dog laid down on the ground and looked up at me. "You can't walk anymore? Is that it?" It barked. "Okay, I'll carry you." I picked it up and carried it home.

When we got there, I filled a dish with water and let the dog drink from it. There was some leftover Spam in the ice box, so I gave some of it to the dog. It must have been hungry the meat disappeared in a heartbeat.

"Okay, like it or not, you need a bath." The dog cocked its head like it was trying to
figure out what I'd said.

I filled the sink with water, picked up the dog, put it in the water, and used a bar of soap to bathe it. When I finished, I grabbed the dish towel, dried it off, and set the dog on the floor. The dirt was gone, and its golden hair was much cleaner now. It shook itself dry and looked up at me with sad eyes. It made my heart ache. I hoped Mom would let me keep it.

"Now look what you did. You got the floor wet and me, too." It scampered off and hid in a corner.

"I wasn't yelling at you. It's not your fault. I can clean it up before Mom gets home." The dog watched as I wiped the floor, my shoes, and pants with the towel. The dog crawled over to me and whimpered. I petted its head. "You're not in trouble." Then I picked it up and let it lick my face. "Now I have to figure out how I'm going to tell Mom."

When Mom came home, I hid the dog in my bedroom on my bed. I'd already fixed dinner for us. She put her things in her bedroom, removed her shoes and sat down for dinner. "What's that dog doing there?" I hadn't noticed the dog until Mom pointed to it. "Well, Francis, do you have an explanation?"

I scratched the back of my head like Dad when he wasn't sure he had an explanation for something. "It followed me home. I couldn't get rid of it, and it was starving."

"What are we supposed to do with it?"

"Can we keep it? Please, Mom? I'll take care of it. I promise." The dog walked over to Mom, sat, and looked up at her. "Please, Mom."

Mom looked down at the dog. "How will we feed it? We barely have enough for ourselves."

"I'll share my meals with it. Look at it, it's so tiny. It won't eat much. Please, Mom."

Mom shook her head. "Okay, but it's your responsibility. What's its name?"

Dang, I hadn't thought about a name. I scratched my head again. "How about Skippy?"

Mom smiled. "Skippy, it is." Mom leaned over and picked up Skippy. "Let's see if it's a male or female." She lifted the dog and looked at its underside. "It's a male."

A stream of urine was the dog's only answer.

"Oh, my goodness!"

I grabbed the dog. "I'm sorry, Mom."

Mom giggled. "It's okay. You did the same thing when you were his age. I'll go change my top and then we can have dinner."

Fortunately, Skippy hadn't peed on Mom's dinner. I got up from the table and hugged her. "Thanks, Mom. You're the best mom in the whole wide world."

"You better not make me regret this."

When Mom came back to eat, Skippy cuddled up on her feet and Mom was smitten.

CHAPTER 17

I WAS AMAZED AT HOW MUCH Grandpa had remembered, especially the part about the dog. It made me wonder why my grandparents hadn't had a dog when I lived with them. I would have loved a dog when I was a teenager. I thought about asking Aaron if we should get one. But that would be a huge commitment, like becoming a parent, and we weren't ready to go that route yet. For now, I'd concentrate on Grandpa's story.

"Listen, all this reminiscing is wearing on me." Grandpa rubbed his chest. "You think we could stop for today?"

"Sure. We can do it again tomorrow."

"How about another day? A lot happened in 1943, and I need time to get my facts together. I want the book to be as accurate as possible."

So did I. "Okay, Aaron and I will check our schedules and then I'll call you."

It was best that we stopped for the day and wait a week. I was concerned for Grandpa's health. And if reminiscing was beginning to wear on him, I didn't want it to become a problem.

The first thing Aaron said once we were in the car was, "Boy that Violet sure was a wild one."

"She sure was," I said.

"Do you think there was anything between Violet and your?"

I glared at him. "Don't even go there."

I knew what he was thinking. I was, too, and I was curious. I thought about talking to Mom about it.

"You know something, Erica? Listening to you grandfather makes me think that millennials like us have no reason to complain. Think about it; we have all the comforts of home, unlike your grandparents."

"What's your point?"

"The forties were hard times, and folks had to make sacrifices. Your great-grandmother had to provide for your grandfather while her husband was off fighting. And your grandfather had to make do without a father. I'm just saying they made a lot of sacrifices." He rubbed his hand on the back of his neck.

"It gives new meaning to the term 'The Greatest Generation.' It wasn't just about those off fighting, it was also about those left behind." Next, he pointed at me. "Think about it. Would you get up every morning, greet the milkman, feed the chickens, make your breakfast, get yourself off to school, and make lunch and dinner?" Then he smirked and added. "Would you ring a chicken's neck, butcher it, cook it, and eat it for dinner?"

"Yuck, no way I would."

"That's what I'm talking about."

I waved my hand at him. "You're right."

"You're damn right I am. And the next time any of our friends start complaining, we'll lay into them. Also, no matter what the implications about your great-grandmother and Violet, your great-grandmother was one hell of a woman."

Mom called me the next day to tell me about Grandpa's cleaning lady.

"Erica, she's reasonable. Only sixty dollars a visit and comes every other week. I had Annamarie go there to help get her set up and to make sure your grandfather was a good boy."

"That sounds great. How did it go?"

"Without a hitch. Annamarie was there. She'll go again the next time to be sure he's not a pain in the ass. You know he can be. When are you visiting him again?"

"Not until next week."

I decided I'd best ask what she thought of Grandpa's comments today. I felt sure that she would tell me not to put everything he said in it and just tell him that I would.

"Mom, Grandpa told us somethings that I'm not sure I should write about."

"You did promise your grandfather that you'd write the story as he told you. Are you questioning that now?"

"Something like that."

"Okay, let's try this. Did your grandfather kill someone?"

"If you call strangling and butchering a chicken killing someone, then yes."

"Oh, I did that, too. Your grandfather taught me how when your father and I were first married. Anything else?"

This next one was more difficult. "It's not about Grandpa, but about Great-grandma."

"Did she have an affair?"

How do I put it delicately? "Sort of."

"What does that mean?"

"It's just things Grandpa implied."

"Okay, I'll make it easy for you. If my grandmother had an affair, I don't blame her."

I gasped.

"Her husband had gone to war leaving her alone with a boy to take care of and to manage on her own. Trust me—it's not easy being alone. I had to do it myself."

I had forgotten that my mother did—which was how we ended up living with my grandparents after Dad died. Mom eventually bought a two-bedroom bungalow and got a job as a secretary at the local bank. I chose to continue living with my grandparents. But did she have an affair? If she did, I never knew, and I don't care.

I hadn't considered the similarities between what Mom and my great-grandmother went through.

"If my grandmother sought comfort in someone's arms, I don't blame her."

The vehemence in Mom's words shocked me.

"And if my father doesn't blame her, then you write what he told you. If you don't, he'll be disappointed. You can always take that part out of your book after he's dead. But trust me, it will weigh on your conscience. It's your decision."

I hadn't expected her to say that, but she was right—it's my decision. And since Grandpa said whatever happened that night was none of his business. I decided it was none of mine.

"Life wasn't meant to be easy, Erica. As you're thinking, think about your grandfather's request and what he wants."

"I will. Thanks, Mom."

The weather was gorgeous Saturday morning, so Aaron and I drove downtown to the Downtown Market. We found a space on Park Avenue and then strolled among the tents beginning at Monroe Street.

Aaron pointed to a tent with displays of books. "Let's visit that one." He grabbed my hand and led me there.

"All books by local authors," called out an older gentleman. "Bet we have something you like to read." He waved us over. "Come in and browse."

Inside the tent were two women. They sat behind tables with books on them. Above and behind them was a writer's association banner.

"You like mysteries?" the man asked.

"Maybe," I replied.

"She's writing a book," said Aaron.

"She is? What's it about?" the man asked.

"My grandfather growing up in the forties."

The man nodded. "How old is he?"

"In his late eighties," I replied.

"How's it going?"

"She hasn't started writing it yet," Aaron said. "She's still doing research."

"Will he read it when it's done?"

"I hope so," I said.

"You might want to start writing before it's too late," said one of the women. "I waited too long and now I can't write my grandmother's story. You may want to think about it."

I detected a note of sadness.

I knew what she meant. I didn't want to think about it. I didn't want to think about Grandpa dying. Why did we come to this damn park anyway?

"I will, thank you."

CHAPTER 18

ITHOUGHT ABOUT WHAT THAT WOMAN said, and I didn't want to be like her. I didn't want to wait too long and have something happen to Grandpa and not be able to write his story. He had been showing signs of deteriorating health lately, and I was concerned that something might happen.

I met with the writing coach Aaron hired for me. She was an attractive forty-year-old brunette named Harriet. She'd written four novels and two children's books. She was cheerful, friendly, and easygoing. I warmed to her instantly. I told her about Aaron's outline, the CD of my recordings, and my notes.

Harriet suggested I find time by myself, sit at the computer with headphones on, and listen to the CD. Don't worry about grammar or structure, and adlib if I felt like it. She suggested I use Aaron's outline as a chapter guide and refer to my notes if I felt the need. After writing five pages, I was to send them to her, and she'd critique them, offer suggestions, and send them back to me. I could use her suggestions however I wanted. We'd meet periodically to discuss her critiques, suggestions, and my progress. It wasn't typically how she worked with other authors, but she was doing it as a favor to Aaron.

She explained that four years ago she was getting ready to leave for an appointment with her pediatrician. Just as she was about to walk out the door, she slipped and fell. The fall prematurely caused her water to break, and she went into labor. Her husband was out of town. She panicked and called 911. Aaron was the first responder on the scene. There wasn't time to rush her to the hospital as Harriet was about to give birth. Having done it before, Aaron calmly delivered the baby. At the hospital, Harriet thanked him for saving the life of her daughter.

So, not only did I have Aaron pressuring me to write Grandpa's story, but now I had the pressure of completing it as a favor to Aaron for what he did for Harriet and what she was doing for me.

I called Grandpa to tell him we would be there Thursday morning.

"Erica, you're not going to believe this." Grandpa sounded elated. "But I went through the memory box and found some more pictures. I've got a lot to tell you and can't wait until you get here."

"That's great, Grandpa. "How's the new cleaning lady doing?"

Grandpa huffed. "Oh, her. She's okay. Annamarie comes by after she leaves and checks to see if she did a good job. So far, no complaints, and Annamarie's not easy to please."

I had to laugh to myself. "You're not easy to please either."

"What do you mean? I'm the easiest person to please."

I shook my head. "Yeah right, Grandpa."

Annamarie was sweeping her porch when we drove past her house Thursday morning. She waved to us as I turned into Grandpa's driveway. Grandpa was waiting on the porch.

"Morning, Grandpa. You could have waited inside."

"I wasn't waiting. I just returned from my walk with Annamarie."

"She waved to us."

"Did you bring the doughnuts?"

"Got them right here, Mr. Teague." Aaron said and held the box up.

"Good, I get first dibs."

"Wait until we get in the house," I said. "Then you can have whatever doughnut you want. Is there fresh coffee?"

"Who do you think I am? A scallywag?"

Aaron and I laughed. We followed Grandpa into the house. Aaron set the doughnuts on the table on the porch. I went into the kitchen to pour us all a cup of coffee. They didn't bother to wait for napkins or paper plates. Like two kids turned loose in a candy store, they each had one gone when I returned.

"What?" I shouted. "Couldn't you have at least waited for me?"

Grandpa shook his head.

Aaron wiped powdered sugar from his mouth with his sleeve. "It's his fault."

"Hey, that's not fair, you scallywag," said Grandpa.

"Why I oughta make you two scallywags walk the plank," I said. We all laughed.

After coffee and doughnuts, I asked Grandpa what had him excited when I called the day before. He picked up the memory box and was about to set it on the table when I stopped him.

I cleared the table, put the plates in the garbage, the cups in the sink, and returned.

Grandpa put the box on the table and took out several pictures. "These are from 1943. Thanks to these pictures, I remembered more of what happened. You ready to take notes?"

" I took out a pad, pen and turned on my recorder. "Whenever you are."

CHAPTER 19

I T WASN'T EASY OWNING A DOG, especially as young as Skippy. It took some time to train him to go outdoors and do his business. But with patience, we succeeded. When Skippy had to go out, he'd sit by the kitchen door and look at it. Sometimes he'd bark to let me know he wanted out. Once Skippy was trained, I let him sleep in bed with me.

One night, I rolled over and Skippy was gone. Thinking he wanted to go out, I got out of bed and went into the kitchen. Skippy wasn't there. My first thought was that he had gone into Mom's room, so I peeked in her room. He was on Mom's bed snuggled against her. Skippy had a mom like me.

Mom started working extra days for the Widow Atkinson baking sweet goods, setting the table, and serving tea to the ladies at her afternoon tea party. Occasionally on a Saturday, Mom did a lunch brunch for some of the Widow Atkinson's friends. Mom brought some of the leftovers home for our dinner and something for Skippy.

Having the responsibility of both my chores and taking care of Skippy was more than I anticipated. Skippy had to be trained not to bark when the milkman and ice man came. And when I fed the chickens, I had to be sure he couldn't get in the coop. He was allowed to get close to the chicken wire, but the rooster chased him away. Skippy decided it was best if he sat and watched from a distance. And, of course, I had to walk him, feed him, and clean up after him. I realized quickly what it was like to be a father and vowed to be a better son when Dad came home.

Skippy soon became an alert dog. When the chickens started cackling, he barked. It meant there was a critter in the yard. I'd get up, grab Dad's bat, go outside with Skippy, and throw rocks at the critter while Skippy kept barking. Fortunately, the neighbors didn't complain as they had the same problem.

We received another letter from Dad in July, but he didn't mention getting Mom's letter. I saw the disappointment in her eyes. Skippy did, too, and offered a paw as his way of consoling her.

Mom said we had to be more frugal with our money. Even though we had the money that Dad had left us, if we didn't be careful we'd run short of money. She started putting money in envelopes and marked each with its purpose. Like gas money, food, household goods, and fun money. That last one was also labeled, 'spend wisely.'

Mom and me occasionally drove into town to shop and get ice cream. Skippy sat in the front seat when we went for ice cream but not when we went shopping. It was too hot to leave him in the truck, and he wasn't allowed in Harris' Grocery Store. We were in and out for ice cream and ate on the drive home. I let Skippy lick my cone.

During the day while Mom was working, Skippy and me went exploring. He'd walk alongside my bike. When he tired, I'd scoop him up and put him in the basket. Skippy sat like he was the leader of the parade only he didn't wave at people. On one of our explorations, we came upon a green belt with a path that snaked through the thick undergrowth and wide enough for a car or truck. We decided to come back another time, maybe at night with a flashlight and investigate.

As the hot summer months went on, I noticed that Mom was acting lonely again. Maybe it was Dad's last letter or just that she missed him so much. Violet had been asking Mom to go dancing with her, but Mom declined. She said Violet drank too much and was too friendly with the men. I couldn't take Mom dancing, and the movies were out because of the Newsreel. I had to come up with something other than taking rides with Skippy and me.

Wednesday after dinner, I made a suggestion.

"Mom, why don't you go dancing with Violet?"

"I told you, Francis, she drinks too much, and I worry about the drive home."

"So, you drive. That way you can leave when you want and if Violet insists otherwise, tell her you won't go. You need a night out without Skippy and me. Have some fun."

Even though I had suggested she go out with Violet, I wasn't sure it was the best idea, but Mom needed to have some fun.

Mom brushed her hand through her hair. "You won't mind if I do?"

"No, I won't." Skippy barked. "See, even Skippy agrees."

Mom smiled. "Okay, I will, but if Violet wants to drive, then I'm staying home. I'll go ask her."

Mom left the house and walked over to Violet's. She was there for a while and then returned with a smile on her face.

"Violet agreed to let me drive. We're going dancing Saturday night."

The rest of the week, Mom was more cheerful. Friday night Mom, Skippy and me went for ice cream.

Saturday morning, I decided to ask Mr. Coogins if there was any chance of me getting some work. I'd work for almost nothing just to contribute to our money situation. Skippy and me rode into town and to the Chevrolet store. When I pulled up with Skippy in the basket, Mr. Coogins had just walked out the door.

"Got a minute, Mr. Coogins?"

He scratched the back of his neck. "You're the Teague boy? Name's Francis, right?"

"Yes, sir."

"You've grown some."

"I have, sir, I'm all of five-feet-four, and I'm thirteen now."

Mr. Coogins grinned. "Good for you." He squeezed my arm. "But you could use some meat on those bones. That your dog?"

I stroked Skippy's neck. "Yes, sir, his name's Skippy. He followed me home one day, and now he's part of the family. Mr. Coogins, I was wondering if things might have changed and you could use me part time. I won't ask for much. Just a dollar or so. Mom and me need the extra money."

"Is your mother still working for Mrs. Atkinson?"

"Yes, sir, she is. But it's not enough. I want to help her. Is there anything you can do?"

Mr. Coogins rubbed his forehead. "Maybe. Business has improved, but if I hire you I can only pay you ten cents an hour and only three days a week for four hours. That's a dollar and twenty cents. I'll make it an even one-fifty. You want it; it's yours."

I almost burst into tears. "I'll take it. When do I start?" One-fifty a week wasn't much, but I was contributing. I suspected Mr. Coogins gave me the work because he was worried Mom might tell Dad what he did when she went to see about working for Mrs. Atkinson. Or maybe he wanted to help Mom and me out of kindness.

He looked at Skippy. "If the dog can keep out of the way, you can start today."

Skippy barked. "He'll find a corner and curl up in it while I do my work. He won't be a bother. But I'll leave him home next time. What days should I be here?"

Mr. Coogins scratched his chin. "How about Tuesday, Thursday, and Saturday mornings?"

"Okay, thanks, Mr. Coogins."

"You're welcome." He rubbed his chin. "Have you heard from your dad?"

"Yes, sir, we've gotten a few letters, but they're mostly for Mom. She misses him a lot."

"I'm sure she does. Grab a broom and start sweeping. And make sure all the tools are properly put away. You know anything about working on a vehicle?"

I knew about maintaining Dad's truck because he taught me, and I taught Mom.

"I can change the oil, check the spark plugs and the battery."

"Good. If the mechanic needs your help, he'll tell you what to do. He's okay but not as good as your dad. I'll sure be glad when he gets home."

"Me, too, Mr. Coogins."

I pushed my bike behind the garage, lifted Skippy out of the basket, and sent him to find a corner. Then I introduced myself to the mechanic, grabbed a broom, and started sweeping. The mechanic's name was Josh, and he let me help him with the maintenance. But my job was mostly to sweep the floors.

When my four hours were up, I called Skippy and then thanked Mr. Coogins.

He reached into his pocket and handed me two quarters. "That's for today. You did good. I'll pay you every Saturday after you're done. Is that fair enough?"

"Yes, sir, thank you. I'll see you Tuesday." I paused. "What time?"

He smiled. "Eight-thirty."

I put Skippy in the basket and rode home. Mom was sitting on the porch.

"Francis, where have you been? I was worried about you."

I lifted Skippy out of the basket and set my bike against the house.

"I got a job, Mom. Three mornings during the week for Mr. Coogins. I make a dollar and fifty cents. Ain't that something?"

Mom placed her hands on her cheeks.

"You got a job making a dollar and fifty cents?" She touched my cheek. "That's wonderful, but you didn't have to."

"I know, but I wanted to help with our finances. Dad would want me to."

Mom shook her head. "Let me give you a huge hug." She wrapped her arms around me and almost squeezed the daylights out of me. "Thank you, Francis, but you put that money in your nickel can."

"I will, Mom."

I didn't want to mention that Mr. Coogins said I could use some meat on my bones because I knew Mom would feel guilty that we weren't eating enough.

"Mom, any chance you could start making pancakes for breakfast?"

"Pancakes? I guess I could. I didn't think you'd eat them with all the cookies and cakes I make. I could make pancakes but not every morning. I'll make pancakes, eggs, and spam on Sunday mornings. And again, twice a week. If you'd like, we can start having macaroni and cheese more often."

I smiled. "Thanks, Mom, you're the best."

Although I said I'd put the money in my nickel can, I put it in Mom's cookie jar.

Saturday evening, Mom walked over to Violet's house. I watched from my bedroom window to be certain Mom was driving and not Violet. Mom backed out of the driveway, and they left.

Since Skippy and I would be alone for several hours, I took him for a ride on my bike. We rode into town, and I used a nickel from my nickel can to buy an ice cream cone. I found a place to sit. Skippy, and I shared the cone. When the cone was gone, we rode back home and sat on the porch watching fireflies. Later, we went inside and listened to the radio before going to bed.

I was concerned for Mom and couldn't fall asleep, so I read a book and watched for the headlights from Violet's car. My eyelids were getting heavy, and I was about to fall asleep when I saw the beam from the headlights on the wall.

Mom and Violet got out of the car. Mom walked around to the passenger side, put her arm around Violet, and helped her into the house. Knowing that Mom was safely home, I fell asleep.

Sunday morning, Mom was up before me and I caught the scent from the kitchen of spam frying. I got out of bed, dressed, and went to the kitchen. Skippy was on the floor and Mom was cooking. I expected to see her bright and cheery after her night out dancing, but she wasn't. At least, she didn't seem lonely.

"Mom, you made pancakes."

"Good morning, Francis. I said I would, and fried spam and eggs. I gathered some from the coop." Mom grinned. "Sit, and I'll fix you a plate. Skippy already had his breakfast.

Skippy barked.

"Thanks, Mom. How was your night out?"

"It was okay. But never again. We went to the jook joint. Violet drank too much and flirted with a lot of men. I told her I didn't like it and wouldn't go with her anymore. She wasn't happy."

I'm sure she wasn't, but I wasn't about to say that to Mom.

"At least you had a night out," I said.

"I guess so." Mom looked at the wall clock. "It's too late for church. Why don't we go swimming? We can take Skippy."

Skippy stood, barked, and wagged his tail.

"I'd like that." I looked at Skippy. "He acts like he knows what swimming means."

"Maybe he thinks it's like taking a bath."

We climbed into Dad's truck. Skippy sat between us and we left for Lloyd Creek.

As soon as Skippy was out of the truck, he took off for the water and leaped in. He paddled out a short distance, turned around to make sure we were watching, and then paddled back to shore. He was a natural born swimmer. Mom and me waded into the water and splashed each other. Mom was enjoying herself. I figured she'd forgotten about Violet and her own loneliness.

Skippy paddled between us, and we swam a little. We were in the water for hours before we decided it was time to go home. I splashed Mom once more for good measure; she splashed me back, then we got out of the water. As we dried off, Skippy shook himself and sprayed us. We laughed then piled into the truck and went home. The rest of the day Mom was more cheerful.

Tuesday morning, I was up real early to let Skippy out and do my chores. I ate a bowl of cereal, and then I was off to the Chevrolet store. Mr. Coogins smiled when he saw me arrive at eight-fifteen. Each morning, I was at work the same time. On Saturday, Mr. Coogins paid me a dollar and fifty cents.

"Make sure this money gets spent wisely. You hear me?"

"Yes, sir, Mr. Coogins, it will." He nodded, and I left for home. Skippy was waiting for me. Mom was, too.

"Francis, you're home. How was work?" Mom said as though she was talking to Dad.

"I got my first week's pay. Well, three day's pay. A dollar and fifty cents."

Mom smiled. "That's good. Now you put that money in your nickel can."

I planted my feet and stood firm. "No, Mom, it goes in your jar or one of those envelopes. I'm earning money to help with our finances." I reached out and handed her the money. "You take it."

Mom hesitated, but she could tell by my expression that I wasn't going to back down. "Okay, if you insist." Then she took the money and wrapped her arms around me.

"You're as stubborn as your father when it comes to money."

"He'd want me to be. But, Mom, can you let me breathe?"

"Sorry." Then she gave me a quarter. "You keep that. I insist."

Suddenly Mom had a tear in her eye and went to her bedroom. I figured she was missing Dad. Skippy and me went for a bike ride so Mom could have time alone.

As the summer wore on, Violet continued going dancing on Saturday nights but not by herself. Mom watched from the window as a car would pull up in front of her house and honk its horn. Violet would get into the car, and it would drive off. There was a different car each Saturday night. Mom would stay up and watch at the window until Violet came home then she'd go to bed.

CHAPTER 20

ONE SATURDAY, MOM LOOKED OUT the window and watched as Violet got in a car with someone, and they drove away from her house. She shook her head and then sat in the living room listening to the radio and humming to herself. I guessed she was both worried about Violet and missing Dad. Believing she wanted to be alone, I grabbed a flashlight, snuck out of the house with Skippy and went for a bike ride. We were going to explore that path we'd seen last month.

When we got there, I stopped and lifted Skippy from the basket. Skippy had grown some and was starting to get too heavy for the basket.

"You have to walk the rest of the way, boy. It's too dark for me to ride. I'm gonna push the bike. Don't want to take a chance riding on the path."

Skippy started down the path, and I pushed the bike behind. We maneuvered our way through the thick underbrush, stopping every so often to shine the flashlight and make sure there were no alligators lurking. The path was covered with leaves, broken branches, and ruts. It was wide enough for a car or truck, and I saw tire tracks. We followed the tracks and eventually the path opened to a clearing. The only sounds were my heart pounding, Skippy's tail wagging, the crunch of damp leaves under my feet, and the crackled cicada song.

I glanced around to make sure there wasn't a ten-foot bear waiting to swallow Skippy and me. There was hardly any light since the moon was shielded by tree branches. Skippy walked to the back of the clearing, stood on two feet and stared out at a stream of trickling water big enough to fish in. We could barely see a few dragonflies resting on the water. I swatted several mosquitos, but not before they bit me. Despite the mosquitos, it seemed like a good spot to come back sometime with a fishing pole and try my luck.

"Hey, what you doing in my spot?" someone shouted.

I almost peed my pants. I let go of the bike and turned around. All I could see were two eyes in the darkness. Maybe it was a ten-foot bear. If it was, it wasn't standing, but on all fours based on the height of the eyes off the ground. Maybe it was about to charge me and eat me for dinner.

Skippy inched closer and barked.

"Who's there," I called.

Skippy barked again, so I shined the flashlight—my only weapon—in the direction of the voice. Whatever it was, I was going to throw the flashlight at it and run like hell, hoping Skippy would be right behind me.

"Turn that light off. Are you daffy? Someone will know we're here. And stop that dog from barking. I mean know harm."

I shined the flashlight right at those eyes again. It wasn't a ten-foot bear, it was a colored boy.

"You scared the shit out of me," I said. "He's protecting me."

"I ain't gonna harm you," the boy said. "Who are you anyway?"

"Me and Skippy was exploring that's all. What's your name?"

"I asked first," the boy replied.

Skippy barked again. I figured the boy didn't mean me no harm, so I answered. "Name's Francis. What's yours?"

"Jackie," he replied and cackled. "Ain't Francis a girl's name?"

"So's Jackie. You want to make something of it?" I raised my fists ready to fight him like I would have Coleman.

"Nah, just foolin. I get the same thing from folks about my name. How old are you?"

"Thirteen, you?"

"Thirteen, too," Jackie said. "You go to school?"

"Yeah, you?"

"I go to the Academy. You got any brothers or sisters? I got three sisters and an older brother. He's in the army."

"It's just my Mom and me. My Dad's in the navy on a battleship." I glanced at his trousers.

"You own a pocket knife?" I said.

"Yeah, you?"

"Let's see it." I said.

"Show me yours first."

I reached into my pants pocket, took out my knife, and showed it to him.

"You call that little thing a pocket knife?" Jackie said.

"Let's see yours."

Jackie squatted and pulled his knife out of his sock and showed it to me.

"How come you don't keep it in your pocket?"

"My Momma cut the pockets off. She said if I don't have pockets, I can't be accused of stealing anything. White boys ain't got that problem."

"Your knife ain't much bigger than mine. I bet you can't cut a watermelon with it."

Jackie grinned. "Who needs a knife to cut a watermelon? I just smash it on the ground and eat what's worth eating."

We both laughed. "How come you're here?"

"I come to..." Jackie turned toward the rustling sound of something on the path. "Get down or they'll see us."

I squatted down. "Who'll see us?"

"Shh... Hear that car coming?"

I saw lights before I heard the car. We both squatted, and I made Skippy lie down.

"Won't they see us?"

"Just wait. They'll turn the headlights off. They always do."

Just then the lights went off. The driver drove into the clearing, made a U-turn, and then parked. "When it's the high school kids, they do the same thing. Now watch."

The driver put his arm around the woman passenger, pulled her to him, and they started kissing. We watched as they seemed to wrestle with each other causing the vehicle to shake.

"You want to peek?" asked Jackie.

"What if they see us?

"We run like hell and don't look back. That's what we do."

I was sure Skippy and me could get away. "What about my bike?"

"The bike? Forget about it. They won't see it anyway. You want to peek or not?"

I could always come back tomorrow for the bike. "Okay."

The three of started toward the car, taking slow steps so as not to make any noise.

We were almost to the running board when suddenly the woman stopped and slapped the man.

We froze and ducked down

Then she got out of the car and started to walk away.

Jackie nudged me to back away.

"Don't look good," he whispered.

We backed farther away. The woman stopped as though she heard something. We got down on our bellies and watched. Skippy got down beside me. The man got out of the car. Jackie and me covered our mouths.

The woman continued walking. When she was just past the car, the man caught up to her and grabbed her arm. She spun around and slapped him.

Then he slapped her. She stumbled backward but didn't fall.

Jackie and me covered our mouths.

The woman reached into her purse, pulled out a gun, and pointed it at him. Then bam! She shot him. He stumbled backward against the car and fell to the ground. The woman put the gun in her purse, turned and started toward the path. Skippy growled. I grabbed his mouth to silence him. She stopped, turned, listened, looked around, and then ran off toward the path and disappeared in the dark. We crept across the clearing to check on the man.

"Think he's dead?" I asked.

"He looks dead. What should we do?"

"Maybe we should go get help I can ride my bike into town and get the policeman."

"You daffy?" Jackie said. "You gonna tell the policeman that you and a colored boy was watching two white people kissing in their car?" Jackie waved his hands. "You know what they'll do to me? They'll string me to a tree. Ain't no way in hell that's gonna happen."

"I could say I was alone, and not tell them about you."

"No way. You ain't leaving me here with a body."

Jackie was right. I couldn't do that either. "So, what do we do?"

Jackie rubbed the back of his head. "Shine your flashlight on him. See if he's bleeding."

I shined my flashlight on him. We didn't see any blood.

"Now what?" I said.

"How about you kick him on his foot to see if he's alive?"

"Kick a body? Are you serious?" On the other hand, I had no other solution. I kicked his foot while Skippy licked his face. "Hey, mister, are you dead?"

"Kick him again," Jackie said.

I kicked his foot again, and Skippy kept licking his face. "Mister, are you dead?"

He opened his eyes. "Get that damn dog off of me." He pushed Skippy away. "Is she gone?"

"Yeah," I replied. "She shot you. You're not gonna die, are you?"

He felt his stomach. "Nah, I've been shot by worse. That little pistol of hers couldn't hurt an ant. I probably got a flesh wound. But my head aches. I must have hit it when I fell. How long have I been out?"

"Not too long," answered Jackie. "What do you want us to do?"

"Help me up."

Jackie looked at me, and I looked at him. He nodded for me to go first and I nodded for him to go first.

"Just help me up before I pass out again," the man yelled.

We each grabbed an arm and pulled him up to his feet. Then we walked him to his car. I opened the door. The smell of the woman's perfume wafted out. He got in the car behind the steering wheel.

"Listen, boys, don't tell anyone what you saw tonight. I don't want trouble." He reached into his billfold and gave us each a dollar. "Can I trust you?" We nodded our heads. He started the car, drove down the path, and disappeared.

"What now, Jackie?"

"You heard him. As far as we're concerned nothing happened." Jackie looked at his dollar. "We each got a dollar, and we wasn't here. Can I trust you to keep his secret?"

"Yeah, let's go home."

I put my dollar in my pocket. Jackie reached down and put his in his sock.

I grabbed my bike, and we walked down the path. When we reached the road, we looked both ways to be sure there were no cars and no people. Then Jackie went his way, and me and Skippy went ours.

At home, I got Skippy out of the basket and then put my bike against the house. I looked in the kitchen window and saw two figures inside. Uh-oh. What if Mom checked my bedroom, saw I wasn't there, and panicked. What if she thought Skippy and me were kidnapped. Maybe she called the police. If she did, someone on the party line would have spread the word and there'd be dozens of cars on the street. She could have gone to one of the neighbors and asked for help. But she would have seen my bike was missing and figured I was out for a ride with Skippy.

Whatever happened, I decided to face the music and go inside. I opened the door and walked into the kitchen. Mom was hugging Violet. When she saw me, she dropped her arms.

"Francis, where have you been?"

Skippy sat down beside me.

"I took Skippy for a bike ride. You were sleeping, and I couldn't fall asleep."

Violet grabbed a tissue from the counter and wiped her eyes.

I looked from Violet to Mom. Mom wasn't yelling at me, which was the first clue something was wrong. And Violet was crying.

"What happened?"

Mom said, "You and Skippy go to bed. I have to talk to Violet."

Things weren't okay, but Mom's tone left no room for argument. Me and Skippy went to my bedroom and climbed into bed. Mom came and closed my bedroom door so I couldn't hear what she and Violet were talking about. Eventually, I fell asleep.

In the morning, Mom made a big Sunday breakfast. I didn't ask about what Violet and she talked about. I didn't want to have to tell her what I'd been up to the night before.

I finished my eggs and pancakes and pushed back from the table. "I'm gonna let Skippy out and check on the chickens. I'll be right back."

"I already checked the chickens, and they're fine. Let Skippy out, and then I want to ask you something."

Dang, was she gonna ask about last night? I'd better come up with something while I was outside with Skippy. I waited until Skippy did his business, cleaned up after him, and went back inside.

"Before you ask, I—"

"It's about Violet," Mom said. "Do you mind if we take her to Lloyd Creek with us to go swimming? She misses her husband and could use some fun."

Yippee ki-yay. I wasn't gonna get questioned, but I was gonna get to go swimming. No argument from me. "No problem, but we can't all four fit in Dad's truck."

Mom touched my cheek with her hand. "Thank you, Francis. If she says yes, I'll ask if we can take her car." Mom left to go to Violet's house.

"I thought we were gonna have to lie, Skippy. But I wonder what Violet was crying about last night." Skippy wagged his tail. I guess he wondered, too.

It took a while for Mom to return but when she did, she said Violet agreed to go swimming with us and we could take her car.

That afternoon, we all piled into Violet's car, and my mother drove to Lloyd. Skippy ran to the water and dove in it. Mom and Violet waded into the water and started splashing each other. I joined in the splashing and smiled as I watched Mom and Violet laughing and having fun. None of us was worried about anything except enjoying ourselves. After a couple of hours, we dried off, piled into Violet's car, and Mom drove home.

Violet hugged Mom and thanked her over and over again.

"You mind if I chat with Violet," asked Mom.

"Go ahead. Me and Skippy will take a bike ride."

Mom and Violet went into Violet's house.

I never asked Mom what she and Violet talked about.

Tuesday after I finished my work at the Chevrolet store, I rode through town and stopped at the newspaper stand. I wanted to see if there was a story about the shooting Saturday night or about someone having an accident because they were hurt when they were driving. There was nothing in the newspaper, so I started for home. When I passed the barber shop, I saw Jackie inside shining shoes. I didn't make any attempt to let him know I had seen him.

Skippy was barking at the door when I came home. I opened the door, and he leaped out at me.

"So, you missed me, did you?"

Skippy leaned back on his hind legs and barked.

"You want to play catch?" He wagged his tail and barked. I grabbed the stick I had set aside and threw it. Skippy chased after it and brought it back and dropped it at my feet. We did it several times before he started panting. "Okay, it's too hot. Let's go inside."

When I opened the door, the sweet aroma of Mom's baking beckoned me to the kitchen counter. On it were the cakes she had ready for delivery. Mom was washing dishes, and I thought…

"Don't even think about it, Francis. Those are for customers. There's some cookies in the jar for you, but don't eat them all."

Dang, I almost made it to the cakes. Instead, I reached into the jar, grabbed a couple of cookies, gave one to Skippy, and ate the rest. Mom had figured out a way to make her cookies without using sugar. In place of sugar, she used some of our canned fruit, ground up raisins, and apple butter. I couldn't tell the difference. She even tried watermelon—an experiment that didn't work. Needless to say, Me and Skippy had a bountiful supply of watermelon cookies.

"How was work?" Mom asked.

"Good. Mr. Coogins lets me do some work on the cars. Just little things. The mechanic does most of it. But I'm learning."

"Good for you. Now that you're home, I can make my deliveries. Skippy waited at the door for you all morning. I'd ask you to come with me, but the smell of the cakes would be too tempting. I'll be back way before dinnertime."

"What are you going to make for dinner?"

"We haven't had chicken in a while. Is there one you could… you know, for dinner?"

Mom couldn't say the words *kill and butcher.* "I'll take care of it."

CHAPTER 21

GRANDPA SLUMPED IN HIS CHAIR and dropped his head back with his eyes shut.

Aaron immediately sat up straight. I did, too. We'd both seen that happen when someone fainted. My first thought was a heart attack.

I started to get up and rush to Grandpa's aide, but Aaron signaled for me to wait.

I said a silent prayer. *Please, God, don't take my grandfather from me.*

I stood. I didn't want to wait; I wanted to help Grandpa.

Aaron extended his palms and mouthed, "Just wait."

Although I was once an ER nurse, Aaron had more field experience dealing with stroke and heart attack victims, so I waited and worried.

If it was a heart attack, it was my fault. Why did I have to write a book about his boyhood? Why did I do this? It was a stupid idea. I knew enough about him. Why did the world have to know about his boyhood?

Because of my dumbass idea, we might witness Grandpa being carried out of his home in a body bag. And if we weren't here, Grandpa would be suffering alone. Thank God, we were here. Hopefully, it's not a heart attack, and I won't have to tell my mother that it was all my fault.

Fortunately, Grandpa opened his eyes. Thank God.

"You okay, Grandpa?" I asked.

He raised his hand. "I'm fine. I just felt a little woozy. Must have been the doughnuts. How about we take a break?"

Woozy? That was more than just woozy. It may have been his hypertension. It might not be a bad idea to stop the doughnuts as a precaution.

"Are you sure you're all right?"

"Stop fretting." Grandpa looked at his watch. "There's cold cuts in the fridge and tomatoes on the windowsill in the kitchen. Make some sandwiches for lunch."

I glanced at Aaron who seemed concerned, too. Maybe it was a good sign that Grandpa

was hungry.

"Did you take your medications this morning?"

Grandpa scrunched up in his rocker. "I took a baby aspirin."

"Not good enough. I'm gonna check your blood pressures. Where do you keep your meter?"

"No need. I'm fine."

"Where's your meter, Grandpa?"

"You're worse than your mother. It's in the cabinet above the coffee pot."

"Don't go anywhere; I'll be right back."

"Where do you think I'd go?" Grandpa said. "Oh, that's right. I have to go to the bathroom. Be right back."

Grandpa rocked forward, then sat back down.

"You need help, Mr. Teague?" asked Aaron.

Grandpa glowered at Aaron. "No, I don't need help. I can pee by myself."

"I meant getting up."

"I know what you meant. I can do that by myself, too."

I wasn't about to let him go to the bathroom by himself, pass out, and seriously injure himself. "Let Aaron help."

"I said I can go by myself."

"Either Aaron helps you or I do. Dammit."

Grandpa waved me off. "No, you won't. Let's go, boy, and don't hold me."

Aaron helped Grandpa stand and walked with him to the bathroom.

"Make sure you sit down," I shouted.

"You gonna watch?"

"Just do it," I snapped.

Aaron shook his head and mouthed, "Bring a glass of water and a wet towel."

Grandpa went to the bathroom while Aaron stood guard by the door. I went to the kitchen.

In the cabinet, I saw the meter and his medications. I set them on the counter near the coffee pot so he'd see them tomorrow and not forget to take them. He may have forgotten to take them for several days, which was why his hypertension acted up. I filled a glass with water, set in on a tray, and added one of his blood pressure pills, his meter, and a damp dish towel. By the time I got back to the porch, Grandpa and Aaron were back in their seats.

Aaron shook his head. Grandpa must have given him a hard time about standing guard at the bathroom door.

I put the dish towel on Grandpa's forehead.

"Give me your arm so I can take your blood pressure."

He held out his arm, and I put the cuff on it, held his hand, and pressed start. Grandpa's face tightened as the meter hummed.

"One-eighty-seven over ninety. Not life threatening, but too high. Your heartbeat's seventy-nine."

"So?" he said.

"So, it means I have to call Mom and have her come and stay with you."

Grandpa sat up straight. "No, no. Don't call your mother. She'll put me…"

Mom really scared him when she threatened to put him a nursing home. But I can't let him be by himself.

"Annamarie is just up the street," Grandpa finally said. "She can stay with me."

I looked at Aaron hoping he had an answer for me.

"Erica, why don't we stay the night. I can go home and get us a change of clothes. That way your grandfather won't be alone."

"You'd do that for me?" asked Grandpa.

"Sure." He glanced at me. "What do you think?"

What did I think? I wanted to say I think *I love you, and you're the most fabulous boyfriend a girl could have.*

"That's a great idea. We'll have lunch when you get back."

"You two eat," said Aaron. "I'll get something at home. What about dinner?"

"Annamarie usually makes dinner for me," said Grandpa.

I didn't want Annamarie involved. She'd panic, want us to rush Grandpa to the doctor, and then call Mom and cause her to panic.

"What kind of food doesn't Annamarie like?"

"She hates Chinese."

Aaron shook his head. He didn't like Chinese either.

"Bring back three salads with chicken. I'll call Annamarie and tell her we're staying the night and having Chinese takeout."

Aaron mouthed, "Rabbit food?" and left.

"Grandpa, I still have to call Mom." He pulled at what little hair he had. "I won't tell her what happened. I'll just tell her we're staying the night to get an early start in the morning."

Grandpa breathed a sigh of relief.

"But we may have to forget about the book. I'm worried about your health, and that's more important than the book."

"No. You have to write the book. Not just for you, for me. I've kept too many things bottled up. I want to get them out." He grabbed my arm. "Please, don't quit on me."

Quit on him? I'd never quit on him. I was quitting on me.

"But, Grandpa…"

"Please, Erica."

My idea for writing Grandpa's story started because I worried something would happen to him, and I'd never get the chance to write a book. Something almost did happen to him, and now he wanted me to write the book about him.

I gritted my teeth. "Okay, but we'll take our time, and if you don't feel up to it, we'll stop. There's no hurry. Agreed?"

After today, there may be a need to hurry. But if necessary, I'd turn what I'd learned so far into a book. Harriet could help me.

"Agreed."

"Good. Now I have to make the beds in the bedrooms."

Grandpa grinned. "Why? Don't you two sleep together at home?"

Seriously? How did he know we lived together?

He winked. "Your mother told me when you first moved in with Aaron. I never said anything because you were old enough, and it was none of my business."

I wrapped my arms around him. "I love you, Grandpa."

"I love you, too. Now go do what you have to."

I got sheets and pillowcases and made the twin-sized bed in the room I slept in when I lived here. It was painted a soothing olive green. My high school and college graduation pictures were still on the dresser. Damn, was I young then. The last time I slept in that bed had been three nights after my grandmother's funeral. I stayed with Grandpa. Mom stayed two weeks longer to help him with Grandma's things and to be there for him, too.

I called Annamarie and let her know we'd be there, and she didn't need to come by. She was disappointed but was glad we would be spending the night. Then I called Mom and told her we wanted to get an early start in the morning. I could lie to Annamarie, but it bothered me when I lied to Mom.

I made Grandpa and me a sandwich.

An hour and half later, Aaron returned with a Publix shopping bag and an overnight bag. I put the salads in the fridge.

"Put the bag the green room."

Aaron nodded toward Grandpa.

I whispered, "It's okay."

Suddenly he had a shit-eating grin. When he kissed me, I tasted fried chicken.

After dinner, we sat on the porch. I knew Grandpa sometimes watched sports, so I put the Atlanta Braves game on. When the game ended, Grandpa said goodnight and went to bed. Aaron and I were both tired so we did too.

During the night, I looked in on Grandpa. I felt comfortable that he was okay.

Friday morning, I rolled over expecting to kiss Aaron, but instead I found just his pillow. I got out of bed, showered, and dressed. When I reached the bottom of the stairs, I was greeted by the smell of fresh brewed coffee. It reminded me of when I was younger and lived with my grandparents.

I poured a cup and joined Grandpa and Aaron on the porch.

"There you are. Why didn't you wake me?"

"I didn't want to bother you," Aaron answered.

"It's about time you got up."

"And good morning to you, Grandpa."

"Whatever. You gonna make us breakfast or should I call Annamarie?"

I guess Grandpa was feeling better. A good night's sleep was what the doctor had ordered, just like Grandma used to say.

"I'm taking orders," I said. "What's your preference?"

"Fried eggs," shouted Grandpa.

"Eggs over easy," yelled Arron.

"I'll make us all scrambled eggs."

"Scallywag," mumbled Grandpa.

"I heard that."

We ate breakfast in the kitchen.

"I'm up to talking about my boyhood if you'll stay and listen."

"Did you take your medications?" I asked.

"Did it. Ask Aaron. And he took my blood pressure."

Aaron nodded and mouthed, "He seems okay."

I trusted Aaron's judgement, but we could only stay that morning. We both had to work that night.

"Okay," Grandpa said. "I'm ready whenever you are."

I cleared the table, put the dishes in the dishwasher, and joined Grandpa and Aaron on the porch.

"Ready, Grandpa?"

"Before I start, let me say this. You've heard some things that may have bothered you, and you'll hear more. I told you before that those were things I'd never told anyone. Use your discretion if you want to use them or not. But I prefer you do. It was a long time ago, and no one is alive that will be bothered by them. I'm not."

What things? Had I made a mistake agreeing to continue?

CHAPTER 22

ATURDAY NIGHTS, MOM AND VIOLET played card
games and listened to music on the radio, sometimes
at our house and sometimes at Violet's. Violet stopped
going dancing on Saturday nights. She told Mom that she had
to conserve gas and started riding her bike more often. As the
summer came to an end, I had to quit my job at the Chevrolet
store. Mr. Coogins said if I wanted to work on Saturday's I could.
It would only be four hours, and he'd pay me fifty cents. I took
the job.

When school started in September in 1943, I entered eighth
grade. For me, it was a big deal because I'd be in high school
next year and everything would be different—including girls. I
hadn't yet discovered them, but one discovered me. She was the
girl who always called me Francis.

That girl would walk by me dressed in a blouse, a plaid skirt
and bobby socks. She'd smile and say, "Good morning, Francis.
Hope you have a nice day."

I'd just say, "You, too," and keep on walking because I didn't
know her name. But I kinda enjoyed her greetings.

Before the first bell rang that day, I stopped by Miss Lucy's to
see if she'd heard anything about her fiancé.

"Morning, Miss Lucy."

She looked up from whatever she was doing and smiled. I
loved that smile. It was more beautiful than the girl who called
me Francis.

"Good morning, Francis. How was your summer vacation?"

Miss Lucy had seemed like her old self.

'It was great. Mom and me…"

Miss Lucy pointed her finger up. "Mom and I, Francis. Use proper grammar."

She always corrected us. Proper grammar was a must with her.

"Mom and I…"

Miss Lucy smiled.

"We got a dog. His name's Skippy. He followed me home the last day of school before vacation." I grinned. "He's teaching us how to take care of him."

Miss Lucy laughed. It was wonderful to see her laughing.

"Have you heard any news about your fiancé?"

Another huge smile. "Good news. He's in a hospital in England recovering from his wounds. His plane was shot down, but he survived. Some good people found him, took care of him, and kept him hidden from the Nazis. They were able to get him to an American unit that got him to England." She crossed her hands over her heart. "Francis, he may be home for Christmas. Isn't that wonderful?"

I wanted to run to her and wrap her in my arms to show how happy I was for her, but I knew I couldn't. I just smiled. "That's wonderful. I'm so happy for you."

"Thank you. Have you heard from your father?"

"Mom got…"

Miss Lucy raised her finger and an eyebrow.

"Mom received a letter from him. She also wrote him, but we don't know if he got it. His letters are mostly for Mom, but he asks about me. Oh, I got my learner's permit, and I taught my mother to drive. Now we can drive together."

Her hand flew to her chest, and she gasped. "You taught your mother to drive?"

"Yes, ma'am. My father taught me before he went away, and he made me promise to teach Mom. Oh, and I worked three mornings a week at the Chevrolet store." I hunched my shoulders.

"Didn't make much, but I contributed to our finances."

Miss Lucy smiled again. When she did, I got a warm feeling inside me.

"I'm sure he'd be proud of you. You best get to your class, and I have some work to do. We'll talk another time."

I had heard that teenagers could hang out at Ma Barnes on Saturday afternoons where they could dance to the jukebox. Being as I was now a teenager, I decided to go. I didn't stay long because I didn't know how to dance and the kids were all older than me. Maybe next year or in my sophomore year I'd come again—if I learned how to dance. I could ask Mom to teach me.

We got a letter from Dad, and he mentioned that he got Mom's letter. He asked her to write often—a few lines to let him know we were okay. Mom wrote him back, but I don't know what she said. Each time we got a letter from Dad, Mom wrote back. Sometimes she let me add a line or two. Mom was always happy when she received a letter, but later I'd hear crying in her room. Skippy would go into her room and lie on the bed with her. He'd been doing that lately.

As the war dragged on, Mom seemed wearier. She played cards with Violet on Saturday nights, but that didn't take away her sadness. Mom really missed Dad, and there was nothing I could do except be there for her.

The Widow Atkinson asked Mom if she could work five days a week. With the holidays coming, Mrs. Atkinson planned on doing more entertaining and she would like my mother's help. Mom agreed as long as it was during the week—but an occasional Saturday was okay. It meant we would have more money and more food and more groceries. It also meant Mom would have to do her baking at night after working all day. And I had to deliver the goods the next day after school on my bike.

That lasted about a month before Mom decided it was too much for her. She decided to do her baking on Friday nights only and make deliveries on Saturday to whatever customers agreed to the new arrangement.

Violet joined us for Thanksgiving dinner. We had a roasted chicken, potatoes, vegetables, and rhubarb pie for dessert. Skippy got to taste everything. After dinner, Mom and Violet cleaned up. Skippy and I went out to walk off the meal.

Just before going home for Christmas recess, I stopped by Miss Lucy's class to wish her Merry Christmas and Happy New Year. When I walked into her classroom, a strange man in a military uniform had her wrapped in his arms. I started to leave.

"Francis, come here. I want to introduce you to my Christmas present." I hadn't noticed at first, but then I saw that the man held a cane in his right hand. "This is Charles Rodgers, my fiancé. Charles meet Francis. He's a dear friend."

My face turned pink. "Nice to meet you, Mr. Rodgers." I held my hand out. He looked down at the cane. "Sorry." I extended my left hand.

"Please call me Charles. I understand you looked after my girl while I was away."

"Nah, I just made sure to say good morning and good afternoon a few times, that's all. It wasn't nothin'."

Miss Lucy frowned. "It wasn't anything, Francis. Remember your grammar."

Mr. Rodgers laughed. "I does it, too, Francis."

"Charles use proper grammar," Miss Lucy said, and we all laughed.

I turned to Miss Lucy. "I wanted to wish you a Merry Christmas and a Happy New Year." I focused on him. "You too, Charles."

"Thank you," Miss Lucy said. "Before you go, I have something to tell you. Charles and I are getting married in the spring. This will be my last year teaching here."

Miss Lucy couldn't have said anything worse. She wouldn't be teaching here anymore, and I won't ever see her again. Miss Lucy broke my heart. It was gonna be the worst Christmas ever.

"Congratulations. I have to go now."

I turned, walked out of her classroom and then ran all the way home. I was sure Miss Lucy saw the disappointment on my face. When I got home, I went right to bed and cried. Skippy hopped up on the bed and snuggled next to me.

When Mom came home, I was still in bed. Skippy had gone to greet Mom. He brought her back to my room. I was lying on my side facing away from Mom, making believe I was asleep.

"Francis, what are you doing in bed at this hour?" She put her hand on my shoulder. "I know you're not asleep. What's the matter, sweetheart?" I rolled over. I figured Mom could tell I was crying 'cause my cheeks were red. "Francis, did someone hurt you?"

I couldn't decide if I should just tell her that Miss Lucy wasn't going to be teaching next year and I'd never see her again. Or say that I loved Miss Lucy and she broke my heart. I sat up and sniffled.

"Miss Lucy is getting married next year and won't be teaching after she does. I'm gonna miss her even though she's not my teacher."

Mom wrapped her arms around me and held me tight.

"I'm so sorry." Mom put her hand on my cheek. "You may not believe this right now, but someday you'll meet a girl your age and fall in love. Right now, you're experiencing a school boy's crush. All boys have them about their teachers. Your Dad told me he did."

Mothers are so smart. I should have known that she'd understand. I got the best mother in the world.

"Dad did, really?"

She smiled. "He did. So be happy for Miss Lucy." She put her hands on my shoulders. "I have good news. Mrs. Atkinson is having a small party for her employees, you're invited. Skippy is, too."

At the sound of his name, Skippy leaped onto the bed, barked and wagged his tail.

"It's the Saturday before Christmas."

I dropped my head because I had to work Saturday mornings.

"I talked to Mr. Coogins," Mom said, "and he said you could take the morning off."

I grinned. Mom sure knew how to make me happy.

"But…"

Uh, oh. There's always a but.

"I need help getting her house ready for the party. I thought maybe you'd like to help me. What do you say, will you?"

I wrapped my arms around her. "You bet I will. Can Skippy help, too?" Skippy barked twice.

"Sure, he can. Let's have dinner. See if there are any eggs in the coop. We'll have Spam and eggs."

"You're the best mom in the whole wide world."

Skippy and I went to see if there were any eggs. The hens had been productive during the day, and I grabbed a dozen. It meant Spam and eggs for the next several days.

The morning of the Christmas party, Mom and I were getting the widow Atkinson's house ready. Mom was baking, and I was arranging chairs and setting the table. Besides Mom and me, the Widow Atkinson's gardener and his family would be there, her chauffeur and his wife, and Mrs. Atkinson's nurse. Skippy was the only pet.

Mrs. Atkinson was putting some last-minute decorations on the tree. Suddenly, I heard Skippy barking and Mrs. Atkinson cried out.

"Oh, dear, I've…"

Skippy kept barking. He came to get me. Barked louder and rapidly wagged his tail.

"You want me to follow you?"

Skippy led me into the living room. On the floor was the Widow Atkinson. I ran to her and knelt.

"Are you okay?"

"I think I twisted my damn ankle." She reached for my hand. "Help me up." I helped her up, put her arm around me and helped her to a chair.

"Get my nurse. She's upstairs." I started to leave. Skippy sat beside her, and she patted his head. "Thank you, Skippy, for looking out for me."

Skippy licked her face, and Mrs. Atkinson smiled.

Mrs. Bronson wrapped her ankle and told her she had to sit during the party.

"Francis, your mother will have to greet the other guests, be the hostess, and hand the presents out. Go tell her, and thank you again."

Mom was happy to fill in since she knew the other guests. Mom was like a socialite greeting the guests, acting as hostess and handing out the presents—which were mostly for the gardener's children. The adults and me got envelopes. Mine had a dollar in it, but I don't know what was in the adults' envelopes. I do know that after the party, Mom said this would be the best Christmas since before Dad left.

Mom went with me and we purchased a bigger tree than last year. We also splurged on Christmas dinner. Violet was invited. Christmas morning, we paid a visit to the Widow Atkinson, wished her a Merry Christmas, and I thanked her for the gift.

New Year's Eve, Violet came to our house. We listened to the Hit Parade on the radio and danced until midnight. Actually, Mom and Violet did most of the dancing since all I could do was wiggle my butt. Mom changed the station so we could listen to Guy Lombardo and the Royal Canadians playing "Auld Lang Syne." At the stroke of twelve, we said Happy New Year, kissed each other and then Skippy and I went to bed.

CHAPTER 23

IT WAS ALMOST NOON WHEN Grandpa finished.
"I'll be right back. I have to go potty," I said and got up and left.

"Mr. Teague..." Aaron stumbled over his words, "may I ask you something?" His brow was suddenly damp, and he wiped it with the back of his hand.

"You want to ask for my granddaughter's hand is that it? If it is, it's not up to me. It's up to her, and you have to ask her." Grandpa smiled. "But you have my permission."

I'd just returned from the bathroom when I overheard Grandpa's words. I scrunched my eyes and worried that he might have given Aaron permission to go without me. Damn, he had better not have.

"Have your permission for what, Grandpa?"

He pointed at Aaron.

I turned to Aaron and crossed my arms. "Well?" I said. "Permission for what? And it better be good."

Aaron grinned. He got up and then dropped to a knee with a ring box in his hands.

"Will you marry me, Erica?"

I blushed. Then I looked at Grandpa. He smiled. I looked down at the ring and then at Aaron's smile and his pleading eyes.

"You damn well better hope she says yes, young man," said Grandpa.

"First, stand up before you hurt yourself," I said. When Aaron got up, I leaped toward him, causing us both to crash to the floor.

He groaned as I landed on him. "I'll take that as a yes." He inhaled. "But could you get off of me, please?"

"You still have the ring?" I asked.

"Yes, now get off of me."

"You still want to marry me?"

"Damn, Erica, I asked you, didn't I?"

"Okay, I'll marry you."

Grandpa burst out laughing. "You two need some help?"

"We got it, Grandpa." I straddled Aaron, lowered my head, and locked lips with him.

"That was sweet, but please get off me." I smiled and rolled off him. "Damn, you coulda broke a rib."

"You sure you guys don't need help?" asked Grandpa.

"Nope, we do this all the time." I stood and helped Aaron off the floor.

After a long hug and kiss, I turned to Grandpa.

"I'd leap into your lap if we were both younger, but we're too old for that. Can you manage to get those tired old bones to stand so I can hug you, too?"

"These old bones ain't that old that they can't get me up."

Grandpa and I hugged for the longest time. When we stopped, I had tears in my eyes. Then I hugged Aaron and planted a kiss on his mouth.

"You two gonna keep doing that? If you are, then you better use the bedroom again." Aaron and I blushed.

"Now listen to me," said Grandpa, "I want to walk you down the aisle, Erica, so get married before I go meet your grandmother in heaven."

"We will, Mr. Teague. You have my word."

Grandpa won't go meet Grandma. I won't let him.

Aaron and I had agreed that we'd wait to get engaged and married. Until we were prepared to take on the responsibilities that came with it. Out went those plans when he proposed, and now he's ready to get married.

Grandpa's crisis was over, and he seemed to be feeling better. I suspect it was because of Aaron's proposal and my acceptance. Whatever it was, I was relieved. After we finished celebrating, we had lunch, then Aaron and I left.

As we drove away from Grandpa's house, I had a lot to think about. Grandpa's crisis, Aaron's proposal, getting married, and Grandpa's request. As for the proposal and getting married, those were easy. But Grandpa's crisis and his request to write what he told me—those were more difficult. Something inside of me said I should leave the parts about Violet out. Maybe I still had misgivings about her and my great-grandmother. I could deal with his health if I didn't push him.

I may need Mom's help with Grandpa's health and his request to leave nothing out. I wasn't sure about that last one. Maybe she'd know better what to do. Especially, about his health. But the last time I asked her about including everything Grandpa said, she told me he'd be disappointed if I did and as for the parts about Violet, she said it was none of her business. It was up to me again.

"Grandpa scared the hell out of me yesterday, Aaron."

"It turned out okay." When we turned onto Washington Street, he asked, "So, what do you think?"

"About your proposal? I already said yes."

"No, you know about…"

"Oh, you mean hurry up and get married. I'm all for it."

"Wait, did you just say you're all for getting married in a hurry?"

Poor Aaron. Although I meant what I said, I was actually avoiding the elephant in the car. "That's what I said."

"Damn. Wait, wait, wait. I know what you're doing. You're avoiding deciding on your grandfather's request." I concentrated on the traffic even though there wasn't any. "Now you're focusing on driving. It's your stall tactic when you don't want to make a decision." He had me down to a tee—which was why I wanted to marry him. "I say you don't exclude anything from the book. It's your grandfather's story, and he wanted you to write it as he told it."

He was right. But still, my gut said he was wrong. "I'm not procrastinating. I'm just not sure."

"What's to be sure about? It's what he wants. I'll bet if you ask your mom, she'll agree." "We'll see. But those things he told us..."

Aaron placed his hand on my thigh, and a warm sensation filtered through me.

"It's like he said. They happened a long time ago, and no one is alive to dispute them.

And your grandfather doesn't care. Besides, he didn't give us graphic descriptions. Just teasers."

"Teasers? Is that what you call them?"

Aaron laughed. "Yes, and they're rated PG."

Maybe he was right, and maybe what Grandpa told us wasn't that bad. After I listened

to the recording, I'd make a decision.

"What am I gonna do with you?"

His face lit up. "Marry me, that's what you're gonna do." We both laughed.

While Aaron was at work, I listened to the tape of the last session with Grandpa. My worries were unfounded. What Grandpa told us wasn't as bad as I'd thought. If Mom didn't object, I was going to include everything Grandpa told us. And in hindsight, the reason Grandpa wanted that lunch break was so he could reiterate his request to write his story as he said it.

I was going to call Mom and discuss the subject with her, maybe even tell her I was engaged. She was sure to freak out when I did. But, I decided against it because she'd want to plan the wedding, and I wasn't about to let her. Aaron and I had only just got engaged, and I still had to write Grandpa's story. I'd call Mom another day.

When Aaron came home from work, we talked about my plan. He agreed that I should hold off calling Mom.

"Maybe we should elope? What do you think?" Aaron asked.

"We just got engaged, and already you want to elope? What's the hurry?" Maybe I should have told him when he proposed that I wanted to think about it. But then Grandpa would have been all over my case.

Aaron laughed. "I was just kidding. I'm in no hurry either." He smiled. "Besides, I want to hear the end of your grandfather's story."

What a relief, we were both on the same page.

I changed the subject.

"So, when you were a toddler did you..."

His mouth fell open. "Did I pee on my mom?"

I wiggled my head. "Yeah, did you?"

"How the hell do I know. It was so long ago that I can't remember. Did you?"

"None of your business." I checked my watch. "Oh look, it's bedtime."

The following Wednesday, we were back at Grandpa's house without doughnuts. During the week, I wondered what revelations we'd hear today. Anything was possible with Grandpa. We settled on the porch with coffee.

"What's this? Grandpa asked.

"It's a sugar-free oatmeal cookie. Your doughnut days are over. Get used to it."

"Pfft."

Aaron grumbled, too, when I bought the cookies and told him the same thing.

"Did you take your pills today?" I asked Grandpa.

Grandpa reluctantly munched on his cookie. "I did. Why? Don't you trust me?"

"Just asking."

Grandpa finished off the cookie and rubbed his hands together.

"You ready for some juicy tidbits?" My jaw dropped. "Hey, you wanted to write my story, so I'm baring my soul."

Oh, oh, what next?

"Whenever you are."

"Where did I leave off, last time?"

"Happy New Year and kisses."

CHAPTER 24

RIDAY NIGHTS, WE LISTENED TO Edward R. Murrow on the radio for news about the war. Italy had surrendered, but the Germans kept fighting in Italy. Our navy was still battling the Japs in the Pacific. Hopefully, Dad was safe.

All we could do was hope and pray like many other families.

Mom continued working Monday to Friday and an occasional Saturday for Mrs. Atkinson. With the extra money, Mom bought more groceries, and we splurged on ice cream downtown. We even shopped at the fish market. Mom still didn't want to see a movie, but she gave me a quarter so I could. It was enough to pay for the movie, a bag of boiled peanuts, and a stop at Candy Jones Candy Store.

The widow Atkinson had grown fond of my mother, and since she no longer needed her car because of rationing, she offered to have her chauffeur drive my mother home periodically, especially during inclement weather.

I continued working at the Chevrolet store on Saturday mornings. One Saturday after work, I came home to find Violet in our kitchen with her arms around Mom. I didn't like that—it didn't seem proper. When Mom saw me, she stepped away from Violet. She had tears in her eyes and ran to her bedroom. Had Violet said something that made Mom cry?

Violet turned around, I saw a piece of paper in her hand.

"Why was my Mom crying, Violet? Did you do something to hurt her?"

Violet pulled me to her chest and pressed my face against her bosom. It was soft and warm and impossible not to draw in her scent. She smelled a lot like the perfume smell in that man's car the night of the shooting. She kept pulling me against her, so close that I felt like a baby nursing at his mother's teats.

"Oh, Frankie, I'm so sorry."

I pulled away and caught my breath. "For what? What did you do to my mom?"

She shoved the paper at me. "I didn't do anything. Here, read this letter."

I grabbed the letter. It had come from the government—I could tell that by the letterhead. I had to read it over and over again to be sure what it said was right. The words just didn't sound like something a kid should read—let alone his mother.

It must have been a mistake. Why would anyone say things like that? They said my Dad was missing in action. Those were the same words I'd seen in Miss Lucy's telegram.

I threw the letter on the floor and shouted, "My Dad's not missing. He's on a battleship in the Pacific. That letter's not right."

Violet reached for me, but I pushed her arm away. "Go home, Violet."

Silently, Violet turned and left, closing the door gently behind her.

I went into my mother's bedroom. Skippy was on the bed next to her. I got on the bed beside her and put my arm around her. I needed words that were different from what was in that letter, and I needed them to be special—extra special.

"It'll be okay, Mom. Whoever sent that letter was mistaken. Dad wouldn't do that to us. You'll see. He'll come home one day, and we'll be a family again." My words might not have been special, but they were the best I could come up with.

Mom turned over on her side. She was clutching her crucifix in one hand. She ran the other palm over my cheek. Whenever she did that, it made me forget my heartaches and setbacks and I looked on the bright side. Could I touch her like that and make her feel the same? I didn't know, but Mom's face didn't look like she saw the bright side of anything or ever would. I wiped her tears with my hand.

"You really think so, Francis?"

I was only thirteen, but Dad would expect me to be brave. If there was a book that would give me directions on how to comfort a woman, I wished I had it in my hands so I could have read it right then.

I held back my tears. "I do, Mom, I really do. I bet Dad's writing you a letter right this moment."

Mom continued rubbing my cheek and then put her arm around me. "You're so brave, Francis. I don't know what I'd do without you. You're the man of the house now." She kissed me. "I'm so ashamed that you had to see me like this. I should be brave for you."

I mustered a smile. "You are, Mom. We couldn't have gotten this far without you. You work hard, cook our meals, clean our house, wash my dirty clothes, and even look after Skippy." Skippy barked, got between us, and licked both our faces. We started laughing.

I guess my words were the right ones.

"Francis, about those dirty clothes..." Oh, no. Me and my big mouth. "I think it's time you learned how to wash your own clothes."

Thank goodness, she said my clothes and not our clothes.

"Okay." Mom taught me how to wash my clothes, and it became a weekly ritual. We didn't have a washing machine like the widow Atkinson. I had to wash them by hand in the washtub, run them through the ringer, and then hang them on the clothesline.

After the holidays, I returned to school. Even though Miss Lucy had broken my heart, I still considered her a friend just like she considered me her dear friend.

After class, I hurried to the elementary school to stop by Miss Lucy's classroom before she went home. I wanted to show her the letter we received from the government. She was bent over her desk writing something. I stood in the doorway and watched. She looked up, saw me there, and called me over.

"Francis, I'm so glad you stopped by."

See, she still cared about me. "I was just in a hurry." I took the letter from my history book. "Mom got…"

"Received, Francis. Use proper grammar."

"Mom received this letter from the government. It says my dad is missing in action. Would you look at it for me?" I handed her the letter.

Miss Lucy's chin trembled and she reached for a tissue. I guess she remembered the letter that she received about her fiancé.

She read the letter. "Francis, didn't you say your father was in the navy?"

"Yes, ma'am. He's on a battleship in the Pacific. Why?"

"This letter is from the Secretary of the Army. It can't be about your father. There must be a mistake."

My eyes nearly popped out of their sockets. "Really? You mean it's possible my dad isn't missing and is still on the ship?"

Miss Lucy smiled.

"It's most possible."

I'm not sure she'd used proper grammar, but I didn't care. She'd given me hope.

I was so happy I couldn't control myself. I wrapped my arms around her, squeezed her tight, and almost kissed her.

"Thank you. Mom will be so happy." I realized what I was doing and stepped back. "I'm sorry, Miss Lucy. I shouldn't have done that."

Her smile made me forget what I did was wrong. "I don't mind. I'm just happy I was here for you, and I'm sure your mother will be glad when she realizes the mistake, too."

Maybe she wouldn't have cared if I'd kissed her, too.

"Thank you, Miss Lucy. I'm gonna..."

Miss Lucy raised her finger with her eyebrow.

"I'm going to run home and tell Mom. You have a wonderful day."

"You, too."

I ran down the hallway, out the door, and all the way home. I felt like I was an ace pilot flying through the clouds a thousand feet in the air and going a hundred miles an hour. Nothing could stand in my way, and nothing could stop me. I was the invincible flying ace. When I landed at home, my mother wasn't there but Skippy was. Since I needed to tell someone, I told Skippy. I don't think he knew what I was saying, but I guess he could tell by my excitement that it was something good. When I knelt, he started licking my face.

When Mom came home, I was waiting at the door.

"Mom, hurry, I have great news."

"Wait until I get inside." She stepped inside. "Okay, what's your great news?"

"I showed that letter to Miss Lucy. And guess what?"

Mom's mouth fell open. "You shouldn't have done that. That letter was for us only."

I handed her the letter. "Look who sent it. It's from the army, not the navy. You know what that means?"

I wanted to tell her to hurry up and read the letter so she could take me in her arms like I had Miss Lucy and kiss me.

Mom read the letter carefully. After she had finished, she dropped it and put both hands on her cheeks. "Oh, my gosh. It's a mistake." Then Mom clasped her hands like she was saying her prayers.

"But that means the letter was meant for another family. I'll ask the mailman to return it. Hopefully, that family will get it."

Another family? That meant no flying ace for that family and they'd be saying lots of prayers. Mom bundled me in her arms.

"You were right, Francis. Dad's probably on that ship, and we'll get a letter from him soon."

"I told you so. But, Mom, I can't breathe."

She laughed. "Sorry. This calls for a celebration. Just a small one. After dinner, we'll go get ice cream."

"That's a good enough celebration for me."

The next day when Mom got home from work, she told me she brought the letter to the post office and asked if was possible to return it to the sender since it wasn't meant for her.

"After the mail person read the letter carefully, she asked me how I spelled my last name. I spelled it slowly for her." Mom smiled. "She said I was right, and it was meant for the Teegue family." She showed me the spelling. I was surprised at the mistake. "Then she said she'd send it back to the sender, and hopefully it would get to the right family." Mom's expression turned grave. "That family won't be happy when they get it as we weren't. I thanked her and left for work. Thankfully, Mrs. Atkinson had given me the time to go to the post office and right that wrong."

I was grateful for Mrs. Atkinson, too, but saddened for that family.

Violet and Mom continued spending Saturday nights playing card games, listening to shows on the Lux Radio Theatre, and dancing to music from Your Hit Parade. Most of the time it was at our house, but Mom didn't allow Violet to drink liquor when she hosted so occasionally they went to Violet's house. While Mom was out, I listened to the radio and read comic books. When Mom came home, she looked like she was in good spirits.

Sometimes Violet wanted to be by herself. On those Saturday nights, Mom would look out the window to make sure Violet's car was in her driveway and that nobody came to pick her up. Mom worried that Violet might still be going out with strange men.

One night, when Mom was at Violet's, Skippy and I rode to that spot where the shooting took place. We wanted to see if Jackie was there. He wasn't, so we rode into town and got ice cream. Eventually, we went back to that spot with a fishing pole and did some fishing. I didn't catch anything, except mosquito and chigger bites. We just wanted to pass the time away outside instead of at home alone.

In March, we got a letter from Dad. Mom smiled as she read it and said there was no mention of him ever having been missing in action. Dad did say that he missed us both and hoped he would see us soon. When Dad left, I was twelve, and now I was about to start high school. I hoped he'd be home before I did.

Mom tried using V-mail to write Dad, but she found the process complicated, so she continued sending letters the old way. Dad occasionally used V-mail. I guessed it was easier for him.

In April, I turned fourteen and Miss Lucy got married.

Hope for the war's end had become more promising when on D-Day, June sixth, Allied troops landed on the beaches of Normandy to begin the liberation of Europe.

I wondered if Mr. Sheren had taken part in the landing.

We didn't know what Mr. Sheren did in the army or if he wrote letters to Violet because she never mentioned him. She might have told Mom, but it was none of my business, and I never asked. Maybe that was why Violet drank so much.

The war dragged on in the Pacific. Our boys were battling the Japs and making strides. Japan's last aircraft carrier forces were defeated by our carrier planes. Maybe this would be the year that Dad would get to come home.

In September, I started high school and every morning that same girl—who was in all my classes—would greet me after she got off the bus. She even walked me to my homeroom occasionally. After all the years we had been in school together, you'd think I'd know her name. But I was never interested in girls, and never paid attention when her name was called at role.   Maybe I did know her name, but I didn't remember it. She was pretty and wore a small bow in her hair. Next time she said good morning, maybe I'd find a subtle way to ask.

I had several new classmates that I'd never met. Some were bussed from the town of Lloyd. Our high school was the only one in Jefferson County. My English teacher was more of a stickler for grammar than Miss Lucy was.

When the coach asked why I didn't try out for the football team, I told him I had obligations at home. Maybe next year. He said if I did, I needed to put some meat on my bones. That was one of the reasons I didn't want to be on the team. I took grief for not trying out from a few of my classmates—mostly Coleman, but I ignored it. Honestly, I didn't think I had the physical coordination for sports.

Violet wanted to be alone more often, so I tried to convince Mom to go to a movie with me. We discussed the pros and cons—actually it was more of an argument. Mom wanted to stay home and make sure Violet didn't go out by herself or with a man. I argued that Violet wasn't Mom's responsibility that Mom had to look out for herself. And a night at the movies with me would do a lot to alleviate her loneliness. Mom reluctantly agreed, but before we left she looked out the window to make sure Violet's car was in her driveway.

I thought that maybe other teenagers would find it odd that I was with my mother and not a girl, but it was more important that I be with Mom than a girl. Besides, I didn't know any girls who liked me enough to go on a date with me.

We got a bag of popcorn and sat in the front row. My worry about other teenagers was unnecessary as there were hardly any in the theater. I guess they weren't interested in *Mrs.*

Parkington—a black-and-white movie starring Greer Garson and Walter Pigeon. The kids were probably at a party at one of the kids' house.

When the newsreel came on, Mom grabbed my hand. The pictures and sound of a naval battle frightened her. She wiped a tear with a tissue. My hand ached from her squeezing it.

I leaned over. "Would you rather we left, Mom?"

"Do you mind, Francis?"

"Why don't we go to the drugstore and get ice cream sodas?"

Mom let go of my hand, and we left the theater and walked to Grey's Drugstore. When we entered, the girl behind the counter recognized us and smiled.

"Evening, Mrs. Teague. Evening, Francis. What can I get for you folks?"

She was the girl who always said good morning to me at school.

"I'll have a vanilla ice cream soda," said Mom.

"And you, Francis? What would you like?"

"Uh…" I couldn't get the words out. Somehow my mouth wouldn't work.

"He'll have the same thing. How do you know my son?"

Why did Mom have to ask? I was already embarrassed.

"Francis and I have been classmates since first grade. Right, Francis?"

"I guess so," I managed to answer.

"My name's Rosalind." She looked at me with a big smile. "But you can call me Rosie. All my friends do."

Mom narrowed her eyes. "I'll call you Rosalind."

Mom didn't like calling people by nicknames.

"Okay." She wore a radiant smile. "Two vanilla iced cream sodas coming up."

At least now I knew her name. Rosalind returned with our sodas.

"Anything else I can get you folks?"

Mom shook her head.

"Okay, that'll be ten cents."

I reached into my pocket and took out a dime—before Mom could—and laid it on the counter. Then I took out two pennies and put them next to the dime.

"Thank you, Francis." Rosalind winked at me.

I was sure my face was the color of a cherry. After we finished our sodas, we said goodbye.

"See you in school Monday, Francis."

I just smiled as we left.

"She's cute," Mom said, "and she has a crush on you."

"We're just classmates." But I had to confess that I was happy if she did have a crush on me.

Mom handed me the keys to the truck. "You drive. I'll be your date tonight."

"Aw, come on, Mom."

She ruffled my hair like Dad used to and smiled.

As soon as we got home, Mom glanced at Violet's driveway. She seemed pleased that Violet's car was in the driveway.

Monday morning when Rosalind got off the school bus, she hurried to catch up with me.

"Good morning, Francis, I hope you had a pleasant weekend."

I turned to find her smiling, so I smiled back.

"I did, thank you, Rosalind, I hope you did, too."

Like Mom had, I'd call her by her given name, not her nickname. She was too pretty not to.

I had finally spoken to her—after being her classmate for going on nine years. Maybe if I had paid attention during attendance when her name was called, I might have known it sooner.

"Do you mind if I walk with you to class?"

I shrugged, pretending I didn't care. "If you want to."

We walked to class together. After classes ended, I considered walking Rosalind to her bus, but she'd disappeared.

Maybe another day.

CHAPTER 25

G RANDPA HAD PACKED A LOT of information into today's session, and I was surprised how good his memory was. He didn't seem forgetful, and he was more at ease. Maybe shorter sessions were best for him.

"That's it for today," Grandpa said. "When can you come back?"

"It'll have to wait until Aaron and I can coordinate our schedules. And, I don't want to overwork you. We're taking it slow. Remember?"

"I remember. It's just…I'm eager to talk about things."

"I know. There's plenty of time."

After last week, I hoped there was.

"I'll call you, Grandpa."

"You do that." He frowned. I could tell he was disappointed.

I gathered my notes, turned the recorder off, and we left.

As we drove past Annamarie's house, she waved to us.

"What do you think about today's session?"

Aaron rubbed the back of his head. "Think it all happened?"

"Hard to say, but I trust my grandfather. Maybe I'll pay another visit to the genealogical society and see if they can add anything."

"I don't think you should ask those people about Violet and Miss Lucy. It may be embarrassing for your grandfather." Of course, I wouldn't. Why would I? He should know better. "I'll say one thing though. Your grandfather and your great-grandmother were survivors. No matter what the implications about your great-grandmother and Violet, your great-grandmother was one hell of a woman and mother." Arron turned and smiled at me. "I'm happy I'm going to be a part of your family, Erica."

I blushed. "And I'm happy that I'll be a part of yours."

"Rosalind may have had a crush on your grandfather, but I bet he ends up having one on her, too."

When we arrived home, and I'd had time to think about what Grandpa told us, I had to decide whether I should call Mom. It amused Aaron that my grandfather had a crush on Miss Lucy. Aaron had previously disclosed that he had a crush on one of his elementary school teachers. I thought it was cute because I had one on my seventh-grade teacher.

"And there's something else, babe," he said.

"What's that?"

He gave me a huge smile. "I love Miss Lucy, too."

I punched him in the arm. "You're such a guy, ain't you?"

"Grammar, Erica. Proper grammar." We both laughed.

I called Mom and told her about the last two sessions with Grandpa but not about what happened the day we stayed overnight. I mentioned the letters, Grandpa's schoolboy crush, the shooting, and Grandpa's reaction to it all.

"The missing-in-action letter reminds of when we got the news about your Dad's cancer. Only that wasn't a mistake." I detected a note of sadness. "The part about his schoolboy crush reminds me of the one you had on Mr. Buxley, your science teacher."

"Wait, how did you know?"

"Your grandmother said your sleepovers with Gina Amendola were a bit noisy."

I panicked. "What else did Grandma tell you?"

"I'll never tell."

Damn, I sure hope Grandma didn't hear Gina and I talk about what happened on our dates in high school.

"Mom, I promised Grandpa that I'd write everything as he told me, but now I'm second guessing that decision."

"Why? Didn't I tell you last time to do what your grandfather wants you to." Same advice as Grandpa gave me. "I'm surprised he's so open with you. Whenever I asked him about his teenage years, he clammed up. Your grandmother said he did it with her, too. You must have a special bond with him. I can't wait to read your book."

Another reason I had to finish what I started. Mom wanted to read it.

"Thanks. Oh, one more thing…"

"What now?"

"The day we stayed overnight, Grandpa forgot to take his medication that morning. He keeps his pills in the cabinet over the coffee pot. I put them on the counter next to it and had him take a blood pressure pill."

"Good thinking. I'll take care of it. Anything else?"

I was still curious about the stack of letters.

"Mom, do you know anything about the letters he keeps in the memory box?"

"What letters?" She sounded alarmed.

"I saw a stack of letters and when I asked Grandpa about them, he said I didn't need to know about them."

I waited. I thought for a moment we were disconnected.

"You don't need to know what's in them." Mom sounded upset. "Their personal, and you'll only upset your grandfather. You best forget about them."

She piqued my curiosity about the letters. They weren't a priority, and I didn't want to upset Grandpa. If they come up in our conversations, I'd ask about them.

"Whatever you say."

"Anything else?" She sounded agitated.

"Nope, that's it," I said.

"Before you hang up, I thought I'd ask one more time…"

Oh boy, was she about to be surprised. "Yes, Mom, I'm wearing the ring now." I expected her to shout yippee, but there was just silence. "Mom…Mom, are you still there? I said I'm wearing the ring now."

"I heard you. I had to get up off the floor and take an aspirin in case of a heart attack. When did it happen?"

"The other day at Grandpa's house. And before you ask, Aaron asked Grandpa for permission. He said it was up to me."

"I'm not surprised; it's the same thing he told your father."

"He did?"

"He sure did. I felt sorry for your dad."

"I felt the same way about Aaron. Grandpa wants us to get married before he won't be able to walk me down the aisle."

"Then I'll have to start planning the wedding. We'll need a church, a place to have the reception, a big cake, and, of course, I'll need a dress. You will, too. I can't wait to be the mother of the bride."

I had known she'd do this. Aaron won't be happy. "Mom, stop. We're in no hurry. I have to finish Grandpa's story and write the book. That's my priority."

"But, Erica…"

"No buts. We're not ready to get married just yet. If you start wedding planning, we'll elope." I heard her gasp, and I'd bet her jaw dropped. "I mean it, Mom."

I had to take a firm stand or things would get quickly out of hand.

"Oh, shit, you're no fun. Okay, but please don't elope."

She couldn't see my huge grin. "As long as you butt-out, I won't."

Our discussion about the engagement and a wedding ended the one about the letters. But they'd stay in the back of my mind.

Later, when Aaron and I had a chance to talk, I told him about my conversation with my mother. Not the one about the letters. He didn't need to know about it. Aaron was of the same opinion as I was. If my mother started planning our wedding, we agreed to elope.

CHAPTER 26

I MADE A TRIP TO THE genealogical society the following Wednesday morning. I wanted to find out if some of the things Grandpa said were accurate.

The same folks were there, all except Rosie and Annamarie. Leena was more than willing to help as were the others.

"So, how's the book coming?" Leena asked.

"It's getting there." I didn't want to tell her that all I had were beaucoup notes and recordings. "I need to do more research, which is why I'm here. I want to look through yearbooks, and I'm looking for activities my grandfather may have participated in—like sports, clubs, and such. I have some more questions, too."

"I don't know about clubs, but as for sports, we had football, basketball and baseball," Leena replied. "Ronnie get her our copies of the Jeffecello."

Ronnie stopped what he was doing and got up. "What years?" he asked.

"I think 1947 and 1948," I replied.

Ronnie handed me the yearbooks, and I went through them and made notes on my pad. Grandpa wasn't in any of the sports teams' pictures, but his senior class picture looked like a younger version of him. I spent about an hour and a half going through the yearbooks and asking questions. I had enough information to use in the event I had to fill some gaps in Grandpa's story.

I considered asking if they had my class yearbook to compare my senior picture to how I looked now. But I changed my mind because I'd lost some weight since then.

"Well, that should do it. Thanks, Leena and Ronnie. I hope I don't have to come back again."

"Come back whenever you want. We'll be here," said Leena. "When will we see the book?"

I cleared my throat. "Uh, it's some ways off, but I'm working on it. When it's finished, I'll come back with several copies"

Most of what Grandpa had told us I was able to verify with the folks at the genealogical society and the yearbooks. I also knew that many of the sites he had mentioned no longer existed, so I had no need to drive around town looking for them. Also, a few of those sites were advertisers in the yearbooks.

Later in the evening, I told Aaron about my trip to Monticello and what I'd learned.

He listened attentively, nodding every so often. "Erica, doing research is good, but it's

just your way of procrastinating. You need to write more. Isn't that what Harriet told you?"

Harriet had been nagging me to send more pages.

"But it's so difficult."

"Everything in life is difficult. Look what your great-grandmother and your grandfather had to endure. And your mother. Finishing the book can't be that difficult."

I was such a coward. Aaron was right. Finishing the book wasn't as difficult as what mother, grandfather, and my great-grandmother endured.

"Okay, no more procrastinating, but I still may need to do some research. I'll keep it to a minimum and only if it's necessary."

He smiled. "That's my girl."

I wrote more chapters and sent them to Harriet. She reviewed what I had written and said she liked them. She approved of the way I wrote Grandpa's scenes, but she suggested when it came to his quotes not to be afraid to make things up. It would help make it sound like him. After our discussion, I took her advice.

I knew my grandfather well enough that I could make it seem like him talking.

I made arrangements with Grandpa to visit him Tuesday morning.

When we arrived at Grandpa's house, he was waiting on the front porch.

He waived and said, "What no doughnuts?"

I held up a paper bag. "Sugar-free cookies."

He raised his brows and swatted at us. "You scallywags can turn around and go back to Tallahassee."

I looked at Aaron and nodded. He nodded, too.

"Let's go, Aaron."

Grandpa held both hands up. "Wait, wait don't go. I was just fooling."

"You sure?"

"Yes, I'm sure."

"And we're not scallywags?"

"No, dammit, you're not. Are we gonna stay here and argue or go inside?"

I smiled. "Lead the way."

We followed him into the house. I went to the kitchen, made a fresh pot of coffee and then sat on the porch with Grandpa and Aaron.

"We'll have the cookies when the coffee is ready, and don't give me no lip. You hear me, Grandpa?"

"Dang, you're no fun."

I opened my backpack and took out my recorder, a pad, and a pen. Grandpa looked at them.

"When are you gonna start writing?"

I thrust my chin out. "I already have."

"How many chapters?"

"Sixteen, and I'm working on more."

Aaron shook his head. He knew I hadn't, but also knew a little lie was best as far as it concerned Grandpa.

"Well, at least you started." He pressed his hand to his ear. "Sounds like the coffee is ready. Get us a cup and bring those dang cookies."

"Aye, aye, captain."

I went to the kitchen, got a tray, poured three cups of coffee, and brought them out to the porch.

"Did you remember to take your pills today?"

Grandpa frowned. "Of course. How could I forget with that damn contraption your mother got me?"

I knew he had because the slot for today's pills was empty. Mom had bought him a pill dispenser. She and Annamarie made sure it was kept filled and checked to be sure he was taking his pills.

"It's for your own good."

"Pfft."

I wondered if anything had happened since the last time we visited. Had he gone anywhere? Like the senior center or to lunch with Annamarie. Anything?

"So, what's new?"

Grandpa's eyes sparkled.

"Last night, Annamarie had dinner with me. After dinner, we listened to a radio station that played songs from the forties and fifties. We danced to a few and we even…"

"Even what?" What was he implying he and Annamarie did?

He grinned. "It was just a little peck on the cheek. What did you think we did? Have sex?"

I blushed. "No, I would never think that."

Grandpa glared at me. "You think we're too old?"

"Grandpa, stop. Can we change the subject? How about you tell us some more about your life in the forties?"

Grandpa laughed. "Gotcha good, didn't I?"

"That's not fair. You almost gave me a heart attack."

Bad choice of words, Erica.

"A heart attack?" You're too young for that. Maybe we better begin before you get gray hair like me."

CHAPTER 27

AS THE HOLIDAYS APPROACHED IN 1944, I wanted to earn more money to help Mom and be able to buy her a Christmas present. She hadn't gotten one since before Dad left.

I walked into town and stopped at every store and gas station asking if they needed help. I forged on until I finally got a yes at the Sinclair station, where I'd pump gas and sweep the floors after school. It didn't pay much, but what little I earned would go in Mom's cookie jar and my nickel can for spending money. I also had the fifty cents I'd earned from Mr. Coogins.

But having a job meant long days. I had to get up real early and do my chores, walk Skippy, make my breakfast, and then go to school. After classes, I went right to the service station and worked until six o'clock. If Mom got home before me, she let Skippy out and then made dinner. If I got home first, I did the same. I always made grits, hoping it would help put some meat on my bones.

Skippy had put on some pounds and was taller than when he'd first followed me home and no longer fit in the basket. He was almost knee high. I'd trained him enough that I trusted him to walk beside me wherever we went.

After dinner, I did my homework. On Saturday afternoons, I had to do my wash—as did Mom—which meant we shared space on the clothesline. And that was embarrassing because I saw Mom's personal items.

Violet came for dinner a few Friday and Saturday nights. Sometimes she made something at her house and brought it with her. Her cooking wasn't as good as Mom's, but I had to admit it was a little better than mine. At least Violet was contributing. She started asking Mom to go dancing, but Mom kept refusing. She told Violet not to go by herself. So far, Violet hadn't. Instead, she came over and listened to *The Grand Ole Opry* on the radio with Mom.

I was doing well in school. My best and the most favorite subject was math. English wasn't a favorite, and I struggled a bit with it. Rosalind got an A on every test. She never once mentioned how her grades were higher, but there was one girl who did. She rode the same bus as Rosalind. I thought she was prettier than Rosalind, but kind of stuck-up.

One Saturday after working at the Chevrolet store, I walked around town. In the window of Candy Jones Candy Store, I saw an ad for a Whitman's Sampler. Inside, I asked how much it cost. The smallest sampler cost less than two dollars. It was a lot of money, but with my earnings and what I had saved in my nickel can, I had enough. I told Candy Jones to keep one for me and I'd be back before Christmas to buy it.

Thanksgiving went by, and Mom got a letter from Dad. Knowing he was still alive was all we needed to give thanks. We also gave thanks that we had managed on our own for almost three years. I'm sure other families had it harder than we did.

Two days before Christmas, I went to the candy store and bought Mom's chocolate sampler. On Christmas Eve, Mom and I purchased a Christmas tree. The widow Atkinson hosted a party for her employees just like she had the year before.

Christmas morning, I gave Mom her gift wrapped in newspaper.

She unwrapped it and clutched her heart. "Francis, you shouldn't have done this. I'm so overwhelmed." She put her arm around me. "It's my favorite candy. This is the same thing your dad gave me the Christmas before he..."

I grabbed Mom's hand. "I remember. You deserve a special present after all you've done for me." Skippy barked. "And for Skippy. We love you, Mom."

Mom set the candy on the table and put her arms around me. "Oh, Francis, I love you, too. And you're the one who deserves something special. I don't know how I would have managed without you." Again, Skippy barked. "You too, Skippy."

We both laughed and our eyes filled with tears.

New Year's Eve, Violet came to celebrate with us, as usual. I danced with Mom and Violet to songs on the Hit Parade. At midnight, we listened to Guy Lombardo welcome in the New Year. I kissed Mom, and Violet kissed me on the lips. It was the first time I'd been kissed on the lips by her, and it felt strange. Skippy and I went to bed and left Mom and Violet to enjoy the rest of the night.

I had made a New Year's resolution to climb the water tower. So, in March, I waited for a weeknight when there was no moon and the stores downtown were closed. I walked into town with Skippy. When we saw the police officer, we hid and made like he was a Jap sentry. When we reached the water tower, I left Skippy on the ground to be the lookout and then I climbed. I thought I'd be the first to carve their initials in the tank, but other initials were already there. I carved mine next to the one that read BT and then climbed down. I raised my hands signaling touchdown and then Skippy and I started for home.

In April, I got invited to a party at the house of a girl in my class. Mom baked some cookies and told me to bring them as a gift for the hostess. I put the cookies in the basket and rode my bike to the girl's house. I wasn't the only boy who'd ridden his bike to the party, but I was the only boy who'd brought a gift. Rosalind was at the party, as was that stuck-up girl. We mostly played games and the girls danced, but the boys just watched.

The girl's mother made hot dogs for everyone. After hot dogs, we all sat on the ground and played spin the bottle. I was the first to spin the bottle, and I hoped when it stopped, it would point to Rosalind because I felt she wouldn't embarrass me since I'd never kissed a girl before. Unfortunately, the bottle pointed at the stuck-up girl.

"Um, can we do this in private?" I asked.

The girl whose house it was said that's not how you play the game, but the stuck-up girl said it was okay. We went to a corner of the yard where we had privacy. Not knowing what to do, I did what I saw Dad do. I held her arms, leaned in, and kissed her on the lips as Violet had did to me. Her lips were sticky and tasted like bubble gum.

"That was nice, Francis. Have you done this before?"

I figured, why should I embarrass myself and have her tell all her friends that it was my first kiss. God wouldn't punish me if I fibbed—just a little. "A few times, you?"

"Me too. Would you like to do it again?"

"Okay." I leaned in, held her arms, and kissed her on the lips.

Suddenly, something was in my mouth. It tasted like a cherry ice pop mixed with bubble gum, and it sure tasted good. Since we had already kissed for the first time, I offered her the taste of a hot dog and mustard. She must have liked the taste of hot dog and mustard because she didn't spit it out. It was my first tongue kiss, and I've never forgotten it.

When we finished, she grinned at me for what seemed like a month until we realized the mother of the girl whose house it was watched us from the kitchen window. The stuck-up girl smiled and waved to her. The woman smiled and waved back. I looked down at the ground as I didn't want her to recognize me and tell my mother what I did. When we joined the others, everyone smiled as we sat down. I couldn't look at Rosalind because I was embarrassed. But even though I was embarrassed,

I figured that kiss was a day-late fifteenth birthday present. And after the party, I had a new appreciation for that stuck-up girl.

The war in Europe was coming to a close. In late April, Italian dictator, Mussolini, was captured and in early May, Germany surrendered. Downtown Monticello was awakened by the air raid sirens celebrating VE Day.

In May, Mr. Sheren returned from the war. He was one of the fortunate ones. We still had no idea what Mr. Sheren did during his time in the army. Personally, I don't believe he actually joined the army. I still think he was a Chicago gangster and was using the war as an excuse to do illegal acts. For all we knew, he might have had another wife and a family somewhere, was living with them, and just came back to get his car.

Two weeks after he was home, Mr. Sheren and Violet knocked on our door. They wanted Mom to go out dancing with them. Mom politely refused.

"What's the matter we're not good enough for you?" he said belligerently.

He was angry and had never spoke to Mom like that before. Maybe something happened during the war and changed him.

Before Mom could reply, I stepped in front of her and put my fists on my hips.

"My Mom's not interested in going dancing. She has to be home with our dog and me."

Skippy came up beside me and growled. "You'll just have to go without her." I stood in front of

him hoping my eyes were menacing eyes and my expression was fearsome. If he didn't back off, I'd hit him with a mighty left—*Kapow*. Then a powerful right would knock him down. I'd jump on him and crush him like a cockroach. He'd beg for mercy. And if Mom wanted me off him, I'd ignore her, even if it meant a scolding.

Mr. Sheren sized me up, and I did the same to him. His head was so small his eyes barely reached over his shirt collar, but his head was big enough that I could smash it like a watermelon. He was nothing more than a piss-ant.

"We don't need her. Come on, Violet, let's go."

Dad had taught me that the only way to stop a bully was to stand up to him but be prepared to fight—which I was. I'd grown a few inches and had put on some weight. I guess Mr. Sheren figured I wasn't that twelve-year-old kid from when he went off to the war. And at fifteen, I wouldn't be easy pickins in a fist fight.

When I turned around, Mom stood rigidly, tapping her foot, her arms crossed and a clenched jaw.

"What did you think you were doing? He might have taken a swing at you."

I put my hands on my hips, puffed my chest like *Joe Palooka*, and grinned. "I knew he wouldn't." Skippy barked. "See, even Skippy agrees. But he might have taken a swing at you, and I couldn't let that happen. Not as long as Skippy and I are here. Besides, he smelled of whiskey."

Mom laughed. It warmed my heart to hear her laugh. I could tell she was upset that Violet had her husband home at last while Dad was still at war. Although Mom hadn't said it, I was sure she appreciated me standing up for her. Dad would have wanted me to.

"Are you going out tonight, Francis?"

"I don't think so. I'm gonna stay home with you." Skippy leaped up on my legs. "Yeah, and you, too, Skippy." I grabbed his paws and made like we were dancing. Mom laughed.

"Would you like me to teach you to dance? I could. We can put the radio on and dance to the Hit Parade."

I'd already been invited to a party where there was dancing, but I didn't dance because I didn't know how. Maybe I'd be invited to another one with dancing. Or, maybe I'd go to the Woman's Club and dance. But not if I didn't know how to.

"Do you think you could? I'm sure clumsy. Remember how I was on New Year's Eve?"

Mom ruffled my hair. "Of course, I can." She nodded toward the living room. "Let's go do some dancing."

We listened to the music of Artie Shaw, Benny Goodman, and Billy Holiday. Mom taught me how to do the jitterbug, the waltz, and the foxtrot. It took some time to get my feet to do what they were supposed to do, but eventually they did. When we danced to the waltz and the foxtrot, Mom grimaced every time I stepped on her toes.

I must have apologized a hundred times that night.

"Don't worry. Your father was just as bad when I taught him to dance."

My brows hiked. "You taught Dad to dance? Really?"

"I sure did." Mom grimaced when I did it again. "Maybe we should take a break. I'll make us some sweet tea."

"Okay."

In the kitchen, Mom sat down, took her shoes off, and rubbed her toes. Then she made sweet tea, and we sat in the living room just listening to the music. I think Mom had enough for one night, but I know she had fun as did I.

Mr. Sheren didn't come by the house again that night or the next day. We didn't see Violet except when she hung their wash out to dry. Mr. Sheren always drove Violet to work and picked her up when she was done. They did go out on Saturday nights. Mom and I spent those nights dancing in the living room.

Occasionally, we heard shouting from the Sherens' house. Mom turned the radio louder so we didn't have to listen.

Eventually, Mr. Sheren went out of town to wherever he worked, maybe to his other family or whatever. That left Violet to ride her bike or walk to work. Mom offered to ride with her, but Violet said that would only work when Mr. Sheren was out of town. On the ride home, Mom had to leave Violet a few blocks from her house. It was a precaution in the event Mr. Sheren was there.

Occasionally, Mom would take Dad's truck and let Violet make a quick stop at the grocery store. It meant she had to carry her grocery bags the few blocks from her house where Mom dropped her off. Violet had told Mom that Mr. Sheren refused to allow Violet to have any contact with us.

CHAPTER 28

"THAT'S ENOUGH FOR TODAY, GRANDPA. Aaron's and I have to work this afternoon." Aaron shifted in his seat and narrowed his eyes. He was confused, and I didn't blame him. We both had the day off, but I didn't want to hear that Sheren had abused Violet. Just the thought of it made my stomach queasy.

During my shift Monday, the last call my partner and I had responded to was a domestic disturbance. When we arrived on the scene, the man was handcuffed. Inside the house, the woman lay on the floor. Her face was covered in blood and her arms and legs showed signs of bruises. I lifted her top and saw bruising on her ribs. We stabilized her and rushed her to the hospital. The ER nurse told us she survived her wounds, but she'd have scars on her face.

Scars on her face could be taken care of with plastic surgery, but the emotional scars would last the rest of her life.

I still get depressed when I think about it.

Grandpa leaned forward and covered my hand. "Something bothering you?" he asked.

Like Aaron, Grandpa had learned to read my moods.

"I'm just tired." Grandpa's touch comforted me. "I had indigestion last night and didn't sleep much." Aaron's head flinched back. He was confused. I ignored him. "Do you mind if we continue another day?"

"Maybe we should." Grandpa wrinkled his brow and looked at Aaron. I supposed he didn't buy my excuse. "I could use the time to refresh my memory about what happened after the war ended in Europe. Could you do me a favor and go on the internet or wherever you go and look up the timeline for the war?" Grandpa scratched the back of his head. "I have one someplace, but I don't remember where I put it. I'll check my bookshelf and see if there's a timeline in any of my books about the war."

Aaron and I had already done that, and I had a copy in my backpack and one on my desk at home. I reached into my backpack and took out the timeline.

"Does this help?" I handed it to him.

He lowered his glasses and looked at it. "That was quick. What else do have in that backpack? A ham and cheese sandwich?"

"Hah, hah. Matter of fact, I do." I giggled. "Would you like a bite of it?"

Grandpa shushed me and glanced at the timeline. "I see you made some notes. You marked my age, year in school, and you even wrote Miss Lucy on it." He evil-eyed me. "You checking up on me? Making sure what I told you was the truth?"

Damn, he was on to me. "Those notes are for my frame of reference. I'm writing a book, remember? I have to make sure I get the facts right for the chapters. Otherwise, I'll end up with gibberish." I smirked. "My memory isn't as good as yours."

Grandpa pursed his lips. "Maybe I'll do the same thing. So, when are you coming back?" He had given me a lot of information, more than I expected. Now I had to review it and make sure I had everything in chronological order. Aaron would help me, and most likely he was already making notes in preparation for when we got home.

Aaron mouthed a week.

"Next week?" I suggested. "That way I can write a few chapters, and you can work on your timeline."

"Sounds like a plan to me." Grandpa's eyes lit up. "Damn, I always wanted to say that. Okay, next week. I'll look in the memory box for more pictures. Maybe it'll refresh my memory of kids I went to high school with."

"How about my secretary calls yours?"

"Okay." He looked at Aaron. "You make sure you call my secretary, you hear me, Mr. Secretary?"

Aron nodded.

"Then I'll see you two next week." He looked at his watch. "Time for a nap before Annamarie gets here. She's cooking dinner for me."

"Grandpa, she always cooks dinner for you. You should take her out to dinner."

"Maybe I will. Who's paying you or Mr. Secretary?"

"Forget it. You're hopeless." I turned to Aaron. "Come on, let's go before he pickpockets us."

As soon as we were in the car, Aaron asked, "What was that about? Today's our day off. And you never mentioned that you had indigestion last night."

I took a deep breath. "I didn't want to hear about that Sheren guy abusing Violet. That's why I said what I did. You remember how upset I was about that domestic disturbance call?"

He put his hand on my thigh. "I do, and I'm glad you got us out of there. I didn't want to hear it either."

"I knew you'd understand."

"But what if he should mention it later on?"

I bit my lip. "Let's not think about it. I'll be up all night worrying about it."

"We don't want that." Aaron rubbed my leg and then winked at me.

"What's that for?"

He grinned. "Wanna tongue kiss, babe?"

I punched his arm. "No. You're impossible." Maybe a kiss would be good to relieve my angst. We were still in the driveway. I checked. Annamarie was no longer on her porch and no one was on the street. "Okay, just once." It worked, I felt relieved.

I pulled out of Grandpa's driveway and drove away. As we drove on West Washington Street, I pointed to a monument.

"That's the monument to Boots Thomas. He was the Marine Corps Sergeant killed in action in the battle of Iwo Jima in March, 1945. Boots was awarded the Navy Cross and the Purple Heart. He was also one of the marines who helped raise the first of two flags atop Mount Suribachi."

"How did you know all that?"

"Everybody in Monticello knows that." I grinned and added, "Besides it's on the monument."

A week later, we returned to Monticello. I had written four more chapters and was beginning to get a rhythm. I wrote and wrote and figured I'd edit it later. Hopefully, Grandpa had done his homework and had looked for pictures and worked on the timeline.

After Grandpa greeted us at the door, I made a fresh pot of coffee and served the guys their cookies.

"Cookies again?" said Grandpa.

"Stop complaining or I'll eat yours."

Grandpa waved me off. "Dang," He lowered his voice. "Scallywag."

"I heard that."

"Pfft," he mumbled.

I ignored him, sat down, took a bite of my cookie and a sip of coffee. Aaron stifled a laugh. "Did you do your homework?"

"Are we back in high school?" Grandpa put a finger to his forehead as though he remembered something. "Oh yeah, we were. That's where I left off. I guess that's where I'll begin. Turn that dang recorder on and get ready to take notes. I might test you later."

CHAPTER 29

MOM CONTINUED TO RIDE HER bike to work as did Violet when Mr. Sheren was out of town. Strangely, I felt sorry for Violet being isolated from her only friends—Mom and me. When you think about it, Mom's only friends were Violet and me. But I was there for Mom, and she could go into town and socialize. Violet couldn't. She was too scared of Mr. Sheren.

The last week of school, I got invited to a Saturday night party at a classmate's house. I looked forward to going, and Mom let me take the truck. Rosalind wasn't there as she had to work at the drugstore, but the stuck-up girl was. I had hoped that we would play spin the bottle and maybe when it was my turn, the bottle would put me and the stuck-up girl together. Unfortunately, we didn't play the game but we did do some dancing. Thanks to Mom teaching me, I was a hit with all the girls. I even danced with the stuck-up girl but not a slow dance. She danced a slow one with another boy. Oh, well, there was still the summer vacation and maybe more parties and the next school year. Plenty of time to dance and play spin the bottle, and who knew what else?

When school ended, I didn't plan on wasting the summer vacation. I started looking for a job. I'd take anything just to make some money. Mom said I should enjoy my vacation, but I wasn't going to let her be the only wage earner. I asked at every store and garage in town. I even rode my bike out to the nursery and the Tung orchard hoping to get work, but neither was hiring teenagers for the summer.

Luckily, the City Garage needed someone to pump gas and do a little work in the shop. Mr. Coogins gave me a recommendation, and I got the job. It paid fifty cents a day. I worked from eight in the morning until two in the afternoon. The owner said the hours and the pay were the best he could do, take it or leave it, so I took it. I had to give up my job at the Chevrolet store on Saturdays. Three dollars for six days work didn't seem like much. But for a teenager it was, and with Mom and me needing extra money it meant a lot. If I got an invite to a daytime party, I would have had to decline.

We had a new president since Roosevelt died while in office. Truman took ending the war with Japan grave. At the beginning of August, atomic bombs were dropped on the Japanese cities of Hiroshima and Nagasaki. On his radio broadcast, Edward R. Murrow said that it wouldn't be long before Japan surrendered. Mom and I hoped so because that meant Dad would be coming home. Japan officially signed the surrender on the second of September. The Monticello city officials set the air raid sirens off, and we all celebrated in the street downtown. The *Monticello News* headline read *WAR ENDS*.

My sophomore year started, but Dad hadn't come home. Not much had changed in our lives. Even though gasoline rationing had ended, Mom still rode her bike to work unless it was raining. I had to quit the job at City Garage because I decided to go out for junior varsity football. Mom gave her permission. We figured Dad would soon be home and he'd take care of us like he did before the war.

Over the summer, I had grown a few inches and put on some pounds. I didn't expect to make the starting team as most of the players had at least a year's experience. We practiced on the football field behind the elementary school. The field was mostly dirt. It was grueling in the afternoon heat, but I survived.

Rosalind continued to say good morning to me after getting off the bus, and we walked to class together. I was invited to a party, and I decided to ask Rosalind what the stuck-up girl's name was. We were standing in the hallway and there was no one in earshot when I asked.

"I'm surprised with you," she said. "Kathleen Shure has been in our class since first grade. Don't you pay attention at attendance?"

My head jerked back. "She has?" I never paid attention when the girls' names were called? Why would I? I didn't care about who they were. Maybe that was why I hadn't known Rosalind's name until she'd told Mom.

Rosalind rolled her eyes but couldn't contain her grin. "Yes, she has. But she likes to be called Katie." Rosalind grinned. "You have a crush on her?"

I waved her off. "I was just asking."

Rosalind smiled. "If you say so."

We walked into class. At least now I knew that stuck-up girl's name if ever I got the nerve to talk to her or she spoke to me. But I'd call her Katie, not Kathleen.

The varsity team's first football game was in one week. The JV coach didn't want the junior varsity quarterback to get hurt, so he put me in as the opposing team's quarterback for the varsity during practice. The defense was practicing their formations. On Wednesday's practice, the defense kept rushing the quarterback, and I ended up on the ground under a pile of defensive linemen. As the opposing quarterback, the coach wanted game-like conditions, and no one was to ease up. That wasn't good for a kid my size. Every time I got knocked down, I got back up and called the next play. My practice uniform looked like I'd rolled in a mud puddle.

When practice ended, the varsity players patted me on the back and told me, "Nice job, kid."

The coach put his arm around me and asked if I was okay.

"I've been hit harder," I said. "It was nothing."

"Well, don't expect to play quarterback anytime soon."

I didn't expect I'd ever play quarterback nor did I hope to see any playing time. But I'd be in a Tiger uniform when the junior varsity played and close to where the cheerleaders would be. Especially one in particular, Katie Shure.

Our high school was almost one hundred years old, and we had the honor of being the first brick school building in Florida. Although the school didn't have a gymnasium, it had a locker room for the football team in the basement, affording us privacy—almost privacy. Imagine a bunch of teenage boys naked taking showers together. That's not what one would call privacy. We left our uniforms, pads and helmets there, but we had to bring our dirty practice clothes home at the end of the week and wash them.

After one practice, I got a ride home from a varsity player in his truck. He made me sit on the bed because his girlfriend sat in the front with him. After the beating I'd taken, he said it was the least he could do. I started regularly riding my bike to school so I wouldn't have to walk home after practice or be forced to sit in the back of someone's truck.

The weeks went by, and Dad still hadn't come home. Mom and I were worried. The war was over soldiers had come home, but not Dad. We got a letter from him, but he didn't mention coming home. We hoped his ship wasn't in a battle before the war ended. What if something serious happened.

By October, the junior varsity had played several games and I'd sat on the bench. My playing time consisted of being the opposing team's quarterback for the varsity during practice and taking a beating. But the more I took, the meaner and tougher I got. Finally, on the last game in November, the coach called my name.

"Teague, go in for Wilson and don't screw up."

I grabbed my helmet, got off the bench, and started for the field. Unfortunately, I tripped, fell, and landed at a cheerleader's feet. When I looked up, staring down at me was Katie Shure. Could she see how red my face was—and it was burning—beneath my helmet? Nothing could be worse than getting a chance to play, falling at the feet of that stuck-up girl, and staring up at her with a ruby red face.

"Teague," Coach screamed, "pick yourself up and get in the game, now."

I managed to right myself as the cheerleaders laughed.

I ran onto the field without tripping and played a few downs before the game ended. I didn't screw up and didn't embarrass myself again.

After the game, I rode my bike home. When I approached the house, two figures were sitting on the porch. As I got closer, I realized one was Mom, and she had her head on a man's shoulder. The man had his arm around her. It had better not be Mr. Sheren, or I'd grab his arm, twist it until it broke and then crush him like the skunk roach he was. Yeah, that's what I'd do.

I got closer and peered over the bushes to get a better look. The man wore a uniform. He looked familiar.

My heart started to race like it knew something I didn't. Could it be? I pedaled up the driveway and reached the front porch before I let myself really believe it. It wasn't Mr. Sheren, but my dad.

Mom looked at peace with him finally beside her. All the image needed was a wedding cake to set them on top of.

Skippy sat beside Dad, soaking in the pets Dad was giving him.

When Dad saw me, he stood.

Beside him, Mom stood, face beaming. It was a long-awaited moment, and it had finally arrived. No more crying in her bedroom and no more me without the one who'd taught me how to work on a truck and to drive it, who'd taught me how to be a man. Dad was home. I got off my bike and ran up onto the porch. Dad was about to lift me into his arms but stopped when I reached him. His face broke out into the biggest grin I'd seen in forever.

"Gosh, Francis, you're not that twelve-year-old I remember. Look at you." He wrapped me in his arms. "You're bigger and heavier and—Wow."

I'd be relieved of the responsibility of being the man of the house. My Dad was home.

My heart pounded so fast I worried it might burst. I was all choked up. "And meaner, too," I said, but my voice cracked. "It's about time you got home. What took you so long?"

Dad laughed and stepped back. "I had to cross the Pacific and hitchhike across the country. Luckily, there was no shortage of rides. Most folks were just grateful to see soldiers home."

"Why'd you hitchhike?"

"Cheaper than a plane or bus. And I made it."

"You sure did." I couldn't keep the smile off my face, though I'd managed to keep from crying, barely. "And we sure are glad." I turned to see my mother, who was still beaming like a headlight. "Ain't we, Mom?"

"Grammar, Francis," Dad said. "It's *aren't* we."

"Sure, Dad, as you say."

My parents laughed. My father was home, and now I had another English teacher. Just what I needed.

Now that I was over my shock, I sniffed and stepped back from my father. "You stink."

"The last ride I got was from a farmer. He made me sit in the back of his truck with the hogs. You'd stink, too."

I laughed. "Was he here when you got home, Mom?"

"Not quite. And when I saw him, I almost ran him over." Mom smiled. "I couldn't believe my eyes." Although she was smiling, Mom had a tear in her eye.

"So, Francis, why are you home so late?" Dad asked. "Don't tell me you had detention."

"I'm on the junior varsity football team. We had a game today, and I got a chance to

lay." I didn't want to tell him about how I'd tripped and landed at the cheerleader's feet.

"Damn..."

"Frank, don't cuss in front of the boy."

Dad made a wry grin. "Sorry, Marion, it's a tough habit to shake after being cooped up with men on a ship for years. Dang, you're in high school?"

"I've been to two partics, danced with girls and even..." Whoops. My parents didn't need to know about that tongue kiss. They both eyed me skeptically.

Skippy barked at the door. "I think he's hungry," I said, mostly so they wouldn't ask what I'd been about to say.

Inside, Mom fed Skippy. Dad showered and then came into the kitchen dressed in his old pants and shirt.

He puffed his chest. "Feels good to finally get that uniform off."

"What would my two men like for dinner?" Mom asked with a huge grin.

"Whatever Dad wants is fine with me." I smiled. "I could kill a chicken."

Dad pondered the situation. It was his first night home with his family. For almost four years, he shared a table with other sailors onboard ship. Now he had a choice of eating dinner in the kitchen or in a restaurant.

"Let's eat here," Dad said. "No need to kill a chicken. But I wouldn't mind fresh eggs, some fresh vegetables from the garden if there are any left." He turned to Mom. "Maybe you could make my favorite omelet."

I think Mom was pleased that he wanted to stay home. Although it had been years since my parents had gone out to dinner, I was sure, just like me, she wanted to have dinner in our home at our kitchen table and just the three of us.

"I'll make you that omelet and with a surprise. Francis, get some eggs from the coop and if there are any vegetables in the garden bring them in, too."

Skippy and I went to the chicken coop, grabbed six eggs, stuffed them in my pockets, and walked through the garden. There were still a few winter squashes. I grabbed them and rolled them in my shirt, and we returned to the kitchen. When I opened the door, my parents were hugging. I backed out the door and let it close silently. I backed a few feet away and called, "Got some squash and eggs. Hey, could someone open the door for me?"

Dad opened the door, I walked in and set the squash and eggs on the table, and then Skippy and I went to listen to the radio so my parents could be alone. Mom made Dad's favorite omelet. She used Spam and as a surprise and made macaroni and cheese. When dinner was ready, we sat at the table as a family. Dad said grace, thanking the Lord for bringing him home safe and in one piece.

CHAPTER 30

GRANDPA RAISED HIS GLASSES AND wiped his eyes. "Excuse me; I have to go to the bathroom." He stood and walked away.

Aaron used a knuckle to wipe his eye. "That was an emotional moment for your grandfather," he said. "Are you gonna write about it?"

I wiped my tears. Ordinarily, I would have answered, *hell no*, but it was my responsibility to portray my grandfather as he was—with all the raw feelings that he experienced.

"I have to. He shared it with us. He wouldn't have told us about them if he didn't want me to write about it."

"You're right," he said.

"Damn right, I am." I adopted a sullen look. "I'd give anything to have a meal with my father. You're lucky you still can."

Aaron had been my emotional rock ever since we moved in together. There'd been a few scary moments when his father had been ill. Fortunately, his father had recovered from his illness.

Aaron grinned. "Want to tongue kiss?"

"No." I would have kicked him, but he was too far from me.

Grandpa returned and sat down. "Sorry about that."

I put my hand on his arm and squeezed it. "It's okay."

Grandpa covered my hand and squeezed ever so gently.

"Would you like to continue this another time, Grandpa? We can come back tomorrow."

"I think that would be better."

The next morning, Aaron and I returned with a bag of cookies and waved to Annamarie. She was sitting on her porch sipping from a glass of what was most likely sweet tea and called us over. We walked across the yard. Annamarie wiped sweat off her brow. She was feeling the heat as we were. We were in the early days of summer, and the mornings were hotter and muggier.

"I had dinner with your grandfather last evening, and he seemed distant. Like he was in a faraway place. Is everything okay?"

I ran my hand through my hair and glanced at Aaron. Apparently, the memories the day before had affected Grandpa more than I realized.

"He was probably tired from reminiscing. Don't fret. He's fine."

"Whatever," she snapped.

Apparently, she didn't like my response. Annamarie could get testy when it had to do with Grandpa. She cared about him. We ignored her and walked away. Inside Grandpa's house, I made a pot of coffee and brought three cups and the cookies onto the porch. Grandpa seemed in better spirits.

"You ready to rock and roll again, kiddo?"

"Yes, but can we do it in the den? It's hot out here."

Grandpa shook his head. "Can't take the heat? What a wimp."

We moved into the den where it was air-conditioned.

CHAPTER 31

THAT FIRST NIGHT AFTER MY father got home, I thanked God for keeping him safe, but I was still angry with God. He could have stopped my dad from volunteering and my mother wouldn't have been so lonely. And, although I was happy that Dad was home, I was angry with him, too. I fell asleep with no worries about my father. Mom had Dad beside her for the first time in almost four years. I'm sure she slept untroubled—as I did.

The next morning, I overslept and was awakened by Skippy licking my face.

"Okay, boy, I'm getting up. Have you been out, yet?" Skippy barked and wagged his tail. I got out of bed and dressed. Mom was in the kitchen washing dishes and humming. I hadn't heard her hum since before the war. "Morning, Mom."

When she turned, her eyes were wide and glowing. "Good morning, Francis. Did you sleep well?"

"Better than ever. Where's Dad?"

Her eyes sparkled. "He's outside working on the truck. Would you like some breakfast? There's still some Spam left."

I closed my eyes, thought about the house just one day before, and then opened them again. Nothing had changed, and everything had changed. What a difference Dad's coming home made in our lives.

"I'll have cereal," I said.

"But there's no milk."

"I'll eat it dry."

Mom turned and went back to washing dishes and humming.

After breakfast, Skippy and I went out to see what my father was doing. Dad had the truck's hood raised and was leaned over the engine and whistling. His sleeves were rolled up. I rolled mine up. Four years ago, he did the same thing, and I was side by side with him, helping work on the engine. Now I hoped that what he'd taught me I had put to good use. I hoped he found the engine in good working order.

"Everything okay, Dad?"

He stopped whistling and backed out from under the hood. Dad wiped his greasy hands on an equally greasy towel, his smile as wide as the truck's grill. "You did good. The engine needs a little work. Sitting idle for so long wasn't good for it." Dad didn't know that we drove it more often than just let it sit idle. He motioned for me to join him. "The plugs need cleaning. The carburetor needs a good cleaning. It's not your fault. You did the best you could, and I'm proud of you."

My father couldn't have made me feel any prouder than I was at that moment. "Thanks, Dad. We had to conserve gas, so the truck mostly sat unused in the driveway. Except when it rained."

"Not anymore since rationing is over. The truck needs to be taken for a long ride. We'll do it Sunday after church."

Just then, Mr. Sheren walked into the driveway. Bad timing. We don't need him ruining a perfectly good morning.

"Frank, you're finally home." Mr. Sheren, as usual, spoke in his blustery voice. "It's about time."

Dad reached for a wrench and pretended to tighten a bolt. "Not now, Sheren. I'm busy." Just like me, Dad was annoyed that Mr. Sheren was interrupting a father-son moment.

"Too busy to talk to your neighbor? Come on, Frank, I just have one question."

Dad stepped to the side of the truck. He held the wrench so tight it made his knuckles turn white. I rubbed my hands on my pant legs. I was worried that Dad was angry and was going to hit Mr. Sheren with the wrench.

"What do you want?"

Mr. Sheren held his palms out, wiggled his hips and shook his shoulders. "What say you and the missus go dancing with Violet and me tonight?"

"I just got home."

"See, that's why you need to go dancing. You gotta celebrate, Frank."

Dad crossed his arms. "Whatever celebrating I do will be with my family, not with you. I'm busy here, so if you don't mind, we'd like to get on with what we were doing before you so rudely interrupted us."

Mr. Sheren's face turned ashen and his eyes bulged.

Way to go, Dad. That told him. If he didn't leave, I'd have Skippy bite him. That's what I wanted to say, but I didn't.

"I should have known," he said. "Your wife didn't want to go with us either the last time I asked her."

I'd seen that look on my father's face once before. A fox had wandered into our yard and was heading for the chickens. The fox had seen Dad, looked at the chickens, back at Dad, and left the yard. Mr. Sheren also made the right decision. Like the fox, he walked away.

When he disappeared into his house, Dad turned to me. "If there's one thing I didn't miss while in the navy, it was that jackass."

We both laughed.

"Dad, what was it like during the war?"

There was that look again, the same one he gave Mr. Sheren, and that was the last time I asked about the war.

"You gonna stand there and ask questions or you gonna help me?"

After lunch, Dad suggested I go to the high school football game. I hadn't planned on going because it was his first weekend home, but his smile told me that I should. When I returned, my parents were walking along the sidewalk holding hands. Skippy walked in front of them. I waited until they were inside before walking up to the driveway. I knew I'd made the right decision going to the game.

That night after dinner, we sat in the living room and listened to the Grand Ole Opry. Floyd Tillman, Red Foley, and others sang songs. But Ernest Tubb's song "Soldier's Last Letter," affected Dad. He got silent, glanced at Mom, nodded, and held her hand.

Dad had brought home a set of Dominoes, and he taught us how to play the game. Dominoes and popcorn became our Saturday night entertainment from then on.

Sunday morning, we sat in the church pew listening to the priest's platitudes about arguing and fighting. He preached the virtue of turning the other cheek, walking away, and forgiving your enemy. Dad clutched his hymnal. Obviously, that priest never had to defend his country, family, or a comrade in arms. Obviously, that priest had never had to face an enemy bent on killing you. I was sure Dad would get up and walk out of the church, but he remained seated until Mass ended.

If Dad had got up and left the church, I would have gone with him. Dad had sacrificed for that priest and the people at the Mass. That priest and those people should at least have appreciated it and said so.

After Mass, we got into the truck. Before Dad had left for the war, I was small and thin enough to sit between my parents. But now I had to sit by the window. Mom sat between Dad and me. I don't think she minded because she scooted close to Dad and smiled at him.

Before leaving the parking area, Dad asked, "How about we take a ride out to Moccasin Gap Road? Maybe go to Bradley's and buy some meat. What do you say, Marion?"

"But that'll use up all our gas."

"It's my first weekend home, and I want to take a ride in the country with my family. I'll get gas tomorrow."

Dad pulled out of the parking area, drove through town, and turned onto State Road 59. We'd gone about five miles when we saw a car parked on the side of the road. The car's hood was raised, and a colored man was standing in front of it. A colored boy was struggling to change a tire, and a colored woman and two-colored girls were standing nearby. I recognized the boy. It was Jackie.

"Looks like those folks need some help. I'm gonna stop and see if I can be of use."

"But, Frank, they're…"

"So what that they're colored folk. That don't mean I can't offer help." Dad parked the truck a little behind the car. "You wait here while I see what's up."

"Can I go, Dad? Maybe I could help change the tire."

"Okay. Grab my toolbox."

I reached behind the seat to get the toolbox Dad kept there for emergencies. We walked over to the car. "You folks need some help?" Dad called.

The man hesitated and backed away. "Boy needs help changing the tire, and I can't get the car to start. We'd appreciate any help you can give."

Jackie recognized me and nodded his head. The woman clutched her purse and motioned for the girls to get behind her. Mom strained to see what was happening.

Dad looked at the woman and girls. "That your family?"

"Yes, sir, that's my momma and my sisters."

Dad tipped his head at the woman. "Ma'am, if you'd like, you can join my wife in the truck. The girls can sit on the bed."

The woman ducked her head. "Thank you, sir, if your wife wouldn't mind, I'd appreciate it."

Dad waved to Mom and signaled that the three ladies were going to join her. Mom waved for him to send them over. "Go ahead, ma'am. My wife's name is Marion."

"Thank you, kind sir. Come, girls let's go." One of the girls winked at me as she walked past me. Jackie noticed and rolled his eyes.

Dad had me help Jackie change the tire. We exchanged glances and bumped shoulders, but we didn't make it obvious to the men that we knew each other. While we worked on the tire, Dad looked under the hood.

"Here's the problem," Dad said.

The man leaned over, nodded.

"Say, what's your name?" Dad stepped back, met the man's eyes. "Mine's Frank."

"Cecil."

Dad extended a hand. Cecil offered his left hand, and Dad glanced at the man's right hand. I followed his gaze and saw the hand was gnarled as though it had been damaged. "What happened?"

Cecil stared down at his hand. "Bayonet fight with a Jap in the war. Severed the nerves."

Dad nodded slowly. "Did you finish him off?"

Cecil made an upward thrust with his right hand. "Gutted him good." Cecil looked at me and toward the truck at Mom. "Don't suppose you was in the war."

I expected Dad would give him that look he gave me when I asked him about the war, but he didn't. "Navy, a mechanic on a battleship in the Pacific." Dad focused on the engine again. "Your spark plug wires are loose. Someone didn't put the caps on all the way. While I'm at it, I might as well check the plugs. Hand me my toolbox."

I handed the toolbox to Cecil, who gave it to Dad. He unscrewed the plugs and looked at them. "You could use new ones, but I'll clean them for you. Next time you have work done, get new plugs."

Jackie and I had finished changing the tire and were listening to their conversation.

"I'm the one to blame." Cecil held up his left hand. "Only hand I can use, and I'm right-handed. Fortunately, I'm a school teacher at Howard."

Dad looked at me. Howard was a school for colored kids. I looked at Jackie. He nodded, and I figured he went there.

Dad replaced the spark plugs. "Okay, that should do it. Try to start it now."

Cecil called out to Jackie. "Jackie, fire it up." Jackie got behind the wheel and turned the key, and the engine fired up. "He's the driver now."

"Good for him," Dad said. "Where you folks headed?"

"Miccosukee. We got kinfolk there. Momma hadn't seen them since Christmas forty-one, just before I left for the war. They're having a social for us."

"Well, it looks like you and your family can go join them." Dad scratched the back of his head. "I was going to ride out to Bradley's. How about I follow you to Moccasin Gap Road and make sure you get where you're headed?"

"If it won't be a bother." Cecil tapped a loose fist against his heart. "I'd appreciate it. Momma would feel better if you did." Cecil called his mother and sisters over. His mother had gray hair, walked like she was tired from being on her feet, and I figured she was years older than my mother. Cecil's sisters were younger than Jackie and constantly smiled. Cecil's mother nodded at him. "Momma, he's gonna follow us to make sure we're all right."

"Thank you, sir; you're a good man. My family appreciates you stopping to help us. Most white folks wouldn't."

"I'm not most white folks, ma'am. It was my pleasure." Dad gestured as though he was tipping his hat.

Dad extended his hand to Cecil, and the two men shook. Jackie nodded at me, and I nodded back. His way of saying thank you, and my way of saying you're welcome. Cecil's family piled into the car, waved goodbye to us, and Jackie drove off.

Dad and I got into the truck, and we followed Cecil's car.

"Nice family," remarked Mom. "That woman has supported her children by herself since her son went into the army. She's had to walk almost three miles a day, six days a week to her place of employment. I don't envy her."

I didn't envy her either, since I knew what it was like for Mom to walk to work. I just hoped now that Dad was home, she could stop.

"She told me that at first she was worried when you pulled up behind their car," said Mom. "She said other cars just drove on by and never gave them a second look. I was wrong when I first questioned us stopping." Mom lifted her chin. "Those same people would think poorly of me because I clean someone else's house."

"Let them, Mom," I said. "You did it for us."

"And because you had to," said Dad with some regret in his voice. "I didn't leave you much choice." I was surprised to hear him say that, but he was right. Mom squeezed my knee.

"Were there any colored men on board the ship, Dad?"

Dad nodded. "Some. And a few worked alongside with me. But they weren't allowed to eat with us." Dad shook his head. "Such a shame."

I could have said I knew Jackie, but then I would have had to say where and I couldn't do that. Jackie and I had a secret.

"It's a good thing that her eldest son is a schoolteacher," Dad said. "I'm gonna follow them up the road and then turn at Moccasin Gap Road intersection. We'll eat lunch at home."

Sitting alongside my parents, I felt honored to be in their company. My father hadn't had to stop and help that family, and my mother hadn't had to keep company with Jackie's mom. When we reached the intersection, Dad waved to Cecil's family, made a U-turn, and headed back to Monticello.

I had forgotten about falling at the cheerleader's feet Friday because my mind was elsewhere over the weekend. But Monday morning, after Dad drove me to school, I realized I had to face Rosalind and the cheerleader when they got off the school bus. After he dropped me off, he then took Mom to work. He had planned on going to see Mr. Coogins and see about getting his old job back. I was glad he dropped me off early because that meant the school bus hadn't arrived yet and neither had Rosalind and the cheerleader. Unfortunately, I still had to face my classmates who'd attended last Friday's JV game.

I walked down the hallway and to my class and sat in the first row and waited for the classroom to fill. I didn't want to see my classmates faces as they entered—most likely snickering. And that stuck-up cheerleader would probably be the lead giggler of the girls. I heard some giggles, cackles, snickers, grins, and jeers as they entered. But, I held my head up high and ignored it all.

Lunchtime, Rosalind joined me at my table. We were the only two there as everyone else avoided me. I kept my head down as I ate my lunch wondering if I should have eaten outside in the schoolyard.

"I heard that your father came home," Rosalind said.

Boy, word sure got around in this town.

"How does it feel having him home?"

"It's awesome. He hitchhiked all the way across the country to get here." I felt like shedding tears. "We got to sit down to dinner as a family for the first time in four years."

"I bet your mother was overjoyed."

"She sure was. Thanks for asking. I thought you were going to ask about…"

She grinned. "About the game? Who cares about that?"

I would have kissed her if I hadn't been a gentleman. "Thanks, I appreciate you asking."

We finished lunch and walked back to class together.

I walked home from school, did my chores and took Skippy for a walk. Dad wasn't home, but eventually, he and Mom arrived together. Dad had picked Mom up from work. They were all smiles and giggles as they got out of the truck.

Dad had met with Mr. Coogins about his old job. Mr. Coogins was willing to hire him but at a lower salary. He reduced Dad's old wage by ten-percent explaining that it was the only way he could afford to hire him. Dad tried to negotiate, but Mr. Coogins refused. Dad took the job but told Mr. Coogins he couldn't start until the following Monday.

With both my parents bringing in a salary, life would be better than it had been before. I decided that I would try to make up the ten percent that Dad was deprived of and went looking for an after-school job.

I excelled at math, played JV football, and had work experience. Using those as my resume, I visited every store in town and wound up with a job at Harris Grocery. I stocked shelves, swept floors, and did whatever else they wanted me to do. I worked until six o'clock every day after school and from nine until four on Saturdays. My pay was ten cents an hour, and I earned two dollars and twenty cents a week. That seemed like a lot of money to me, and it made up some of what Dad had lost. Plus, I got to work inside.

When Thanksgiving came, Mom wanted to invite the Sherens, but Dad was reluctant. Mom explained that she was concerned about Violet and would like to give her a chance to socialize with someone other than Mr. Sheren. Dad gave in, but with a condition. There'd be no alcohol in the house. If the Sherens wanted to drink, they'd have to be satisfied with apple cider like us. Dad didn't trust the Sherens when it came to drinking. Mr. Sheren declined the invitation. It didn't bother Dad, but Mom was upset.

For Christmas, the three of us took Skippy and went to the nursery and bought the biggest tree we could fit in the bed of the truck. We decorated it on Christmas Eve. Christmas morning when I took Skippy out for a walk, the weather was unseasonably warm unlike last Christmas when the ground had been blanketed with frost, and I saw my breath.

We celebrated Christmas breakfast and dinner together. We said a blessing before dinner thankful that we were all together again. Dad gave Mom a Whitman's Sampler as a gift. I gave her a box of Cracker Jacks. It was all I could think of. Skippy gave us all kisses. But, I got the best present. Watching Mom smile as she opened Dad's gift, and then the two of them hugging each other, made me believe there really was a Santa Claus.

New Year's Eve we celebrated with apple cider and popcorn. The Sherens had gone somewhere to celebrate, and when they arrived home, I heard a commotion coming from their driveway. I was in my bedroom reading and looked out the window. They appeared to be arguing. Violet said something, and Mr. Sheren slapped her.

I rushed into the living room and told Mom and Dad what I saw.

Mom stood, eyes wide. "Are you sure?"

"I just saw it."

Dad stood, too. "I'll go see what's going on."

"No Frank, let it be. You'll only make matters worse for Violet."

Dad and I did a slight head shake. We were confused. Dad reluctantly sat down, his eyes darted at the front door and he considered going anyway. I wanted to go, too. Mom stood by the door like a sentry and prevented either of us from going. She must have known something that we didn't.

CHAPTER 32

ONCE AGAIN, I WORRIED THAT Grandpa was going to give us details about Sheren abusing Violet. So far, he had only slapped her that once in public, but what had he done to her in private? I didn't want to know, and I didn't want to hear any more, so I interrupted Grandpa.

"Grandpa, I think you've talked enough for today. Let's do it again next week." I silently prayed he would agree so I'd have the week to prepare myself. "I could use the time to write some. Don't you agree, Aaron?"

"I could use a break, too," he said.

Grandpa looked from Aaron to me. "Okay, if you want to." Then he smiled. "Have your secretary call mine and schedule an appointment."

I gratefully grinned. "I'll do that. Aaron, did you hear that?" Aaron seemed like he was daydreaming. "Aaron, did you hear that?"

He woke. "Huh? Oh yeah, I'll call your secretary, Mr. Teague."

We all laughed, and my mood changed. But, I really was going to write more chapters at home. In fact, I had a lot of stuff to write.

I loathed having to come back to my grandfather's house to hear about how Sheren abused Violet. I didn't know what I'd do if that happened. If I left it out because of my angst, Grandpa would be disappointed that I hadn't kept my word to write what he told me. I could wait until after he died before finishing the book, but that would be deceiving him and I couldn't do that. I could ask Aaron, but I'm sure he would want me to honor my grandfather's wishes.

Then I remembered what my high school track coach once said. "Suck it up, Blass. You wanted to be on the team, now quit whining and get with the program." So, I guess I'd suck it up and get with the program.

We said goodbye to Grandpa and left. Annamarie was coming down the sidewalk as we came out of the house.

She waved to us. "Erica, how's the book coming?"

"Fine. I've done a lot of writing. But it's a long way from being finished." I still felt uneasy about the abuse thing and wanted to go home. I glanced at my watch. "We have to run. Maybe another time."

She put her hands on her hips. "Have a safe drive."

With that, Aaron and I were on our way back to Tallahassee. I was quiet during the ride. Aaron must have suspected something was bothering me because he let me keep my thoughts to myself. It was one of the reasons I loved him. He understood me and let me have my moments.

That night, we discussed what we had learned that day. I decided to ask his opinion about the Sherens.

"I'm worried what my grandfather might say about Sheren and what he did to Violet, and if I should include it in the book?"

Aaron scratched his arm. "You made a promise, and you should keep it."

"Yeah, you're right. But…"

He placed a hand on my arm and rubbed it. "I know, babe, I feel the same way." He tilted his head. "What if he mentioned something else about your great-grandmother and Violet? Then what?"

My stomach churned. "Hopefully, that won't happen. I couldn't handle anymore turmoil. I hadn't expected anything like this. I just wanted to write about Grandpa, not all that other stuff." I took a deep breath. "Maybe I should stop…"

Aaron put his arm around me. "Maybe you should talk to your mom."

I sighed. "Last time I did that, she told me to stay with it. There's no point in calling her. She'd say the same thing."

He kissed my forehead. "Don't quit, stay with it. You know I'm always here for you, and you could always lean on me. Besides, maybe it won't be so bad."

I leaned against him. "I guess we'll know next week."

"Say, did you work after school when you were in high school?"

"I was a cashier at the Piggly Wiggly, but I earned way more than my grandfather," I said, grateful that Aaron had changed the subject. "How about you?"

"I worked at a local hardware store, and I stocked shelves, swept the floors and did whatever I was asked to do." Aaron smiled. "Guess we were typical teenagers like your grandfather."

I called Grandpa and arranged to visit him Wednesday morning. He agreed with one condition. No, two conditions—that I bring Aaron and doughnuts. Aaron I'd bring, but doughnuts no way.

We stopped at Publix and purchased three sugar-free oatmeal cookies and one doughnut. The doughnut was for Aaron—which he ate on the drive to Monticello.

Grandpa was waiting for us on the front porch.

"Hurry up. I've been waiting all week for a doughnut." He evil-eyed Aaron. "I bet you already ate one, didn't you?" Aaron smirked. "I thought so, but it had better not be one of mine. Give me that bag." Grandpa snatched the bag from Aaron and peered in. "Where are the doughnuts? Those are cookies."

"I told you no more doughnuts. It's cookies or nothing."

Grandpa shook his head. "Cookies are as bad as nothing."

I snatched the bag from his hand. "Okay then, Aaron and I will eat them. You get nothing."

"Never mind. Let's go inside, and I'll eat a damn cookie."

"We're not sitting on the porch. We're going into the den." I grinned. "So what if I'm a wimp. It's too hot for the porch."

"Pfft," Grandpa mumbled.

"Pfft, yourself," I said.

I made a fresh pot of coffee, poured three cups and brought the cookies into the den. The air-conditioning felt great. Aaron grabbed a cookie and munched on it. Grandpa reluctantly ate his.

"Thanks for waiting for me," I said. "When did I become the maid service?" They both waved me off.

After I ate my cookie, I was ready to take more notes. Aaron was supposed to take notes, too, but lately he'd become more interested in listening to Grandpa. But I still brought him with me because my grandfather insisted that I do and because...Well, if you had a brown-haired, blue-eyed guy as your fiancé, you'd want him by your side too.

"You ready to begin, Grandpa?"

Grandpa wiped his mouth with the back of his hand. Why he didn't use the napkin was a mystery to me. Aaron did the same thing. I guess it was a guy thing.

"Ready," he replied.

CHAPTER 33

FTER THE HOLIDAYS ENDED, I was invited to party on a Saturday night at a classmate's house. I wasn't sure I wanted to go because the kids who'd be there were the same classmates who'd ridiculed me about my mishap at the football game. Especially that stuck-up cheerleader, Katie Shure. Rosalind wouldn't be there because she still worked Saturday nights at the drugstore. I hemmed and hawed about what to do. Finally, I decided not to go. Instead, after a game of Dominoes with my parents, I walked into town to get a milkshake at the drugstore.

"Francis, what are you doing here?" Rosalind asked. "Why aren't you at the party?" I considered being honest and saying because you're not there, but she might take it the wrong way and think I had a crush on her. To be frank, since I'd gotten to know her better, I wouldn't mind dating Rosalind. But I wasn't going to tell her.

"I didn't feel in the party mood. Besides, you know how those kids feel about me."

Rosalind smiled. I loved her heart-warming smile.

"Well, that's their problem. You know how I feel about you."

Oh-oh, what was happening here? Did she have a crush on me or was I making something out of nothing?

"Could I have a vanilla milkshake, please?"

Rosalind winked at me. "Sure thing. Coming right up." She walked away and came back shortly with my milkshake. "Enjoy it." Another wink and now I wondered if she was toying with me or her wink was something more than just friendly.

After I finished my milkshake, I waved goodbye to Rosalind. "See you Monday, Francis." Another wink along with that heart-warming smile.

I walked home, and for some reason felt like I was walking on air. What was happening to me?

Mr. Sheren was out of town more often than before the war, and Violet had only her bike as transportation. Dad drove her and Mom to work. I walked to school. If Dad finished his job in time, he'd pick up both ladies and bring them home. Violet asked that he drop her off at the end of the block so she could walk home in the event Mr. Sheren was there. Dad was confused by her request, but Mom explained it to him. Dad didn't like the reason.

I started waiting for Rosalind until she got off the school bus, greeted her, and walked her to class. Stuck-up Katie Shure glared at me, but I ignored her. I didn't walk Rosalind to the bus after school because she had band practice, and I had to work at the grocery store. However, I did go for milkshakes several Saturday nights.

Mr. Sheren had returned from one of his trips after three weeks away. He and Violet went dancing that Saturday night but came home earlier than usual. I had already returned from the drugstore and was listening to the radio with my parents.

Suddenly, there was a pounding on our door.

"What the hell," yelled Dad.

Mom started to get up, but Dad gestured to her chair. "No, you sit, I'll get it." Dad walked into the kitchen and carefully opened the door. Mom looked at me with concern. I was concerned, too. We couldn't see who pounded on the door.

"What's going on, Violet?" asked Dad.

When Mom heard who was at the door, she went to see what was going on. I followed her. When Mom saw Violet covering the left side of her face, she shoved dad aside and extended her hand.

"Come in. What happened? Did he…" I guess Mom knew what happened. "Frank, get some ice."

Dad chopped a sliver of ice from the block in the icebox. He wrapped it in a dish towel and handed it to Mom.

"Sit down and put this on your eye."

Violet's knees buckled. She was about to collapse, but Dad and I grabbed her in time and set her in a chair.

"Thank you." Violet's voice trembled. "I'm embarrassed. You shouldn't see me like this." Violet placed the towel against her eye. Dad's face reddened. I gritted my teeth. "I don't know what set him off this time."

"This time?" Dad looked from Violet to Mom and back. "What do you mean this time?"

"Frank, please, you'll upset her," Mom said.

"The hell with upsetting her. I want to know what's going on." Dad's nostrils flared. "Has he done this before?"

Mom placed a hand on Violet's shoulder. "Yes—"

"That's it," Dad said. "There's not going to be any next time. I'll take care of this."

"No, please, Frank you'll only make it worse," Violet said, voice wary.

"Worse for who, Violet? You or him? No man beats his wife and gets away with it. I'm going over to your house and have a talk with him."

Violet stood and grabbed my father's arm. "Wait. He's got a gun, and he's drunk."

That got Dad's attention. "Where'd he get a gun?"

"It's mine," she said, voice shaky. "It's a Derringer. I kept it in my purse to defend myself. But he grabbed it away from me."

My parents' mouths fell open. "Grabbed it from you?" Mom's voice was a mixture of awe and fear. "Were you going to shoot him?"

Violet sniffled. "Yes."

Dad's voice held only anger. "Have you ever fired the damn gun?"

Violet returned to her seat and clutched at her blouse. "Once."

Something came to me. A memory. I smelled her perfume, saw the way she clutched her hand to her chest. I remembered the woman who Frankie and I had seen shoot the guy by the car. Violet was that woman. When I'd gotten home that night, Violet was with Mom. She must have confessed her crime to Mom, and my mother had kept her secret just like Jackie and I had.

"I don't care. I'm going over and have a talk with him."

"Can I come too, Dad?"

"You stay here and mind the ladies. Skippy, you help him."

Skippy barked and sat at my feet.

Fifteen minutes later, Dad returned and in no harm. "He won't be bothering anyone tonight. But, Violet, you're not going home. You'll stay with us."

"She can have my bed, Dad. Skippy and I can sleep on the couch."

Dad shook his head. "No. I'll sleep on the couch just in case he gets any ideas. Violet, you sleep with Marion. Go on now, all of you. No questions, just do like I said."

Mom and Violet went to Mom's bedroom, I went to mine, and Skippy stayed with Dad.

The next morning, I was up early and went into the kitchen to check on Dad. He was sitting at the table with a cup of coffee. I got a glass of orange juice. Violet and Mom came out of the bedroom.

"He's gone, and I don't think he'll be coming back anytime soon," Dad told Violet. "You're safe now. But just to be sure, you'll spend the next few nights here. I'll drive you and Marion to work."

"I don't think she'll be going to work for a few days," said Mom.

Violet's eye was swollen shut.

I stood, unsure what to do. "Let me get some more ice."

That night, Dad and I listened to the radio while Mom and Violet talked in the bedroom. When I went into the kitchen to let Skippy out, I overheard some of their conversation. Violet told Mom about how she shouldn't have come south with him and was going back to her people and was passing as white. Whatever Violet meant by passing as white was lost on me as I didn't hear the rest of the conversation. I was sure Mom knew.

Violet didn't go back to work. She went home during the day and spent nights with us. I felt sorry for Dad sleeping on the couch. His back must have ached, but he wouldn't trade places with me and sleep in my bed.

At the end of the week, Violet asked Dad if he would take her to the train depot in Lloyd.

"Where will you be heading?" asked Dad.

"Back home."

"And where is home?"

"Mississippi."

So far, the conversation was very brief, extremely brief, and I wondered if we'd learn more about Violet.

"Won't he be there?" Dad asked.

"No, he's from Detroit. That's where I met him." My jaw dropped. At least now I knew Mr. Sheren wasn't a Chicago gangster, but he could be a Detroit gangster.

Violet focused on the floor and sighed. "We were never married."

Now Mom's jaw dropped.

All those years, my mother had trusted Violet, and she broke that trust by keeping secrets from my mother.

"We were just pretending. Will you still take me to Lloyd, Frank?"

"Of course, he will," replied Mom.

"Do you have enough money for a train ticket? It might be expensive," asked Dad.

Violet fidgeted her hands and bit her lip. "I have some money that I saved for an emergency, and this is an emergency."

Dad scratched his chin, contemplating Violet's options. "Let me drive into town first and ask how much a bus ticket costs. Where in Mississippi are you going?"

She glanced at Mom, at me, and then back at Dad. "Tupelo. I have fifty dollars. Hopefully, it's enough."

"Don't worry," Mom said. "We'll make sure you have enough." My mother was a forgiving person.

Dad raised his eyebrows, turned, and left the house.

While Dad was in town, Mom took Violet into the bedroom and closed the door. She didn't want me to hear what they were discussing. Most likely, Mom wanted to know why Violet hadn't told her about not being married to Mr. Sheren. A few minutes later, Mom and Violet came out of the bedroom. Mom had her arm around Violet and a hand on her shoulder. Violet wiped her eye with the back of her hand.

Dad returned from the Greyhound station with the cost of a bus ticket to Tupelo, Mississippi.

"You've got more than enough for a one-way ticket, Violet. There's a bus leaving Monday morning."

Violet placed her hand on her chest. "Thank heavens. I only need to go one-way. I'm not coming back." Her face and neck turned red. "If he comes back, tell him to do whatever he wants with the house. It's in his name, anyway." She clenched her jaw. "And you can tell him to go to hell."

Apparently, there was no love lost between Violet and Mr. Sheren. Violet went home, packed a bag, and returned to spend the weekend with us—which meant more backaches for Dad.

Monday morning, Dad went outside to start the truck and put Violet's bag in the back. Mom was feeding Skippy. I was in my room getting ready for school. Violet came into my room to say goodbye.

She wrapped her arms around me and squeezed me against her. Her bosom pressed against my chest. I felt an excitement in me. Her face was close to mine which added to the excitement. It made my heart race.

Violet stepped back and put her hand on my cheek and rubbed her thumb over it. I thought about doing the same to her but didn't.

"So long, Frankie boy. Thanks for looking out for me." I thought about that night in her bedroom. "You're gonna make someone happy one day."

"Thanks for being Mom's friend."

When she brushed her lips against mine, it was electric.

Violet winked, smiled, turned and left my room. As I watched her walk away, I wanted her to stay.

I rode my bike to school hoping to get there in time to see Rosalind before class. Unfortunately, I missed her.

My parents took Violet to the bus station. Violet was gone, Mr. Sheren was gone, and the identity of the mystery woman was solved.

CHAPTER 34

"**M**R. TEAGUE, DID SHEREN EVER come back?" Aaron had rudely interrupted my grandfather. If he hadn't, I was going to because I was upset about what Sheren had done to Violet.

The most distressing emergency a paramedic had to respond to was a domestic violence call. Some of the women I treated were lucky to have lived. I won't describe what they looked like except to say that they were beaten to within an inch of their lives. After treating them and taking them to the hospital, I always asked for time off and considered getting drunk. That a man that a woman had loved, in many cases, pledged her life to, would do such a thing. And in most cases, the women would keep going back. It made me sick. It made me question humanity. From what Grandpa told us, Violet was one of the fortunate ones.

"What?" Grandpa's head snapped back. "No, he didn't."

"What happened to his house?"

"His house stayed vacant for a year before another couple moved in," Grandpa said. "We didn't see much of them; they kept to themselves. As long as they didn't bother us, we didn't bother them." Grandpa rubbed his chin, a habit he had when thinking of something to say. "Come to think of it, they only stayed a while and then another couple moved in." There was that habit of his again. "There was always a different couple that stayed for several months at a time."

"You think they were Sheren's family?" Aaron asked.

Grandpa smiled. "You mean his gangster family?" Aaron's eyes lit up. "Could have been. Who knows?" Grandpa turned to me and put his hand on my arm. "You okay, kiddo?"

"Yeah, I guess."

"What do you mean you guess?"

"I think Erica needs a break," said Aaron. "Will it be all right if we come back another

day?" Aaron glanced at me and could tell what I was thinking. *Thank you, thank you, Aaron.*

You are my savior and read my mind.

"No problem," Grandpa said. "I could use a break, too." Grandpa thrust his chest out. "I turned sixteen in April and got my driver's license. Dad went with me and just as Mom did, I passed the test on the first try. I continued working at Harris Grocery Store until school started and my junior year." Grandpa smirked. "Some exciting things happened my junior year. I'll tell you about them next time."

I put my hand on his and smiled. "Thanks, Grandpa. Want my secretary to call yours?" At least I still had a little humor left in me.

"Sure." Grandpa looked at Aaron. "You got that secretary?"

Aaron saluted. "Yes, sir, Mr. Teague."

"Good, now get the hell out of here, both of you."

"What about lunch?" I asked. "Want me to make you something?"

"Annamarie left potato salad in the refrigerator. I'll eat it and make a bologna and cheese sandwich." Grandpa waved us off. "Now go, go on, go."

I kissed my grandfather on his forehead, and we left.

On the drive home, we stopped at Bradley's Country Store for a late lunch. We both ordered six-inch sausage dogs with mustard and relish, two bottles of water, and chips. We sat out on the porch in the rockers.

"You okay, babe?"

I took a bite of my sausage dog and then a drink of water before I answered. "I'm not sure I want to write about the Sherens."

"You have to. You promised your grandfather, and he trusts you to do what he asked. You don't want to break his trust, do you? Besides, it wasn't as bad as I expected."

For sure, I didn't want to break my grandfather's trust. And I wanted to ask Aaron how much worse he'd expected it to be? Had he expected Sheren to kill Violet?

"It might have been," Aaron continued. "and your grandfather spared us the details." Aaron could have been right. I hadn't considered that possibility.

"Maybe," I replied. "But if there is any more domestic violence, I'm leaving it out, and I won't let my grandfather talk about it. No matter what he says." Aaron knew better than to argue with me at times like this, and that was the end of the subject.

Just then, an elderly gentleman stepped out of the store. Aaron got up and stopped him.

"Excuse me, sir, do you live around here?"

The man looked Aaron up and down. "All my life down the road a piece. Why?"

"I was wondering if Centerville Road was a dirt road back in the forties?"

He pointed down the road got that old timer look and said, "You know, lots of folks don't know, but this here road's Moccasin Gap. Centerville ends back at the fork. Both Moccasin and Centerville were unpaved roads until sometime—" he scratched his head. "Sometime in the sixties, I think. The plantation owners and farmers liked them for their horse and wagons." Aaron seemed surprised, I wasn't. The man smiled. "Any more questions? I'd like to stay and chat, but I gotta get this food home or the missus will give me the dickens."

"No, sir, thank you. You've been quite helpful." The gentlemen stepped off the porch, got in his SUV and left.

"What was that about?"

"Just wanted to verify something your grandfather said when he said he went to Army Day." Aaron munched on his sausage dog and sipped some water. "What do you think of your great-grandparents? They didn't have to help those folks on the highway. Did you ever meet them? And what about Violet passing as a white woman and hiding the fact that she was a colored woman?"

Sadly, I had not met my great-grandparents, and I wish I had. Just like my grandfather felt after they had helped Cecil and his family, I was proud that they were a part of my heritage.

"That was a shocker." I shook my head. "My great-grandmother trusted Violet and she broke that trust by keeping it a secret."

"Not the first time she did it," Aaron said. "Remember when she admitted that she cleaned someone else's house? That should have been a giveaway. So, did you ever meet your great-grandparents?"

"I never met them, but my mother did. Now I understand why my grandparents took Mom and me in and cared for us after my father died. They were following in the footsteps of my great-grandparents of caring for others."

"Maybe that's why you became a nurse and then a paramedic." He reached over and grabbed my hand. "You care about people. It's what attracted me to you."

Damn, my man knows what to say and when to say it. "It's what attracted me to you. Something told me you were one of the good guys." I gave him the biggest smile that I could. "It's also why I love you."

Aaron grinned. "Aw gee, I love you, too." We both laughed. "It seemed your grandfather had a crush on Rosalind and she had one on him. What do you think?"

"Sounded like it." It did, but that wasn't what Rosalind told me when I first met her. She said she had a crush on Grandpa, but he had a crush on the cheerleader. Maybe she didn't want to admit it in front of the folks at the Genealogical Society. I gave him a naughty wink. "Let's hurry home." We rushed to the car and sped home.

The next week after my secretary called my grandfather's secretary and arranged an appointment, we drove to Monticello before stopping to buy sugar-free oatmeal cookies. We didn't dare come emptyhanded. And, as he had done lately, he was waiting on the front porch for us.

"Good morning, Grandpa, we brought…"

"Never mind the BS, just get those dang cookies over here. Can't you see I've been waiting all week for them?"

Aaron started up the porch steps and stumbled. Grandpa reached out to help him, but Aaron was just fooling my grandfather and righted himself.

"Dang, boy, you put a scare in me. What would I do without cookies and coffee?"

Aaron shook his head. "And a top of the morning to you, too, Mr. Teague."

"Yeah, sure, and a top to you too. Now, hand me those cookies before you fall and make a mess of them." Aaron handed Grandpa the bag.

Apparently, Grandpa had given in to the fact that the cookies replaced the doughnuts.

"And good morning to you too, Grandpa."

"What the heck? Are we gonna keep this up all day? Before you know it, it'll be lunchtime. If you want me to tell you more, then you best get inside and make a fresh pot of coffee. Then I'll confess to what happened to me since the last time you interrogated me."

I narrowed my eyes. "What? I didn't interrogate you. Oh, never mind."

CHAPTER 35

ESIDES GETTING MY DRIVER'S LICENSE, not much happened the rest of my sophomore year. I had a license, but no car or truck to drive. Dad offered to let me use his truck an occasional Saturday night. Since I had no one to go out with me, I declined his offer. I could walk into town if I wanted to see a movie or stop by the drugstore for an ice cream soda and chat with Rosalind.

I continued working at the grocery store after school and on Saturdays. During summer vacation, Mr. Harris hired me to work full days from ten until six. Now that Dad was home and working, I was able to save half my earnings. Hopefully, one day I'd have enough to buy a used truck.

Sometimes on Friday nights after work, I'd walk to the high school basketball court and hang out with friends. A few girls joined us, but it was mostly guys. The older boys sometimes smoked cigarettes, passed a bag around and took a drink from the bottle. I didn't drink. For all I knew, there was just a bottle of soda pop in the bag. I was invited to a few parties but never attended because I knew Rosalind wouldn't be there.

When my junior year started, I had to quit my job at the grocery store because I went out for the varsity. I didn't expect to make it because I felt I has too short and didn't weigh enough. There were some pretty big guys on the varsity. The coach remembered the beating I'd taken in his practices the year before. It was probably why I made the team—the coach needed another tackling dummy.

I continued walking Rosalind to class in the mornings.

One day, the band was practicing in the corner of the football field—not far from the locker room. After dressing for practice, I ran out onto the field while attempting to snap my helmet strap and not paying attention to where I was running. I accidentally knocked the sousaphone player to the ground. Of course, it had to be a girl. I offered to help her up and almost got hit in the head by the bell when she stood and turned around.

"I'm sorry. I wasn't paying attention. "Of all the band members I had to bump into, it had to be Rosalind.

"Nice tackle, Francis. You should ask the coach if you could play defense."

Embarrassed? That's putting it mildly. It probably meant another day of hiding from my classmates—at least those that who were on the team or in the band.

"Teague, get your butt over here. It's football practice, not band practice," yelled the coach and just in time to save me any further embarrassment. "And what are you doing over there, anyway?"

"I gotta go, I'm very sorry."

She slapped me on the back and smiled. "Go get 'em, tiger. Grrrr."

I snapped my chin strap and ran to join the team taking extra precaution not to trip.

"Nice way to meet a girl, Teague," said the quarterback. The other team members patted me on my butt and laughed. I grinned.

The next day at school, I waited and walked Rosalind to class. I expected she'd comment about yesterday. If she did, I was prepared to face the music.

"Good morning, Francis. Ready for another school day?"

Holy cow, she didn't mention my almost killing her. Or, was there more to come?

"Are you?"

Rosalind winked at me. "Yes, and band practice, too."

Okay, here it came.

"Are you going to the party Saturday?"

Party? What party? I thought she was about to launch into an embarrassing monologue about watching where you're going and how to snap on your chin strap.

"Are you?" It was a foolish question since I hadn't even known there was a party, and also since I knew she had to work.

"Course not."

If she wasn't going, then I wasn't, even though I hadn't been invited. "I don't think so. I have too much homework to catch up on because of football." Why did I have to mention football?

"If you get some time, stop by and say hello." She winked at me again.

"I'll try."

Surprisingly, none of my classmates, teammates or band members mentioned my embarrassing fall. I guess they were accustomed to my accidents.

Saturday night, Dad offered me the keys to his truck, but I said I'd rather walk. I had planned on passing through town and stop at the drugstore and have an ice cream soda. Dad had been offering me the use of his truck on Saturday nights lately. I figured out a long time ago that my parents were just trying to get rid of me so they could have the house to themselves. I was always happy to accommodate.

"Evening, Francis," Rosalind said when I walked in. "Would you like your usual vanilla ice cream soda?"

Dang, she could either read my mind or was used to me always ordering the same thing. Maybe I'd fool her and ask for a strawberry ice cream soda.

"If it's no bother."

"Not at all." She winked and smiled. "Coming right up."

Why did she have to go and do that? Couldn't she leave out the wink and smile? Didn't she know how that made me uneasy?

"Here you go." Another wink and smile. "I put an extra scoop of ice cream in it just for you." When she smiled again, I felt my heart flutter.

"Thanks. Uh, Rosalind…"

"Yes, Francis."

"How do you get home after work? Do you walk?"

There was that smile again. "Why, do you want to walk me home?" Walk her home? I just wanted to know how she got home, that was all. I wasn't asking for her hand in marriage—which meant I'd have to meet her parents and ask her father's permission. "Just kidding. Don't look so nervous. Besides, it's a long walk." Thank goodness, I was off the hook. "My Mom brings me to work, and my Dad picks me up. But if you ever want to take me home, I'm available." Oh, man, there was that smile and that wink.

"I was just curious." I could have said I'm available. Just then someone else walked in. "You've got another customer."

Rosalind walked off to tend to her other customer. I finished my soda and waved goodbye.

"See you Monday, Francis." This time it was just a smile, but I walked home feeling like I was floating on air.

My parents came to every home game, except one. In fact, hardly anyone showed up for that game. Not even the cheerleaders or the band. You couldn't blame them because of the torrential downpour. We were playing Quincy, a non-conference team. Both teams sloshed through the mud and rain. At the end of the game, our team had won by a score of 7-6. The only mud that I got on my uniform came from the pre-game workout.

We were undefeated when it came to the last home game. My parents were there and cheered for me as I ran onto and off the field at the beginning and halftime. Our defense was tough, and our offense readily scored. Late in the fourth quarter, the coach called my name.

"Teague, go in at tailback and stay away from the ball. Just stand there if you have to."

I almost said, "Me, coach?' Instead, I put on my helmet, buttoned the chin strap, ran onto the field taking extra precaution not to trip, and joined the team in the huddle.

"Teague, you want the ball?" asked the quarterback, Bucky Barnes.

Do I want the ball? Was he kidding? I'd spent the entire season getting splinters in my butt from sitting on the sideline and being the tackling dummy for the defense. Of course, I wanted the damn ball. Who wouldn't want an opportunity to score a touchdown and have the cheerleaders fall all over you? *You bet I want it.* That's what I wanted to say.

"Teague, you want the ball or not? We haven't got much time."

I mumbled, "But coach said..."

"Forget what he said. You want the ball or not??"

"Uh... yeah, sure, Bucky."

"Okay, you guys, here's the play. Teague gets the ball on hike."

We came out of the huddle, another first for me. I stood behind the halfback and could barely see over his giant butt as I surveyed the offensive line. I knew they'd open a hole big enough to float a battleship through. I'd follow the halfback through that hole, who I was positive would block for me. Once in the open field, I'd show my dance moves. Zigging and zagging waving off tacklers and then sprint down the field and cross the goal line. The whole team would pile on me congratulating me for scoring a touchdown.

Bucky yelled, "Set, down."

I was ready for when he would say hike. Nothing was going to stand in my way to have a memorable moment. But, suddenly, instead of Bucky saying hike I heard a whistle and the ref yell, "Game over!"

Are you serious? I was about to have a memorable moment. One that would have the cheerleaders hugging and kissing me and the team carrying me off the field. But, no, I got nothing. I took off my helmet and felt like a two-year-old attempting to walk across the room for the first time. I felt like I'd fallen flat on my face.

Bucky placed a sympathetic hand on my shoulder. "I tried, Teague. Maybe next year."

"Thanks." The way I felt, there might not be a next year.

I walked off the field alone with my head hanging so low it almost scraped the bare ground. Someone was calling my name, but I couldn't tell who it was because my head was pounding and my veins felt like they were about to pop. I kicked up some dirt several times as I made my way to the locker room. While the team celebrated, I showered, dressed, and quietly slipped out of the locker room. When I came out, my parents were waiting for me. Mom wrapped her arms around me.

"We're proud of you, Francis." Only mothers knew when their baby needed consoling—and this baby damn sure needed it.

My Dad ruffled my hair. "There's always a next time, son." Fathers have a different way of consoling their children.

"Thanks, you guys."

Dad held up the keys to the truck. "Want the truck tonight?"

My big moment was gone as was a victory celebration. Why not enjoy the use of the truck? If there was going to be a victory party at the Women's Club, I might go and do some dancing. Maybe the game wasn't over yet for me.

"I'll take it." I could tell my parents were pleased that they'd have the house to themselves. They always were.

I stopped by the Women's Club and stayed a while. Danced with a few sympathetic cheerleaders, but certainly not stuck-up Katie Shure. Everyone was in good spirits celebrating today's victory. I eased my way out the door and headed for the truck, figuring I'd stop by and say hello to Rosalind.

She greeted me with a curious look. "Francis, were you at the movies?"

"I stopped by at the Women's Club for the victory dance."

Rosalind narrowed her eyes. "Oh, you want an ice cream soda?"

What no smile and wink? Rosalind didn't seem pleased that I went to the dance. Maybe it was because she had to work and I was out dancing.

"Sure, if it's no bother."

"Be right back." She turned and abruptly walked away.

I wondered why. She usually smiled and winked, not just walked away. She brought me my soda and walked off. After I finished my ice cream soda, I waved goodbye to her.

"See you Monday, Rosalind." She returned my wave with a limp hand. I worried she might ignore me Monday.

Monday morning, I waited to walk Rosalind to class. When she got off the bus, she walked past me without saying hello. She ignored me at lunchtime and all day. When classes ended, I hurried to walk her to the bus since I no longer had football practice. But she was nowhere to be found. She was either already on the bus or still had band practice. I shrugged my shoulders and walked home.

The next morning, I waited again for Rosalind. This time instead of walking past me, she smiled and took my hand.

"Good morning, Francis. Are you ready for another day?"

What a difference from yesterday. Her greeting made me feel warm and fuzzy all over. Thank goodness because she was my best friend—actually, my only real friend.

"Hope it's better than yesterday."

"It already is," she said and then smiled and winked.

Hallelujah, the storm was over, the sun was shining brightly, a new day had begun and Rosalind wasn't mad at me anymore. I squeezed her hand.

"I'm glad," I said.

Rosalind winked and squeezed my hand.

Not much happened after football season had ended except that I applied for my old job at Harris Grocery Store and got it. Oh, and if you ever look through a yearbook for 1947, you won't see my individual team photo. I skipped the photo session the day they took pictures. There was no way I'd have the inscription under my picture say, *almost played a down.*

As the holidays approached, it felt strange not having Violet around to join in our celebrations, especially Thanksgiving. I actually missed her. I think Mom did, too, because occasionally I'd see her look out the window at Violet's house.

For Christmas, Dad and I bought a large tree and decorated it.

A few days before Christmas, my parents were whispering. I couldn't hear what they were saying. Periodically, one of them would glance at me. Was it possible that the man Violet shot came forward after all this time and told the police that it had been her, that Jackie and I were witnesses, and the police wanted to interrogate me? I hoped it wasn't

"Francis, your father and I have been talking, and we've decided…" said my mother.

"What your mother and I have decided is that…"

"Let me tell him, Frank," said Mom. She had a smile big enough to stuff a football in her mouth. "Mrs. Atkinson's gardener is getting a newer truck and wants to sell his old one. It's almost fifteen years old and needs some repairs. I already spoke with him, and he'll sell it to you for a reasonable amount. Are you interested?"

"Damn…dang, right I'm interested." I caught myself just in time because Mom gave me her eye and I wasn't about to lose my chance to own a truck.

"Dad and I will talk to him about what he'll take. You could have the truck by Christmas Day."

"I'm going with you. I want to see the truck before I buy it."

My parents and I talked to Mrs. Atkinson's gardener. It was a 1933 Dodge Commercial Canopy truck. It had plenty of scratches and dents, and the back smelled of manure. Dad cranked up the engine, and it belched. He tried it again, and it sputtered and started.

"Needs a good tune up and maybe more work on the engine," Dad said, "but we can handle it. Check the tires, Francis."

"Back tires look a little worn," I replied. "The front could use new ones."

"How much are you asking for it?" Dad asked the gardener.

"Seventy dollars."

I didn't have seventy dollars. All I had saved in my nickel can was twenty-five. With a little persuasion from Mrs. Atkinson, the man agreed to thirty-five dollars. Dad loaned me ten dollars. I gave the gardener the money and drove off with the truck. It sputtered and coughed, but it got me home.

Mom got a Whitman's Sampler for Christmas, Dad got lots of kisses, and I got a truck. It was the best Christmas ever.

CHAPTER 36

D AD AND I WORKED ON my truck Sundays after church. I wanted to work on it after work, but Dad said it was too dark and not safe. He was the mechanic, so I reluctantly agreed. He could have taken it to work with him, but Mr. Coogins would have objected since it was a Dodge, not a Chevy. We eventually got the truck in working condition, and I was able to take it to school and Skippy got to ride with me on Sunday afternoons.

Now that I had my own means of transportation, I felt bold enough to ask Rosalind if I could drive her home after work—provided I didn't have to meet her parents. I decided my seventeenth birthday was a good enough reason to ask her.

Saturday night after work, I took a bath, changed into clean clothes, looked into the mirror, and combed my hair. Sporting clean shirt and trousers, I was ready to meet my waiting damsel, only she didn't know that she awaited me.

I parked my truck and strutted into the drugstore expecting her to run around the counter, leap into my arms, and say, "Take me away from all this, oh, knight in shining armor." Unfortunately, she was waiting on a customer. No problem. When she did see me, she'd collapse into my arms. I took a seat and waited impatiently until she finally saw me.

"Francis, you're all decked out. Is there a dance at the Woman's Club?"

No, I'm here to rescue you fair maiden and take you to Shangri-La with me. That's what I wanted to say but didn't. Instead, I mumbled, "Not that I know of. I was thinking of…" My mouth suddenly froze shut.

"Thinking of what?" Her mouth formed a huge smile. "Oh, you were—"

Was she clever enough to know why I was there or was it the way I was dressed that gave me away?

"Of ordering a vanilla ice cream soda." At least I got something out of my mouth but not the words I wanted to say.

Rosalind's lips formed a grin. "I'll go make it for you. Don't go anywhere."

Go anywhere? I wasn't going any place but here unless I conjured up the courage to ask if I could drive her home.

She returned with my soda and set it in front of me. "Anything else I can get you?" Then she had to go and smile and wink. Did she have to do that? I was already about to pee my pants.

"Not now, but maybe later." Way to go, Francis, give yourself an option and time to conjure up the courage.

"I hear you got a truck. Is that it parked out front?" Damn this town; everyone knew your business.

"I got it for Christmas."

"Be right back."

She asked me about my truck and then took off. How was I supposed to tell her why I was really here?

Rosalind returned holding a cupcake with a candle in it. "You just had a birthday. This is my way of celebrating it with you. Happy Birthday, Francis."

She wore a pink ribbon in her hair, and my face turned the same color. "Thanks." My heart pounded when she smiled.

"Maybe sometime you could take me for a ride?" She cocked her head and winked.

I almost choked on my drink. I was supposed to ask her she wasn't supposed to ask me. Rosalind wasn't my waiting damsel; she was my femme fatale.

"How about tonight, after work?"

Rosalind frowned. "Can't. You have to meet my parents first. Especially my Dad."

Incomplete pass. *Way to go, Teague. That's why you were the other team's quarterback. You couldn't complete a play. Wait, did she say meet her parents first? No, no, Teague, you don't want to do that. You know what that leads to? First, you go steady, then you get engaged, later married, then a family, and you're working your butt off for the rest of your life. No way, you're just a teenager in high school.*

"How about tomorrow afternoon?" Rosalind said.

Think of something, quick before you're married. "I can't. I have something I must do with my parents." *Good thinking, Teague.*

Rosalind shrugged. "Maybe some other time." Then she left me alone to ponder whether she meant for me to ask her again or for me to just forget it.

Whatever she meant, I had no idea, so I left money on the counter and left.

Sunday after church, I took Skippy for a long ride out to Lloyd Creek. The temperature was mild, but when I opened the door, Skippy jumped out, ran to the water and dived in. Fortunately, we were the only ones there. After Skippy had finished swimming, he came ashore and shook himself dry. I found a stick, tossed it, and watched Skippy go after it. He was having a ball, and I didn't want to spoil his fun, but we had been there long enough and had to go home.

Monday morning, Rosalind ignored me. In fact, she ignored me all week. The price I had to pay because I wasn't ready to meet her parents, get engaged, marry her, and raise a family with her. I had my whole life ahead of me and marriage wasn't something I wanted. Maybe my thinking was irrational. Or was I fantasizing? Whatever, there was plenty of time for Rosalind to get over what bothered her.

Eventually, Rosalind got over her annoyance with me and we were friends again. I hadn't considered again asking if I could give her a ride home after work. I wanted us to be just friends as we parted the school year. Over the summer, I would only see her on Saturday nights if I stopped by the drugstore for an ice cream soda.

CHAPTER 37

AFTER GRANDPA HAD FINISHED REMINISCING that day, we took him for lunch. Seemed a good reward for all he'd remembered.

We'd just dropped him back at his house and were headed away when Aaron said, "Dang, Erica."

I furrowed my eyes. "Dang? Are you mimicking my grandfather or is he rubbing off on you?"

Aaron grinned. "He's rubbing off on me. I love that guy, and he's funny, too. I think he had a bigger crush on Rosalind than she had on him. What do you think?"

"I think you're right. He was smitten with her."

"Think they're gonna?" He winked. "You know. Get it on?"

I knew what that wink meant, and I elbowed him. "Don't even think about going there if you value your life. "

He raised his hand. "Just thinking, that's all. But, you have to admit."

I elbowed him again, harder this time. "I said don't go there. My grandfather wasn't like that." I pressed my lips together. "If you want to go there with me tonight."

Aaron grinned. "I surrender. Think he'll go out for football again? He sure took a beating. I wouldn't."

"My grandfather's not a quitter. He'll go out again. Bet on it."

"I wouldn't take that bet." He raised his finger. "I got another question. Will you write exactly what your grandfather said? You know like about him and Rosalind? Or will you make things up?"

"Is that what writers do—make things up?"

"I don't know. I'm not a writer. Your grandfather didn't tell us everything, so you should make some things up and fill in the blanks. He won't mind." Aaron chuckled. "Maybe that's what writers do."

"Maybe I should," I said. "But you'll have to help me, Mr. Secretary."

Another grin. "Of course, I'm right," he said. "That's why I'm your secretary." Aaron raised his hand. "Or we can go downtown and ask that old guy at the writer's tent."

I shook my head. "Not a good idea. He'll probably want to co-author and want royalties. We'll have to be satisfied with my secretary."

We both laughed.

A week later, we returned to Monticello—with cookies. After the usual pleasantries and, of course, after I'd made coffee and served the cookies, Grandpa continued where he'd had left off.

CHAPTER 38

NOT MUCH HAPPENED DURING THE summer. Mr. Harris hired me full time to sweep floors, stock shelves, and as a part-time cashier. He paid me fifty cents a day, which was better than what most teenagers earned. I saved most of my earnings in my nickel can and kept some for Saturday nights at the movies, ice cream sodas at the drugstore and, of course, gas.

There were no hurricanes that summer but a few storms that caused mild damage. My parents went dancing every other Saturday night at the Women's Club. They hadn't gone dancing since before the war, and I could tell they enjoyed themselves. They were all lovey-dovey when they got home.

When vacation ended, I quit my job at the grocery store to go out for varsity. Hopefully, it wouldn't be another season like the last one with me being the tackling dummy and spending long lonely Saturday afternoon's watching the team play while I got blisters on my butt warming the bench.

Monday morning, I met Rosalind when she got off the bus. She had a red bow in her hair and looked pretty. We walked to class together.

I made the varsity team and practice was the same as usual. I played the opposing team's quarterback and—you guessed it— the tackling dummy. But one day during practice, I decided to shake up the defense. With the ball comfortably in my hands, I dropped back, scrambled to the left and threw a left-handed spiral down the field. The defensive linemen stopped, turned and watched it soar through the clouds only to land in the hands of a linebacker a few yards from scrimmage. I thought I'd thrown that ball a mile, maybe more.

The coach whistled. "Teague, you try that again and you'll run wind sprints until they have to carry you off the field. Understand me?"

I understood him, but I didn't care. I'd run wind sprints every day during practice just to do something other than be a tackling dummy.

"Understood, coach." I turned my head and smiled. But my victory celebration could result in a long season of frustration like last year. Maybe I wouldn't get another chance to almost play a down.

"Nice pass, anyway, Teague," said the defensive tackle.

"Thanks, Big." Everyone called Big Petarski, Big. That's because he was big, really big. Bigger than King Kong.

Same as last year, my parents went to all the home games, watched me warm the bench, and consoled me after. But I was always the first one onto the field at the beginning and halftime.

The last game of the season was homecoming and against Perry. At halftime, both schools' bands provided a color guard and firing squad as military honors for the alumni of Monticello High School who lost their lives during World War II.

Both teams struggled. At halftime, we were up 7-0. But during the second half, Bucky Barnes completed two touchdown passes, and we went ahead 21-7. Late in the fourth quarter, the coach called my name.

"Teague." Was it going to be the same as last year when he sent me into the game with time running out, and I almost played a down? I hoped not. I'd rather stay on the bench than be humiliated again. "Think you can go out there and make like a statue?"

Make like a statue? Is that what he thought of me after all the punishment I took for the team? I'd show him. I wouldn't just stand there like a statue, I'd be the best statue he'd ever seen.

"Sure, coach, whatever."

"Then get the hell out there."

I strapped on my helmet, made sure none of the cheerleaders were near me and that I had a clear path and ran onto the field. There I was in the huddle. Only this time to be a statue.

"You want the ball, Teague?"

Again with that? Of course, I wanted the ball, but coach said to be a statue.

All the guys were watching me, waiting.

"Well, Teague, yes or no?"

I planted my feet in a wide stance and tightened my jaw. "Give that damn ball to me, Bucky. You watch what I'll do with it."

Bucky slapped my shoulder. "That a boy, Teague." The players waited for Bucky to call a play. "Let's make it simple. On hike, you guys give him a hole. Teague, you follow the fullback."

We got out of the huddle and lined up on the ball. Just like last year, I surveyed the offensive line. I knew they'd open a hole for me and the fullback would plow through it with me behind him on his butt.

Bucky called out, "Set, down." I knew it would happen, that the ref would yell the game was over, that it couldn't actually happen. And then, Bucky yelled, "Hike."

I almost peed my pants, and my hands were drenched in sweat. The fullback started to his right. I was behind him following his butt. Bucky reached out with the ball and shoved it into my gut so hard I let out an *oomph*. I wrapped my hand and arms around it and held it closer than a hug.

The offensive line opened a hole big enough for the whole team to go through. The fullback cleared a path as he knocked down every linebacker. I went through the hole and had a wide-open lane to the goal line. With both hands on the ball, I willed my legs and feet to move like a thoroughbred coming out of the starting gate. I saw the end zone. I imagined me crossing it. The team would pile on top of me like the defense did in practice only this time they'd be celebrating my touchdown. The cheerleaders would rush out onto the field and hug and kiss me. Especially stuck-up Katie Shure, who'd probably tongue-kiss me.

Suddenly. I was blindsided by the Perry safety and knocked to my knees. I fell flat on my face and ate dirt, but I held onto the ball. The referee blew his whistle and yelled, "First down!" Then he looked at his watch and yelled just like last year, "Game over!"

Big Petarski rushed over and scooped me into his arms. "Way to go, Teague, you made a first down."

I hadn't scored a touchdown. The team wouldn't pile on me. The cheerleaders wouldn't hug and kiss me. Stuck-up Katie Shure wouldn't get a tongue kiss from me. But, I made a first down. I was *Superman.*

"Thanks, Big," I tried to sound cool, but I could feel my stupid smile giving away my feelings.

Both teams shook hands and ran toward the locker rooms. I pranced off the field waving to my parents. Rosalind honked her sousaphone and, of course, smiled and winked at me. I pumped my fist in the air and felt like I was the greatest champion of all time.

The coach grabbed me. "That wasn't a statue, Teague."

I grinned. "Sorry, coach, you can punish me next year." He shook his head and walked off. Oh yeah—there wouldn't be a next year. But that meant no more chances to almost play a down, make a first down, be *Superman,* and possibly tongue-kiss a certain cheerleader.

In the locker room, everyone congratulated me. Bucky picked up a ball and handed it to me. It wasn't the team ball, but it was a ball.

"You deserve this, Teague, for all the punishment you took the past three years."

"Thanks, Bucky."

Big Petarski hoisted me in the air. The whole team shouted, "Way to go, Teague."

Three long years of punishment at the hands of the defense was worth every bit of that moment. Just like last year, I skipped the individual team pictures. Even though I had a first down to my credit, I still didn't want the inscription under my name to read, *tackling dummy.*

Bucky had invited me to a victory party at his home.

"If you want, Teague," Bucky said, "you can bring a date." Bucky smiled. "How about the sousaphone player?"

How I wish I could, but I couldn't. "She has to work. Can I come alone?"

Bucky patted me on the arm. "Sure thing. There'll be other girls there."

Before leaving for the party, I checked myself in the mirror. I noticed a few whiskers on my chin and under my nose. I borrowed some of Dad's shaving cream and his razor and made them disappear like magic. I was extra careful not to nick myself and have to show up at the party with blotches of tissue paper on my chin. Next, I spat on my hands and rubbed them on my head making sure every hair of my crew cut was in place. Satisfied, I left for Bucky's house.

The entire football team and the cheerleaders were there and welcomed me. Bucky's parents cooked hot dogs and hamburgers for the crowd and provided plenty of soda and then left for the movies. As soon as his parents were gone, Bucky gathered us all in the living room for a game.

The guys and girls took turns spinning the bottle. When it landed on someone, the two went into the bathroom for privacy and to kiss. When it was stuck-up Katie Shure's turn, she spun the bottle, and it pointed at me. She grabbed my hand and led me to the bathroom and closed the door.

"Would you like to kiss me like that last time?" she asked with a wicked grin.

Would I? She was damn right I would. "Sure."

We put our arms around each other and dang if she didn't tongue kiss again. Only this time it lasted longer than I expected.

Katie didn't seem like she wanted to stop. Maybe she had kissed like that with other guys. Whatever, I wasn't about to stop her.

When Katie finally quit, she winked and said, "Did you like it?"

"Want to do it again?" I asked.

She put a warm hand on my cheek. "Can I trust you not to tell anyone what we did in here?"

I crossed my heart. "Trust me."

She smiled. "Okay, once more." She shoved me against the door and brushed up against me. When she tongue-kissed me, I felt a tingling all over me. I felt excited like I was when Violet hugged me and said goodbye.

When the kiss ended, Katie ran her hand down my arms. "I trust you." She grabbed my hand and placed it on her breast. It was soft, so I squeezed it. Katie smiled. "Don't be a stranger, Teague." She opened the door, grabbed my hand, and we joined the party.

Bucky gave me a thumbs-up. Big Petarski and two other linemen did the same. Katie was no longer stuck-up to me.

The next time I saw Rosalind, I wouldn't tell her about the party and kissing because I was sure she'd be angry with me. Maybe I'd make up a tale about going out to dinner with my parents to celebrate my first down so that she wouldn't be mad. But I bet Rosalind had spies in town, and they'd report that I wasn't at any restaurant with my parents. Maybe I should say that my truck broke down and I had to spend the weekend fixing it.

Monday morning, I waited for Rosalind when she got off the bus. I reached for her hand. She

crossed her arms.

"How was the party?" she snapped.

"Uh—It was okay. I didn't stay long."

Katie got off the bus, walked past us, winked, and finger waved me.

Rosalind glanced at Katie's back and threw daggers at it. "And the kisses?"

Katie must have broken our trust and told her. She was no-longer just Katie to me. She was now Loose Lips Shure. When Rosalind walked away, it was like an Arctic chill blew down from the north. I followed her to class. She ignored me all day and all week. I guess I had it coming.

Saturday, I didn't go into town. I stayed home with my parents. Mom sat in her chair knitting—a pastime she'd recently taken up. Dad sat in his chair reading the newspaper. I sat on the couch.

I leaned forward. "Dad, can I ask you something."

He put down the paper. "Sure thing," he said.

I told him about Rosalind and me, but not about the party and Katie. "What should I do?"

"Uh..." Dad seemed unsure how to answer.

Mom lowered her knitting and listened.

Dad looked at her and stood. "Maybe you should ask your mother. Excuse me. I have to go to the bathroom."

I was flabbergasted. Dad had been in the war, he stood up to Mr. Sheren and here he was afraid to talk to me about my problem with Rosalind.

Mom sat beside me. "Girl trouble?" she said.

I was too embarrassed to make eye contact with her, so I looked down. I wanted to do like Dad did and excuse myself.

"Want to talk about it?" Mom asked, concern in her voice.

I hadn't planned on telling either of my parents what happened, but my mother was there for me in the past when I needed her.

I glanced at her, felt embarrassed and looked down. "I was at a party." I looked up and she grinned. I took a deep breath and blurt out, "There were girls and kissing." I looked away. "Rosalind wasn't there. Now she won't talk to me."

"Oh, my," Mom said and put her hand to her mouth.

I felt like a foolish child.

"Remember when I told you one day you'd meet someone and you'd feel the way you did about Miss Lucy?" Her voice was calming. Remembering Miss Lucy caused my heart to ache. "Rosalind could be that someone. When I first met her, she seemed like a nice young lady." I looked at Mom. She smiled. "Rosalind was probably jealous."

"What should I do?" I asked.

"Give her time. If she really likes you, she'll forgive you."

I felt an ache in my heart.

"It may take some time, but in the meantime, be a perfect gentleman. Don't do anything to make her jealous, like kiss other girls. She'll let you know when she forgives you." Mom smiled. "How about some cookies and milk?"

Dad was standing in the doorway listening. Mom walked toward him. I saw him smile and mouth, "Thank you." Mom placed a hand on his shoulder and went into the kitchen.

I sat and contemplated Mom's words.

I had started my old job at the grocery store where I worked after school and on Saturdays. Rosalind still hadn't talked to me or let me walk her to class for what seemed like a year but was several weeks. There was no reason for Rosalind to ignore me. It's not as if we were married or going steady, and she hadn't ever kissed me. All we ever did was hold hands. I was seventeen, would be graduating come spring, owned a truck, played a down of football, and made a first down. I was *Superman* for a day. I deserved to be kissed by a stuck-up cheerleader, other girls, and I deserved to have fun. But like Mom told me, I was a perfect gentleman and continued to walk behind Rosalind to class.

I also stayed away from the drugstore on Saturday nights. I took Skippy for Sunday afternoon rides in the country. He loved having me all to himself and sitting beside me. When my parents and I went for rides, Skippy sat on my lap. When it was just Dad and me, Skippy sat between us with his head held high like King Arthur flanked by knights of his roundtable.

On a Saturday night in December after a movie, I walked by the drugstore. I was sure Rosalind saw me look in the window, but she acted like she hadn't.

The next time I saw Rosalind I planned on walking up to her, say I was sorry and ask if we could be friends again.

Monday morning when I saw her, I started toward her.

"Good morning, Francis." She smiled and winked. "How was your weekend?"

The Arctic freeze had melted. I was dumbfounded. "Uh... it was okay," I replied. "How was yours?"

Another smile. I felt warmth inside me. "I worked Saturday night. Sunday, I helped my mom with housework. What did you do?"

Had she seen me Saturday night? "I took in a movie. Afterward, I stopped at the candy store. Sunday, I took Skippy for a ride. Guess we both didn't do anything exciting."

Rosalind smiled. "Want to hold my hand and walk me to class?"

Did I? If I weren't a gentleman, I'd have kissed her. My heart fluttered. I took her hand and we walked to class. We did it every day from then on. I couldn't meet her after class because I had to go to work at the grocery store. Mom had been right. There was something different about my relationship with Rosalind.

For Christmas, Mom bought me a dress shirt and two pairs of new trousers. Apparently, I was going through a growth spurt, and Mom said my old trousers soon wouldn't fall below my knees. One pair was for school, the other for church. I used the old ones when I worked on my truck and around the house.

The Saturday after Christmas, I visited Rosalind at the drugstore. She seemed different than the last time I was there. I ordered my usual vanilla ice cream soda. She set it in front of me and asked, "Are you going to the New Year's Eve dance at the Women's Club?"

"Nah, my parents will be there, and I don't want to spoil their fun. I'll just stay home alone with Skippy."

Rosalind's precious smile and wink returned. "My parents aren't going, and neither am I. Be right back, I have a customer."

Gee, Rosalind would be spending New Year's Eve with her parents, and I'd be with Skippy. It didn't seem fair for either of us. We were teenagers; we should have been celebrating together. Rosalind returned.

"Katie Shure is having a party, and she invited me," Rosalind said.

Loose Lips Shure was having a party and invited Rosalind? That's a surprise.

"Would you like to go with me?"

"Does that mean I have to meet your parents, especially your Dad?"

Another grin. "They won't bite. They were teenagers once like us. Are you afraid to meet my Dad?"

I wiped my forehead with my napkin. Meeting her dad would be like running smack into a dear on a moonless night.

"You are, aren't you?" Again, with the grin. "And here I thought you were a big brave varsity football player." She grinned. "It's not like you're going to ask my Dad for my hand in marriage." She paused and furrowed her eyes. "Are you?"

I choked on my soda, picked up my napkin, and wiped my mouth. "Dang. Why'd you go and say something like that?"

She laughed. "Because I wanted to see your reaction and it was worth a million dollars just to see the look on your face."

I wiped my brow with my napkin. Rosalind handed me a whole bunch of napkins. "So, do you want to take me to the party or not?"

I regained my composure and realized she was having fun with me. She just asked for a date, and to be honest with you, I wanted to date her. We'd known each other for years, held hands, but never dated. It was time we did.

"Sure. I'll meet your parents because I want to date you. There, I said it."

Rosalind blushed and fanned her face with her hand. "Whew. I thought you'd never ask."

I felt like a giant, an enormous giant, bigger than Big Petarski. Rosalind may have asked first, but I got to decide, and now we were finally going to date. "Me, too. What time should I pick you up?"

"The party starts at eight, so you best be at my house at seven-thirty. Katie doesn't live but a few minutes from my house."

I got up to leave.

"And bring an enormous diamond engagement ring. That way Dad will know you're serious."

I stumbled from my seat and almost tripped and fell. The last thing I heard was Rosalind's laughter as I walked out the door.

CHAPTER 39

AS MUCH AS I HATED to, I had to interrupt my grandfather. I didn't want to overwork him. I already had enough material to fill several chapters, and I was behind in my writing. Besides, I needed a break to compose myself. Grandpa had kept us on the edge of our seats with the latest developments. Especially with what I now deemed as the big event of the story—the date with Rosalind. When Grandpa mentioned the bathroom kiss, Aaron almost fell off his seat. I had to grip the arms of mine. We wanted to hear about the special event that took years to happen. But, although we would be left dripping with anticipation, I had to do what was in the best interest of my grandfather.

"Maybe we should finish another day?"

Grandpa snapped his head back. He was surprised.

Aaron slumped in his chair. I knew he was disappointed.

"You talked enough for today."

Grandpa breathed. "I could use a break." He cocked his head at Aaron, who was still slumped in his chair. "What's his problem?"

"You overwhelmed him."

Grandpa smiled. "He'll have to wait until next time to find out what happened New Year's Eve. You, too."

I shrugged. "I can wait."

Grandpa looked like he didn't believe me.

"Is next week okay?" I turned the recorder off and put my pen and notebook in my backpack.

"Works for me." He looked at Aaron. "Hey, Mr. Secretary," he shouted.

Aaron bolted upright.

"Have your secretary call mine."

"Uh," Aaron said as though he'd been awakened from a nightmare. "Yeah, sure, Mr. Teague.

Grandpa and I chuckled.

"You ready, Aaron?" He was still dazed. Grandpa and I smiled.

Aaron raised a hand. "Yeah, I'm ready."

"Can I get you anything before we leave, Grandpa?"

"No thanks. I'm gonna walk over to Annamarie's house and have lunch with her." He winked and smiled. The old devil.

I kissed him. "Let's go, Aaron."

Aaron walked behind me as if he were sleepwalking. The last thing I heard was Grandpa's laughter.

And just as I expected, as soon as we were in the car, Aaron had a million comments.

"That Katie girl was some tease," he said. "We had a name for girls like her."

"Slut," I said. "And she wasn't that pretty."

Aaron raised his eyebrows. "How do you know?"

I grinned. "Her picture was in the yearbook."

"How about Rosalind? Was she pretty?"

"Cute," I replied. "Any more questions about girls?" I put the key in the ignition.

"Nope." He rubbed the back of his neck. "You think your grandfather and Rosalind will, you know, on New Year's Eve?"

I slapped his arm. "No. My grandfather wasn't like that." My forehead furrowed. "Get your mind out of the gutter or…"

"Okay, already, my mind's out of the gutter—as to your grandfather." He winked.

I knew what he was thinking. "Okay, just once." We leaned toward each other and tongue kissed. "Whew." I took a deep breath and started the car. "Now, can we go home?"

"You're the driver."

A week later, Aaron and I eagerly made the trip to Monticello. We purchased a bag full of cookies at Publix. The cookies were our way of guaranteeing Grandpa would have the stamina to tell us about the date and what happened at midnight. It was hot and humid out when we arrived.

Grandpa must have anticipated our eagerness because he was waiting on the porch with his chest thrust out and a smirk on his face.

"Bet you can't wait to hear about what happened New Year's Eve?" he said.

Aaron and my jaw dropped.

"You bet we can't," I replied.

Grandpa waved us toward the door. "Then let's go inside. I made coffee. We'll have it in the den." He shook his head. "I knew you two sissies wouldn't want to sit on the porch."

Inside, we had coffee and cookies and then Grandpa began.

CHAPTER 40

NEW YEAR'S EVE, MR. HARRIS closed the store at four so he and Mrs. Harris would have plenty of time to dress for the dance at the Women's Club. I was glad because it gave me time to stop at the florist and buy a bow for Rosalind. I got there just as the owner was about to lock the door. I looked at all the bows. Some were made of shiny ribbon. Some weren't. I knew Rosalind liked to wear shiny ones in her hair, so I bought a bright red one to match her smile. I paid and drove home.

I got the ironing board out and pressed my pants and ironed my shirt. Next, I took a shower and dressed. I stood in front of the mirror checking for whiskers. I borrowed Dad's razor and shaved off the few I found. I put a sprinkle of Dad's aftershave on my hands and dabbed it on my cheeks. Then I spat on my hands and combed my crew cut. I was all decked out and ready to party. I said goodbye to Mom, Dad, and Skippy and left to face Rosalind's parents.

When I arrived at her house, I was so nervous that I considered driving by and going home. Instead, I reconsidered, parked my truck, grabbed the bow, and sat there. I needed time to muster up the courage to face her father. If he knew about Loose Lips Shure, would he think me unfit to date his daughter? I thought about my big day as a varsity football player and the moment I had waited for. The coach telling me to get out there, taking the ball and scoring a touchdown. I'd have been a hero, the team would have carried me off the field, and the cheerleaders would have hugged and kissed me.

I didn't have a football, and I wasn't going to be a football hero. But I had a bow. A touchdown would be meeting Rosalind's parents and giving her the bow. I could do that. I'd already been a hero once, and I could be one again for Rosalind.

I strode up to Rosalind's front door and stopped. Should I or should I not ring the doorbell? I scratched my chin, reached for the doorbell and hesitated. I reached again. Hesitated again. Finally, I rang the bell.

Rosalind's father opened the door. He seemed bigger than Big Petarski. He had a menacing look on his face. I considered turning around, running back to my truck, and driving off like *Batman* without *Robin*.

"You must be Francis? Come in. Rosalind's waiting in the living room with her mother."

With her mother? Does that mean they were going to grill me like Dick Tracy did a criminal? I thought about leaving, but I had to be Rosalind's hero.

"Thank you, sir."

He glanced at the bow. "That's a pretty bow and Rosalind's favorite color. You've got good instincts like your father."

Oh, no, he knew my father. What else did he know? Hopefully, nothing about that last party I'd attended.

"Thank you, sir. How do you know my Dad?"

He grinned. "He's worked on my car at the Chevrolet store. A good mechanic. Once in a while, I'd stand beside him and watch as he worked. I wasn't supposed to be in the shop, but he tolerated my presence." His eyes narrowed. "If you're anything like your father, then you're okay for my daughter." He tilted his head toward the living room. "First, you have to satisfy my wife."

Here I was worried about her father, and it was her mother I had to worry about.

He smiled. "Don't worry; she doesn't bite."

I followed him into the living room. Rosalind stood next to her mother dressed in a blue party dress with a pink bow in her hair. Her mother stood with her arms crossed, her lips pursed, and her eyes narrowed. She resembled my sixth-grade teacher when I arrived late for class after lunch.

"So, you're Francis Teague?" Rosalind's mother said. "I've heard about you."

Oh, great, Rosalind told her about that party.

She smiled. "You're the boy that made a first down. My daughter told me all about you. I see you brought her a bow. We'll have to remove hers and use yours."

Rosalind winked and smiled. Her mother removed the bow, took mine and put it in Rosalind's hair. "Now she's ready. You kids have a good time."

"Thank you, ma'am. Ready, Rosalind?"

"I am." She kissed her parents on the cheeks and reached for my hand. I took it and led her outside, casting a glance over my shoulder to find them smiling at us.

I escorted Rosalind to my truck and held the door for her. Rosalind waved to her parents as they stood in the doorway. I waved, too, walked around to the driver's side and got in beside her.

"See, that wasn't so bad. Was it?"

"I guess not. You look pretty."

"Thank you. Would you like to kiss me now or at midnight?" I almost hit the gas pedal and smacked into a tree. "Just kidding, but we'll see at midnight."

Katie Shure lived a few blocks from Rosalind. Her house was gigantic. Way bigger than Rosalind's and mine. It was lit up like a Christmas tree. Both Rosalind and Katie lived far enough from town to ride the bus but close enough to have electricity.

Katie's mother greeted us at the door. She was prettier than Katie and didn't seem stuck-up like her daughter. We said hello, thanked her, and joined the crowd in the living room. The entire varsity football team was there as were the cheerleaders. The girls wore party dresses and the guys trousers. Some came with dates, others paired up at the party.

Katie's parents had set up a buffet on their dining room table. There were sliced ham, cold cuts, salads, bread, and an assortment of cookies. There was more than enough to feed the whole crowd three times over.

Rosalind and I danced the jitterbug. I was amazed at how she could dance. Big Petarski played some slow romantic songs such as *My Funny Valentine* and *Them There Eyes*. Rosalind and I danced to those, too.

When Big played *Someone to Watch Over Me*, Rosalind rested her head on my chest as we swayed to the music. It felt wonderful holding her in my arms. I felt her heartbeat. She probably felt mine. It was a magical moment.

"Can we take a rest and get a bite to eat," Rosalind asked.

I didn't want to let her out of my arms, but I said, "Sure. We can dance again later."

Rosalind smiled. My heart fluttered.

We wandered into the dining room, fixed plates of food and cookies, grabbed glasses of punch and went out onto the porch to eat.

"Thanks for bringing me, Francis. I'm having a wonderful time." She said it without a wink but a beautiful smile.

"I'm glad you invited me."

We chatted a while, and then I put our plates in the garbage bag and we returned to dancing.

Loose Lops Shure was dancing with Big Petarski. They not only danced the jitterbug but danced to slow songs, too. Could you imagine King Kong and Fay Wray dancing the jitterbug? I couldn't, but there they were.

Rosalind and I were dancing cheek to cheek to *Almost Like Being in Love* when everyone started counting down. She looked up at me longingly. I gazed into her hazel eyes. We said nothing. Just stared into each other's eyes. My heart was beating rapidly.

Suddenly everyone shouted, "Happy New Year."

I lowered my head, pressed my lips to hers, and let them linger there for an eternity.

I don't know how much time passed before someone put the music back on. I ended the kiss but didn't move away from her as the song changed to *You Go to My Head*. Rosalind and I drifted off to a mystical island.

"Can we do it again?" Rosalind asked.

I put my arms around her and kissed her again. She put her arms around me and pulled me close to her. I heard the thump-thumping of both our hearts as I squeezed her up against me.

I never forgot that night.

CHAPTER 41

JIMMINY, CRIMINY I THOUGHT MY grandfather would never get to the kiss. I fanned myself and considered leaping across the table and jumping Aaron's bones. Aaron was slumped in his chair and looked like he'd welcome it.

Grandpa sat smugly back in his rocker, Aaron looked like he'd just run a marathon. Me. I finally felt like I'd just finished my yoga class. Namaste.

"What did you and Rosalind do after the party?" I asked, hoping he'd tell us.

He bolted upright. "A gentleman never reveals what he does with his lady." Grandpa looked at Aaron, who was taking deep breaths to control his emotions. "Right, Aaron?"

Aaron sat up straight. "Uh, yeah. Whatever you said."

Grandpa and I laughed.

"How about after the new year? Did you and Rosalind...?"

Grandpa threw daggers at me.

"Did you date?" *Damn, what did he think I was going to ask?*

"Yeah. But our dates consisted of me visiting Rosalind at the soda fountain and driving her home after work." He raised a finger. "And don't ask if anything happened. We also went for Sunday afternoon drives with Skippy." Grandpa smiled. "In case you're wondering, I hugged and kissed Skippy." Aaron and I laughed. "Rosalind and I held hands when I walked her to class after she got off the bus.

"Was there a prom?" I asked.

"Nah," Grandpa replied, "but we had a graduation dance at the Women's Club. Rosalind and I attended." Grandpa had a twinkle in his eye. "She wore a white dress that her mother made her. It fell just below her knee and had some kind of pattern on the right shoulder. I wore black trousers, a tie, and a jacket I borrowed from Dad." Grandpa grinned. "You're not going to believe this, but Big Petarski was there with Katie Shure as his date.

"After graduation, Rosalind continued working at the drug store. I got a job at Florida Power and Light as an apprentice lineman. Turns out, Mrs. Atkinson and Mrs. Coogins knew some important people, and with their recommendations, they got me the job. At first, I thought I'd get to climb the poles, but I was just a get this, get that, wash the truck, and any other menial task they gave me. Eventually, I got to climb the polls.

"We dated regularly until September when Rosalind left to go to the University in Gainesville." Grandpa raised his glasses and wiped his eye.

"Did you see her after that, Grandpa?"

"When she came home for the holidays." His eyes closed then opened. "Unfortunately, she met a beau at school." Grandpa breathed a heavy sigh. "We drifted apart." Another heavy sigh. "I dated a few girls but never more than a couple of times."

I felt sad for my grandfather. I'd have been heartbroken if something like that happened between Aaron and me.

"Later, you were drafted into the army, weren't you?" I asked.

He thrust his chest out but had a vacant stare. "In 1951. That kid, Jackie, was also drafted. We were both in Korea at the same time." He waved his hand. "But that was a long time ago, and you don't need to know about it." Grandpa was just like his father— not wanting to discuss the war. "Jackie is now a retired lawyer in Jacksonville. I took advantage of the GI Bill and enrolled at Florida State University. I commuted from Monticello." Grandpa shook his head. "But after I went into the army, the vegetable garden was left unattended, and the plants rotted. Dad dismantled the chicken coop, and what chickens were left he sold to a farmer.

He no longer felt like taking care of them and could easily buy chicken and eggs at the grocery store."

"What happened to Skippy?" I asked.

His shoulders drooped. "Old age. I never replaced him; I just couldn't. Damn, that dog was special to me." Grandpa wiped his eye.

"Anyway," Grandpa said, "I graduated from Florida State with a degree in engineering. I got a job with an engineering firm in Jacksonville." Grandpa's eyes were suddenly wide and glowing. "I met Florence Rodgers—your grandmother." Grandpa chuckled. "I called her Flossy. She was a high school English teacher." He rocked his head back and forth and laughed. "Imagine that, an English teacher of all things?"

I shot Aaron a look. Was he thinking of Miss Lucy?

"We dated for two years until I asked for her hand in marriage."

"Did you have a big church wedding, Mr. Teague?" asked Aaron.

"No, we had a civil ceremony and wore street clothes. We got us an apartment and later started a family. We had..." Grandpa paused. "Your mother came along, and the apartment got a little crowded." Grandpa bit his bottom lip. "Dad took ill, so we moved back to Monticello to live close to my parents. We bought this house. I was fortunate to get a job with an engineering firm in Tallahassee. I commuted back and forth." Grandpa lowered his head. "Mind if we take a break?"

"Sure," I replied. "How about I make us sandwiches?"

"Good thinking." He seemed relieved. "Be right back." Grandpa got up and went off to the bathroom. I think something he was about to say from his past may have upset him, and he wanted to compose himself.

"Is he okay?" asked Aaron. "He seemed like something was bothering him."

I pursed my lips. "I think it may have had something to do with his father's illness. Or something else. Wait and see." I stood. "I'll make us lunch."

"How about…"

"Cheese and baloney," I said. "Works for my grandfather and me." Aaron's eyebrows hiked. "Besides, that's all there is."

If it hadn't been for Annamarie, the refrigerator would be empty. I made three sandwiches, poured three glasses of sweet tea and put it all on a tray. I returned to the porch and set the tray on the table. Grandpa returned, and we ate lunch.

Grandpa swallowed the last bite of his sandwich, wiped his mouth and said, "Two years later Dad died of cancer." His chin trembled. "The doctors said all those years working as an auto mechanic might have caused it. Personally, I don't think they had a clue." Grandpa rubbed his face with his hands. "Two years later, Mom died of a broken heart."

I rubbed my hand down his arm. "Take your time, Grandpa, we're in no hurry."

Grandpa crossed his hands over his stomach and rocked back and forth. "Anyway, your mother married, and then you came along. The rest you know—end of story."

My heart felt for him. Such a sad ending. I closed my eyes and placed my hand over my heart. Aaron's jaw went slack.

CHAPTER 42

END OF STORY? MAYBE FOR my grandfather. But not for me. I still had quite a bit to write and would have liked to write about his married life, being a parent, then being a grandparent raising his granddaughter. But most of that, I already knew from living with my grandparents and from my mother. Besides, the book was meant to be about Grandpa's adolescence.

I packed up my backpack and stood to kiss Grandpa goodbye.

"What's the title gonna be?" Grandpa asked.

I was exploring options.

"How about Huckleberry Hound?" I said.

Grandpa's head jerked back. "Huckleberry Hound? Who the hell was he? Some scallywag?"

I belly-laughed. "Just kidding. I haven't decided yet. How about Scallywag?"

"Scallywag. You're joking, ain't you?"

"Maybe, we'll see. Got any ideas?"

Grandpa rolled his eyes. "You're writing the book," he replied. "You pick the title. Just not Huckleberry Hound or Scallywag. I trust you."

"Whatever you say," I said. "I'll think about it, but I like Huckleberry Hound."

Grandpa's mouth fell open.

"You'll have to wait until the book is published to find out what title I picked. Trust me, you'll like it."

The book was put on hold in September when Hurricane Hermine ripped through Tallahassee and Leon County. Aaron and I had to work extended hours until the crisis ended. We went without electricity almost a week. Once power was restored and we were back to regular working hours, I returned to writing the book.

Harriet reviewed what I had written up to now. She had me add more emotion and tension to several chapters to make the book more intense. She wanted the dialogue to sound authentic. I felt I was exaggerating, but Harriet said it was necessary. So, I did.

Aaron and I were married in a civil ceremony at the entrance to the Monticello-Jefferson County Chamber of Commerce building. It was the site of the old Catholic church that my great-grandparents, grandparents, and mom and I attended. Aaron's parents came to town for the ceremony but didn't stay long. At least my grandfather, my mother and I got to meet them.

Grandpa didn't get to walk me down the aisle, but he did walk me up the steps to the entrance of the Chamber of Commerce building and gave me away. Our wedding party consisted of fellow paramedics who had time off and could attend. We didn't walk under a traditional wedding arch. Instead, we walked under a ceremonial arch of oxygen masks presented by our fellow paramedics.

Mom brought her boss with her. She looked happy, and they looked good together. I was happy for her and ecstatic that she wasn't annoying me about not having a grand wedding like the Duchess of Cambridge.

Annamarie also attended. The reception was at my grandfather's house. Mom had the food catered, and she even had a cake—a small one compared to what she wanted, just four layers. No hard alcohol was permitted, but Grandpa allowed beer for the paramedics and the bride and groom. Grandpa and I danced to Louis Armstrong's *What a Wonderful World*. I felt like I was fifteen and back in high school, like we were back at the father and daughter dance. I put my head on his shoulder and we swayed to the music.

With Harriet's help, I completed the manuscript. She worked diligently with me and pushed me across the finish line. We polished the dialogue so it sounded like Grandpa talking, and I kept my promise to Grandpa to include everything he told us. Harriet had me intersperse my chapters between Grandpas.

Before sending the manuscript to be published, I offered Grandpa the opportunity to read it. I wanted his approval.

"Nah," Grandpa said. "I trust you. You know what you are if you break a trust?"

"A scallywag." When we said the word together, we laughed.

I learned a lot about myself as I wrote my grandfather's story. Our lives had some similarities. We both overcame obstacles— Grandpa more than me—and we persevered. Grandpa had his mother to support him. I had him. If I ever had a child, I'd use the book as a guide to parenting. It would help us overcome obstacles and persevere. If I had a girl, I'd use it to help her be independent.

My great-grandfather joined the navy and left my great-grandmother alone to care for her son. My Dad died and left my mother alone to care for me. Grandpa taught his mother to work on his Dad's truck and to drive it. He did the same with me. Grandpa worked at a grocery store during high school. I worked at the Piggly Wiggly. He witnessed a shooting; I treated several gunshot wounds. Grandpa had an awkward time with girls in high school. My romantic exploits weren't as awkward.

EPILOGUE

A MONTH LATER, AFTER GRANDPA AND I last talked about the book, Aaron was watching television while I worked on the manuscript. All I had left was to hit submit, and the manuscript would be on its way to eventually become published. Just as I was about to hit submit, my mother called.

I started to tremble when she said my grandfather was rushed to the hospital. She said more and I heard her, but I slumped into my chair.

Aaron saw me. "What's up? Hey, why are you crying?"

"It's..." I sniffled and wiped my hand across my nose.

"It's what? Is it your Mom? Your grandfather? He's not?"

My chest tightened as tears rolled down my cheeks. "No," I sobbed. "They were having dinner at a restaurant here in Tallahassee when Grandpa said he felt lightheaded. He suddenly clenched his chest and slumped over." I sobbed. "He was rushed to the emergency room. Mom said I had to hurry and get there."

Aaron bundled me in his arms, and I cried on his shoulder.

"Let's go. We'll take my truck. Did your mom say what's wrong?"

"Grandpa had a heart attack."

We reached the hospital, and the volunteer at the information desk advised us that my grandfather was in the Cardiac Intensive Care Unit. Once we had his room location, Aaron and I took the elevator and hurried to find him. Mom and Annamarie were already there.

Mom's eyes were red and puffy, and she rocked back and forth. Annamarie had her face in her hands. They both looked like they had been up all night crying. When Mom saw me, she wrapped her arms around me.

"I'm so glad you're here," she said. Her voice trembled.

"How is he?"

Mom slowly shook her head. "It's not good, Erica. You can see him after…"

After what I wondered.

I looked into my grandfather's room and saw a man standing by his bedside. I thought he might be a priest saying last rights.

"Who's that with Grandpa?"

Mom put her hand on my arm. "I'll explain later."

When the stranger finished talking to my grandfather, he walked out of the room and smiled at me. "You must be Erica. You've grown since the last time I saw you. Go see your grandfather. He's sedated but might be able to hear you. We'll talk later."

"Thanks," I said. The man seemed strangely familiar. That was the second time someone had said they'd talk to me later.

Aaron waited outside the room with my mother.

I walked into the room and stood beside Grandpa. His eyes were closed. Looking at him was difficult. He was hooked to a monitor, attached to a breathing apparatus, and had IVs in his arm. It reminded me of my father's last days in the hospital. I'd also seen many a patient the same way when I was an ER nurse. I knew Grandpa's condition was worse than not good.

I placed my hand on his arm. I had hoped Grandpa would open his eyes and recognize me, but he didn't. I felt the tornado of tears begin to swirl. I put my hands on his.

"I'm sorry, Grandpa. I shouldn't have listened to you. I should have stopped writing the book instead of letting you convince me to continue. If I had, maybe you wouldn't be in this room. Maybe you'd be fishing with Aaron." My cheeks were wet with tears.

"Don't do this to me. I need you. Mom needs you, Aaron needs you, and Annamarie, too. We all need you. Dammit, don't you die on me, you old scallywag."

I felt his fingers twitch. Suddenly, the monitor started beeping. I stepped aside as a trauma team rushed into his room. I left the room, joined Mom, and we watched through the glass partition.

It was like a scene from a television show. A doctor started chest compressions. He'd stop, lean back and then shock him again. He did it several times. The five of us watched in horror as they worked on Grandpa. After the last shock, the doctor stopped.

I barely saw the flatline on the monitor. The doctor covered Grandpa with the sheet. I buried my head in Aaron's arms.

The doctor came out of the room and spoke to Mom. I saw his lips moving but couldn't hear him. The strange man took Mom in his arms. I still didn't understand why he was still there.

Suddenly, Annamarie gasped, mouthed something, then dropped to the floor. A floor nurse rushed to her side, reached into her pocket, took out an ammonia inhalant and revived Annamarie. The nurse and the doctor helped her up and set her in a chair. I watched the nurse say something to Annamarie and leave. The doctor left, too.

Mom and the strange man were exchanging words. I saw their lips move but couldn't hear them.

The whole scene was surreal, like an out-of-body experience. Aaron put his arm around me, and it brought back into the moment.

I'd just lost my grandfather.

Mom was in the arms of a stranger. Who the hell did he think he was? Did he think he was going to take her away from me?

"You okay, Erica?" the stranger asked. He reached out to touch my arm.

I brushed his hand away. "Who are you?" I snapped.

"Erica, what's come over you?" Mom said.

I glared at her. "Who the hell is he?"

Mom closed the gap between us and leaned in. "Not now. Don't you have any respect for your grandfather?" She sounded angry.

Other patients were in their rooms. Visitors and nurses roamed the floor. Mom was right; this was neither the place nor the time, but I hated to give in.

"Where then?" I snapped back.

Aaron and the others watched our exchange. I had no idea what they were thinking, and I didn't care.

"There's a waiting room outside of the CICU down the hall," Mom said, her voice lowered so the others could barely hear. "We'll talk there."

Mom, the stranger, and Annamarie left to go to the waiting room. Aaron and I followed.

When we walked in, it was empty. Mom and the stranger had placed chairs in a semi-circle. We all sat. Mom sat next to me.

"Okay, who is he?" I asked.

Mom started to speak, but the stranger held a hand up and interrupted her.

"I'll explain, Marion."

What the hell? Why had he called my mother Marion? What gave him the right?

"Erica, I'm your Uncle Frank."

"No, you're not. I don't have an uncle." I glared at Mom.

"Let me explain it to her. Dad wanted me to."

I looked at Aaron. I'd bet he'd rather be in the hall away from the drama. Annamarie's face was expressionless. She looked down. She probably wished she was home.

"Explain what?" I snapped.

"When you were three years old," Mom said, "your grandfather and your Uncle Frank had harsh words concerning your uncle's lifestyle."

"I'll take it from here, Marion," interrupted Uncle Frank. Mom seemed annoyed.

I grimaced. Was it gonna be a tennis match between them?

He continued. "We argued, but we were both bullheaded and opinionated. I moved to California and have a life there. I shouldn't have stayed away so long. I should have been the bigger person and apologized to Dad. Your mother would have told you, but he made her promise not to."

Again, Mom interrupted. "It was a stupid argument and a dumb promise. I shouldn't have kept it."

He patted her knee. "You had no choice. But that was in the past, and all's forgotten." His words and voice sounded familiar. Like Grandpa's. Maybe he was my uncle.

"Your mother called me at the behest of our father. He wanted to make amends and asked if I would come to Monticello." He had a tear in his eye.

"I flew in several days ago, and it was the smartest thing I ever did. We didn't have much time together, but what little we had was wonderful." I was still confused. He held a hand up. "Before you ask, I was at my mother's funeral. Your grandfather didn't know I was. I wrote my parents but never received a reply." That bundle of letters I had seen in the memory box had to be his. It was probably why Grandpa didn't want me to see them.

"Your mother and I corresponded over the years." He smiled. "I know all about your life growing up. She sent me pictures." He looked at Aaron. "I saw your wedding picture." Mom brushed his arm, and he glanced at her before focusing on me again, "I've been following your life only you didn't know it."

"You're not angry at us, are you, Erica?" asked Mom.

I was angry at both her and my grandfather. I took a deep breath. "I don't know what to say."

"Then let me help you," Mom said. "Your grandfather asked me to give this to you." Mom reached into her purse and handed me an envelope.

I looked at Mom, Uncle Frank, and Aaron. "Do you know what's in it?"

"Yes, but it's meant for you," Mom replied.

I opened the envelope and took out a single sheet of paper. It was a note from Grandpa.

"Dear, Erica, you're probably wondering who the gentleman is with you. I asked your mother to explain him to you. A long time ago, I made a mistake that I've regretted ever since. Your grandmother and your mother tried to convince me to change my mind, but I was too stubborn.

As you were writing my story, I realized I could no longer keep my mistake a secret. After your mother explains, you'll probably think that I broke your trust, and you'd be right if you called me an old scallywag. I wouldn't be surprised if you had me walk the plank.

Forgive your mother for not telling you sooner. She was just obeying my wishes, the same as your grandmother.

Please forgive this old man and thank you for helping me see the light. Unfortunately, you may have to add another chapter to your book.

Love, Grandpa"

I felt the tears on my cheeks and didn't bother to wipe them.

Grandpa and Mom had kept the secret about my uncle from me. They shouldn't have done that. Grandpa admitted he was wrong and asked my forgiveness. He had been there for me after my Dad died and became my surrogate father. He was wrong, as was my mother. And a scallywag he might be, but he was my scallywag. No one could ever take that away from me. How could I not forgive him?

I'd lost my grandfather but gained an uncle. My anger subsided.

"I'm not angry, Mom. I'm disappointed, but I'll get over it." Mom flinched. I looked at Uncle Frank. "I wish I'd known about you sooner."

"We both do," he said.

"Now that we're all together, how about we all get something to eat?" Mom said. "It's been a long night, and I'm hungry." She smiled. "Uncle Frank's treat." He smiled.

Aaron nudged me. "How about coffee and cake or whatever we have at our house? It's not far from here."

"Sounds like a plan," Uncle Frank said. He sounded just like Grandpa.

Aaron and I drove home. He dropped me off and then left to buy an apple pie at Denny's. I made coffee, and we all sat around and talked past midnight before Mom, Uncle Frank, and Annamarie left.

Later that night, Aaron and I cuddled up in bed while I wept.

There should have been three generations of family gathered around a Christmas tree at Grandpa's house for the holiday. Instead, there was a pall of death. Grandpa was cremated. His ashes were buried with my grandmother near my great-grandparents' gravesite. Afterward, we had a memorial service at the Catholic church in Monticello.

Just like Grandpa lived his life, he had a simple gravestone: On it was chiseled. "FRANCIS DAVID TEAGUE 1930-2016."

I wished Grandpa had lived long enough that I could see his face on Christmas morning. That's when I'd planned on telling him he was going to be a great-granddaddy. He would have said, "What, another scallywag? Ain't one enough?"

And that's how my grandfather's story ended.

Oh, and one more thing. Aaron and I got a dog—a one-year-old mutt named Skippy.

ACKNOWLEDGEMENTS

THIS BOOK WAS A WORK of fiction, and the story was derived from my imagination. The events and characters were fabricated.

I don't remember much from the early forties because I was born eight months before Japan bombed Pearl Harbor. But I do remember the late forties, fifties and beyond. And I have to confess that most of Francis' embarrassing moments were from my own experiences.

As part of my research, I spoke with several septuagenarians, octogenarians, family, neighbors, friends, and strangers. Of course, there were numerous websites that I used in doing my research.

My thanks to Dee Counts and the members of the Monticello Keystone Genealogical Society, a group of wonderful folks who were happy to share their memories. Also, to everyone I spoke to over the telephone who were eager to help. Most of the places that I mentioned no longer exist and if it weren't for Dee and her associates, I wouldn't have known about them.

I'm also grateful to those who chose to remain anonymous. Their input was invaluable.

A special thanks to Robin Patchen for her patience and understanding as she guided me through the errors of my ways as a writer, and Erica, too.

I hope you enjoyed reading the book as much as I enjoyed writing it.

Visit my website at www.georgeencizo.com to learn more about me and my books.

Made in the USA
Coppell, TX
26 October 2021